The Forgotten Beast

THE FORGOTTEN ONES
BOOK ONE

FREYA VICTORIA

First paperback edition November 2023

ISBN 979-8-9893882-0-2 (paperback)

ISBN 979-8-9893882-1-9 (ebook)

ISBN 979-8-9893882-2-6 (audiobook)

www.freyavictoria.com

*For those of us who tried over and over again to write our first book.
You can do it, it just takes the right inspiration.*

"To see you was instantly to love you. Entering your apartment, tremblingly, my joy was excessive to find that you could behold me with greater intrepidity than I could behold myself."
—— **Gabrielle-Suzanne Barbot de Villeneuve**

POTENTIAL TRIGGERS IN THIS BOOK

The Forgotten Beast is a Beauty and the Beast retelling. I want you going into this knowing what you're getting. Ultimately, I want you to protect your mental health and there are absolutely no hard feelings if you need to DNF The Forgotten Beast. If you would like a more thorough explanation of any of these, you can find it on www.freyavictoria.com on the book page for The Forgotten Beast or you can go to the Trigger Details at the end of the book so you can decide if it's safe for you or not.

This book includes situations with alcohol, anxiety, assault, blood, cheating, death, decapitation, depression, gore, hospitalization, hostages, kidnapping, murder, physical abuse, profanity, sexually explicit scenes, torture, violence, war

Contents

PART ONE

Thanksgiving Week

CHAPTER 1

Evergreen

I sit in the dust on the floor of my parents' attic. Thirty years of collected Christmas ornaments, garlands, figurines, and other knickknacks my parents have stuffed up here throughout their marriage lie around me. As I decide which ones to bring downstairs to decorate this year, I run my hands over the surface of each ornament.

This is my favorite part of this time of year, looking through all the ornaments my parents bought or were given for each milestone over the course of their marriage. Starting with some ornaments given to them by a friend when they were engaged, which read simply *First Christmas Engaged* followed by *First Christmas Married* with the respective years. Ornaments for the birth of my brothers and me, our first teeth losses, and our first real home as a family. There are ornament cars that represent each of our first cars, and ornaments to represent each of our graduations, and everything in between and after.

Every family has their traditions. Mine is to come back to my parents' home in Jackson for Thanksgiving. Even though I'm grown and have my own home to decorate, I would prefer to come home and help decorate the house I grew up in.

This is the home my mom decorated every year growing up.

It's the house my father would come home from work to everyday and kiss my mom on the cheek. He would ask about her day, knowing that a day dealing with us kids was more than a full-time job. It's the house I had my first broken arm and broken heart in.

Every year, I come back for Thanksgiving and stay for the weekend, helping my parents sort through all the decorations. We decide which ones we'll display this year. Which items should go where, and, are we going to use the nativity this year or the Santa and reindeer set? Are we going to have a live tree or pull down the massive Costco pre-lit tree my mom got on sale one year? These are the traditions I love and will treasure forever.

My life has been full of predictable turns. I grew up with parents who stayed married. Had brothers that gave me a hard time, but nothing more than you'd expect from brothers. But, I haven't really *lived*. Sure, I went to college. Yeah, I graduated and moved into a place of my own in Laramie. Even got a job to support myself. But, I haven't traveled anywhere. I haven't truly seen anything. I've been on this planet for twenty-four years and have spent most of that time within a six-hour radius.

As I look around the attic that extends for most of my parents' house, I remember Christmases that have come before. I remember the fights over who gets to hang mom's favorite ornament or the tree topper. Fights over who gets to set up the Christmas countdown, or who gets the first taste of the pumpkin roll mom makes every year. These are the memories I come back for every year.

My brothers are both married with kids. They now help their wives set up their homes for Christmas, where they also collect a new ornament each year. I continue to come back here, reveling in the time alone with my parents, the time I know will be gone way too soon.

This is the first year I've done this by myself. Mom sprained her ankle, so I'm up here alone sorting through the Christmas stuff while she sits at the bottom of the ladder. She's occasionally asking and answering my questions about which decorations we want to bring down.

I'm just about done here. Taking one last glance around to make sure there isn't another box I've missed, I notice a large, dusty chest tucked away behind all the Christmas decorations. I move some boxes out of the way so I can open it. When I brush some of the dust off, I notice how well made the chest is, inscribed on the top are the words *The Forgotten Ones*. I try to open it and realize it's locked, which means most likely there aren't any Christmas decorations in here. I carefully brush the rest of the dust away with my hand amid much sneezing and coughing. The chest is made of wood, and as I run my hand across its surface, it is smooth, worn that way by time.

"Are you okay up there?" my mom yells up at me.

"Yeah... I'm fine... I'll be down in a minute," I say as clearly as I can amid the coughing and sneezing from the dust cloud surrounding me. I decide I'll ask my mom about it after getting the boxes down from the attic by myself.

It takes me several trips and much struggling before I'm able to get all the supplies and decorations down. Mom helps me as much as she can on her bum ankle and we start opening the boxes and sorting everything in the order we'll need them to put up the decorations. There's nothing better than organized chaos.

This year, we thankfully decided on a live tree, so I didn't have to haul down the giant fake tree by myself. Dad's at work while "us girls do our thing" here at the house. I secretly believe he always schedules himself the day after Thanksgiving to make sure he doesn't have to help with all the decorating.

"How about we take a break and get some hot cocoa? You can catch me up on what's been going on with you lately," my mom asks as she gets up from her spot on the floor. She hobbles into the kitchen to get the cocoa ready. Though, I'm not sure what she thinks might be going on with me. It's always the same: work, home, hanging out with Huxlee, my boss and best friend. The occasional trip back to my parents' house is about as exciting as it gets for me.

"Sure, Mom, sounds great," This is another tradition I come home for, homemade hot cocoa. We always drink out of the same Christmas mugs we got as a Santa gift one year. They are matching, of course, so we each have one to drink the delicious, warm, creamy chocolate drink from. I get up and follow her into the kitchen, dusting off my ass as much as I can while walking.

My phone dings when I'm almost to the kitchen and I pull it out as soon as I walk through the doorway. I grin when I see the most recent text in my "Besties Group Chat."

HUXLEE

Did you survive the dust?

ME

It's not that bad.

JEN

Bull! Why do you think we leave so early?

ME

Really? I thought it was to keep the kids on a normal-ish schedule.

I set my phone down and look up as Mom pulls out various canisters and pans. She hobbles around their large kitchen on her boot. She's made the cocoa so many times, she eyeballs the recipe before putting it onto the stove to warm for us. I don't even think my mom has a package of instant cocoa in this house.

"Hey, Mom, what's that large box up in the attic?" Why I decided to refer to it as a box, I'm not sure.

She looks at me and smiles as she stirs the cocoa on the stove. "What box, honey? You're going to have to be more specific. We've been storing boxes up there as long as we've lived here," she replies with a chuckle.

"The one that was behind all the Christmas stuff, yay big, says 'The Forgotten Ones' on the top of it." She brings her gaze to mine, a frown marring her brow. "I thought maybe it had more Christmas stuff in it, but it's locked."

"Oh, that box," she answers flippantly, quickly gazing back down at what she's doing. "No, there are no Christmas things in there. Don't worry about it. The things in there are private and for my eyes only."

Clearly, my mother was never a child, or at least never a curious child. Saying anything to keep your kid out of something, even one who's 24 years old now, is essentially a dare. Now I will stop at nothing to see what my mother might be hiding in the fancy, dusty, hidden chest. I will just apparently do it behind her back now. With her sprained ankle, it's not like she can follow me around the entire time I'm here. I will stop at nothing to get that chest opened before I leave on Sunday night.

As soon as she's done mixing and warming the cocoa, she pours us each a cup. Then I grab the container of homemade cookies that sits on the counter, and we move to the table. That's one thing I can always depend on the weekend after Thanksgiving. There will be all the leftover baked goods from the big Thanksgiving affair my parents always host.

Once we're both sitting, she continues, "I'm sorry you have to do all the decorating by yourself this year, Callie." Then she motions to me and conspiratorially whispers, "Next year, I'll do my best not to have an accident that takes me out for the holidays." She finishes with a laugh. I grab a napkin from the holder in the center of the table and pull out two cookies to set on it.

"It's okay, I know you didn't do it intentionally. I can't imagine you hurting yourself on purpose." I smile and take a sip of my cocoa, the warm chocolate lighting up my tastebuds. "We'll get this done, even if you're just decorating the lower branches on the tree and handing me ornaments out of the box." Picking up a cookie, I dip it in the cocoa and take a bite.

"Callie, you know you're supposed to dip those in milk, right?"

"But have you ever tried it?" I plunge the cookie into my

cocoa again, accidentally dipping too far. When I pull the cookie out, I stuff the rest in my mouth and lick the hot cocoa off my fingers.

Mom grabs her own cookie and daintily dips it into her cup. After she takes a bite, a smile crosses her face. "Wherever do you pick up these things, Callie girl?"

"Eh, thought it might taste good, so I tried it just now. Turns out, I was right." We burst into giggles and continue to chat, eating more cookies and sipping our drinks.

CHAPTER 2

Deck the Halls

As soon as we're done with our cocoa, we both get up and move to where we've unpacked the boxes. The first thing we do every year is give everything—decorations and shelves especially—a good dusting before we start decorating. Even though we follow the same routine when we put all the stuff back every year, a year in a box would cause anything to get gross.

Mom chatters away while I use her duster and clean all the surfaces. My mom has always gone all out and decorated the entire house, so while I work in every room, I also secretly look for the key to the mysterious chest.

I've worked my way through the living room, kitchen, and several other rooms in the house, and am now slogging my way through my mom's craft room. This room has so many shelves it's taking me a long time to clean everything. My determination to finish this outweighs any discomfort I feel breaking a sweat. It gathers across my forehead and under my boobs the most, but I can feel it across my arms as well.

My mom hobbles her way to the bathroom and I'm frantically searching through all of her drawers looking for the key. As I hear her coming down the hallway talking the entire way, that's when I finally find it. I quickly snag the key and put it in my pocket for later, then close the drawer as quietly as I can right as my mom walks into the room.

"So, Callie, what do you say we take a break for some Thanksgiving leftover sandwiches?" She stands in the doorway with her hands on her hips. My cheeks flame, hoping she didn't see any of that. I feel guilty as hell.

"Sure, give me a minute to finish up in here and I'll be right there."

She smiles at me before turning around and heading toward the kitchen, I assume.

I quickly make sure everything looks normal after my search, and then finish dusting the last couple of shelves before following her to get some lunch. If she didn't see me snag the key, I don't want to give her any reason to suspect anything is amiss.

These sandwiches are another favorite of mine after Thanksgiving. My mom uses leftover rolls, layers of cream cheese, and cranberry sauce, along with leftover turkey, salad, and cheese, and we pick our own sides from whatever is left. She's almost finished making the sandwiches when I enter the kitchen.

I take in a deep breath as soon as I cross into the room. It smells like Thanksgiving all over again, as all the smells and flavors are brought together in our delicious sandwiches. "Mmmm, smells wonderful, Mom. Thank you so much for making lunch." My mom is the best cook I know. She's won many a contest for her cooking in Jackson, taking top place every time for her pies.

"You're welcome, sweetie. I figured it was the least I could do since you're cleaning my house today." She focuses on what she's doing as she talks. Considering she's got one of her giant knives out, slicing the sandwiches in half diagonally, I prefer her paying attention to her task. I'm the klutz of the family, *and* the most likely to slice my hand open accidentally.

"I don't know what you're talking about, dear. You're the perfect housekeeper," my dad speaks as he walks into the kitchen. We both startle when he speaks, neither of us having heard him come in.

"What, not working a full day today, Dad?" I ask sarcastically. He absolutely never misses Thanksgiving leftover sandwiches.

"And miss eating lunch with my girls?" He feigns offense before coming over and giving me a kiss on the top of my head. "Never. The house is looking wonderful, very holiday appropriate."

"Oh, Jerry, we haven't even started the decorating yet. Callie just finished getting everything cleaned and ready for the decorations to be put up. You've arrived just in time to help!" If only I could accurately capture the smirk on my mom's face and the look of terror on my dad's, I'd have the perfect Christmas meme.

"It's a shame I have to go back into the office after lunch then, and have to miss all the fun getting everything ready for Christmas," he smoothly says. As if we don't know he has just been twiddling his thumbs in his office all morning.

My dad is an electrician, he owns his own company, and while he gives his guys days off after the holidays, he could definitely take any calls from home and not have to go into the office. He does this so he doesn't get roped into helping us, just for us to complain he's doing it wrong.

"Whatever you say. Don't think you've got us fooled one bit, though. We'll make sure to eat all the good pie before you get home." I giggle as he gives me a mock angry face.

My phone chimes in Huxlee's special text tone. While my mom says goodbye to Dad, I pull it out to see what she's said.

HUXLEE

I hate Black Friday. My sister brought me tea. TEA!

ME

RUDE! I'll be back soon, don't worry!

HUXLEE

You're my favorite employee.

I roll my eyes as I tuck my phone back in my pocket. I'm her only employee. Except when I'm out of town and her sister pitches in. Usually when I get back, Huxlee is ready to fall at my feet and beg me to never leave her again. She actually did that. Once. And since I never let her live that down, she has made no mention other than the little texts now and then when her sister is in town.

Once Dad's gone, it's time to get down to business. Mom and I rinse the dishes off and put them in the dishwasher. Then we move into the living room where I put all the boxes to start organizing. The living room is always the room that gets the most decorations.

I start by grabbing the outdoor lawn ornaments—we went with the Santa and reindeer set this year, since we did the nativity last year. It takes me a little while, but I manage to wrestle the large things out of their boxes and drag them outside. Finding the extension cords and timers to plug everything into is another challenge. Usually my dad keeps things like that in the garage, so I make my way in there and start digging through everything.

I must be making more noise than I thought. On my fourth box of random cords, my mom calls out, "What are you doing in there, Callie?"

"Just looking for the extension cords and timers," I yell back.

"Oh, honey, those are up in one of the Christmas boxes. It must be one of the ones you left up in the attic."

After getting up from where I was digging through the latest box, I close it and put it back where it came from.

Climbing up the attic stairs again for trip number who knows how many for today, I decide I'm going to take a look in the mysterious chest while I'm up here and Mom is distracted.

I can hear her singing to the music playing downstairs. Another tradition of ours is to turn on a massive playlist of all the Pentatonix Christmas albums. I know I'm safe at least until the end of "Deck the Halls" which plays loudly from my Bluetooth speaker. Slowly making my way over to the chest, I pull the key out of my pocket, insert it into the lock, and with a slow turn, the chest softly clicks open.

The wooden top is heavier than I expected, and when I look in, I see dozens of journals. They are several rows deep, and appear to all be leather-bound, some older than others, possibly going back a few generations.

I assume these are some kind of family heirloom-type journals but, my mom's reaction to my asking about the chest has me suspicious there might be something in here she doesn't want me to see. Slowly, I run my hands across the spines, deciding which journal I want to grab.

All the journals are labeled on the spine with letters. I run my finger across a few of them. They must be initials for something since there doesn't appear to be any actual pattern I recognize to words. After the letters, there is what looks like a year. I dig down into the bottom row of the books and pull out what must be the oldest journal. On its spine it reads *MM 1740*. It's hard to see all the journals at the very bottom though, so I might be wrong. Clutching the journal in one hand, I close and lock the chest with the other.

Next to me, I notice another box labeled *Christmas* I hadn't seen before, and open the lid. Right on top of the box is the extension cords and timers I was looking for. I pull them out, close the box back up, and shove the journal into the back of my pants, pulling my shirt down to cover it before heading down the ladder.

Once I get downstairs, I peek in on my mom and she's sitting in a chair pulling ornaments out of a box and decorating as high up as she can reach on the bottom of the Christmas tree.

She glances up at me and I smile and hold up the cord and timer. "Found it in a box up there, I'm just going to use the bathroom real quick and then finish setting up outside."

"Okay, sweetie, no rush at all. I've made it into a game to see how high I can reach to place ornaments. See!" She stretches her arm up as high as it can go to hook the ornament on the branch above her.

"Nice, Mom! See you in a few."

I walk backward out of the room so she doesn't see the lump under my shirt. My purse is in my old room where I always stay when I come here. Quickly, I shove the leather-bound book deep into the front pocket of my purse. Thank God my purse is the size of Mary Poppins' bag.

I decide I probably should use the restroom just so my absence, and the sound of the toilet flushing, makes my story seem more plausible. Once I'm done, I grab the extension cord and timer and make my way outside. "I'll be back in a minute, just have to plug these guys in and get the timer set."

"Okay, see you in a few," she replies distractedly, as she's again trying to reach up as high as she can before doing a little happy dance in her chair. I smile at the ridiculous motion before walking out the door.

After finishing outside, I come in to see she has finished decorating the bottom of the tree and is currently teetering on her good foot to hang some garland.

"Hey, Mom, I can get that." I gently take the garland from her. The prickly texture tickles my palm as I reach up and drape it around the tree.

"I hate being so useless at this time of year. You shouldn't have to decorate the entire house by yourself. This stupid sprained ankle has completely ruined Christmas," she grumbles, getting progressively more emotional as she sits back in her chair.

Gently I say, "Hey, it's okay, you didn't know you were going to sprain your ankle. Besides, I love decorating for Christmas, and now I get to set up everything the way I've always imagined they should be."

She blows her nose and laughs. "Oh, really? And what exactly would you change?"

"Well, first of all, Rudolph doesn't deserve to be in the front of the outdoor display this year. He really should stop being so selfish and give someone else a turn. This year, it's Dancer's turn to lead the sleigh." We both burst into giggles, resulting in us snorting and then laughing so hard we're holding our sides and crying happy tears. The smell of the live tree surrounds us as we continue to decorate its branches before moving on to other decorations.

We spend the rest of the day talking and laughing while we set up the other Christmas decorations. Dad comes home about the time dinner is ready.

"Well, hello, ladies, I can most definitely tell a difference in the house now! But what's up with Rudolph?" he asks as he comes through the door. We burst into giggles again. Dad thinks he's hilarious, but really, he tells the same jokes every year, minus Rudolph. This is the first time I've unseated him from his place.

Once we're done with dinner, I head to my room, snag the journal out of my purse, and look at the cover. Someone spent a lot of money on these beautifully crafted journals. All the ones in the chest appeared to be of the same quality.

I carefully run my hand over the smooth cover before untying the leather strip holding the book closed. Bringing the book to my nose, I inhale the smell of the wonderful old pages and old, worn leather. That old book smell is one of my favorites. I can never get enough of it.

Gently, I open the journal, admiring the handwritten words on the pages. I slowly flip through and glance through the text. Someone wrote this journal a long time ago. The dates on the cover indicate this one was written in 1740.

Where did my mom get this and why doesn't she want me to know about it?

Inhaling the scent of the pages deeply one more time, I flip back to page one and start reading.

CHAPTER 3

Sleigh Ride

The handwriting is beautiful, very classic-looking. The short, slightly-hard-to-decipher words have a masculine feel to them.

I was forced into this world with nothing more than the clothes on my back and the leather journal in my hands. I suppose while I'm trapped here, I'll make use of my time.

I'm sitting on a large rock by a stream, possibly a river. It's wide, and the water flows like the river that runs by my house back home. There are trees all around me, short ones and tall ones, wide ones and thin ones, so many trees, so many smells. And the flowers, the flowers are the most beautiful I've ever seen. More beautiful than the flowers that grew in my benefactresses' garden. Though, I suppose you couldn't really consider it her garden, since she was rarely the one tending to it.

This appears to be some kind of written account of someone's life, or possibly just someone making shit up. But transported to this world? What? I wonder again how my parents came to own this. I continue reading while the author continues to detail his life in this new world. He explores the world and on his first night, he sleeps under the stars. On his journey, he's written so far that he has seen no structures or anything other than trees and flowers, and the occasional small creature skitters by. I picture the world in my head and imagine I'm taking the journey with him.

I'm torn from the story when I hear, "Goodnight, honey," from my mom as she moves down the hall. I look at the clock and realize I've been reading for several hours.

"'Night, Mom, love you." I stand and grab my pajamas to get changed and ready for bed. Once I'm done washing my face and brushing my teeth, I pick the book up, get comfortable in bed, and continue reading.

As the author continues to explore his world, he outlines the landscape surrounding him, and more creatures he sees. But one thing continues to be clear to me: there are no other people in this world, at least none he comes across. I continue to wonder if possibly this is someone's beginning of a fiction novel, one which they were writing their first draft by hand. But, the way it's written definitely makes me think this is the journal of someone with a very active imag-ination. Transported to new worlds? It has to be made up, right?

I look at the clock and see it's the middle of the night. Getting up, I decide I'd like a cup of tea, so I make my way to the kitchen. When I'm settled back into my bed with my warm tea, I continue reading while I slowly sip the drink.

My tea finished, I decide to hide the journal under my mattress and get some sleep. I have another couple of days here with my parents and I want to make sure I'm awake for whatever activities they may have planned for us.

The sun streaming in through my window wakes me up in the morning. I gently reach under the mattress to make sure the journal is still there. Although really, who would have come in here to take it in my sleep? My mom told me not to worry about it so, I'm sure she hasn't even wondered if I disobeyed her.

I get out of bed and make my way to the bathroom to get ready for my day. Deciding I should probably take a shower since I don't know what we're doing today, I stand under the spray and enjoy the warmth of the water pouring over my body.

"Sweetie, are you coming out soon?" my dad calls from the hallway.

"I'll be out in a sec, Dad," I yell back as I turn off the water and reach outside the curtain for my towel.

I love that my parents have changed very little in the time us kids have been out of the house. They've kept everything almost exactly the same, even down to the towel I have wrapped around myself. As I dry off and get ready for the day, I can't stop thinking about the journal and how I will count the minutes until I can get it back out and read more.

Once I've made my way into the kitchen, my mom says, "Good morning, sweetie, we were thinking we'd go to the holiday in the park event today, what do you think?"

"Of course! You know I love seeing all the vendors and eating the yummy food every year," I agree, genuinely looking forward to it.

Usually, I'm the only one in my age group as my parents' town is all getting older, but I love getting to see the people I rarely get to. I can also usually get some delicious hot chocolate and other warm, sweet delicacies.

I finish getting my shoes and socks on and we all load into my dad's truck to head to the town square. Downtown Jackson, Wyoming, is set up like those cute old towns, all on a square with a statue in the middle.

One thing I notice while we're looking for a parking spot is this year someone has brought in a horse and sleigh for people to ride. I have never ridden in a sleigh before, but I hope the long line is a good sign that I'm going to love it.

"Hey, I think I'm gonna go find out the wait time for the sleigh rides. I'll catch up with you guys later," I say.

"Okay, honey, we have our phones on us. Call us if you can't find us," my dad says and winks at me. Seeing several people I recognize from town, I wave and smile at them as I pass.

I stop and grab a hot chocolate before making my way to the line for the sleigh ride. My phone goes off with an incoming text message. Realizing it's a little childish to be so excited about riding on a sleigh, I glance around to see if there is anyone else out here on their own. I feel better when I see several other adults on their own. What I really notice, though, is the couple arguing right in front of me. I pull my phone out to see who texted me. It's the Besties Group Chat.

JEN

Anyone want to come decorate my house?

STACY

Not feeling the spirit? Maybe a nap?

ME

I think I may take a sleigh ride

HUXLEE

Is that what kids are calling it these days?

I'm staring down at my phone when I hear the woman in front of me speak in a high-pitched, shrill voice, "I told you I wanted to spend today with my friends! How could you drag me *here* instead?" She's yelling at him because he wants her to spend time with him when she wants to go spend time with her friends? I think all of us within earshot see the writing on the wall for this relationship.

I tuck my phone in my pocket and look off to their right, pretending not to listen in.

"Annette, calm down. You're making a scene. You know very well why I didn't want to go with you there. I'm not an idiot. I see the way you and John look at each other every time we're around your friends," he snaps.

"Masey, you know I don't have eyes for anyone but you," she responds in a sickeningly sweet voice. God, I even want to ditch this bitch and I've only been in their proximity for five minutes.

He rolls his eyes. "Annette, stop. Everyone here doesn't need to be privy to our relationship issues."

"What? You're blaming *me* for this?" she speaks even louder than she was before. "How dare you! I can't believe I've even wasted any of my time with you. We've never even fucked. John is sooo much better!" After she says this, she stomps her foot like a toddler and marches off.

But in true narcissist fashion, she turns back around. "Aren't you coming, Masey?"

"No, I want to spend time here at this holiday event. You enjoy your time with your *friends*. Tomorrow we need to talk when we've both had some time to cool down."

She stomps back over to him and hisses loudly enough for us to hear in his ear, "Just know I won't be screaming your name tonight when I'm with John. He really knows how to hit *all the right spots*." This woman is trying too hard to convince him this John is the better guy. But then again, the scorned ex always has to have the last laugh, right? Because I'm sure she's already planning how she's going to blame him for all of this. That's what narcissists do, right? It's sad that this is the most exciting thing I've been a part of in as long as I can remember. And I'm just a spectator to the demise of their relationship. Even my own boyfriends, who have mostly been boring, have all parted ways on amicable terms.

My parents instilled in us that you date to get married. No guy I've ever dated has fit the bill of someone I could even stand to be around for more than a couple of dates. It has made for a lot of time between guys, even a reputation of being a stuck-up prude in college. Is it so bad that I knew I wanted to be able to have a damn conversation for more than five minutes with the person I plan to spend the rest of my life with?

He grasps her biceps and pulls her into him, whispering something in her ear. Annette's face transforms as she tries to pull away from him. Finally, he releases her and her face morphs into anger.

The silence is palpable as we all watch her storm off muttering expletives the entire way. Masey takes a deep breath and looks around to see who witnessed their spectacular drama. I think the fact we are all looking everywhere but at him clues him in to the fact we all heard.

He faces the front of the line, a new stiffness in his broad shoulders. The sleigh pulls up, and he's next up.

"All aboard," the driver says as a couple gets down from the sleigh. But when Masey gets up into the sleigh, the driver turns to me. "Ma'am, are you going to join him?"

"What? Oh, no, we're not together," I explain, cheeks heating in embarrassment. I want to crawl into a hole and die there.

"It's the rule, ma'am, two at a time, unless you're riding with someone else. You and this gentleman here are about to go on one amazing sleigh ride." The driver looks like what I would imagine Santa Claus to look like, big belly, red cheeks, and white hair and beard, to boot.

I look up at Masey to see if he's okay with me tagging along on his ride. If I were him, I'd probably just want a few minutes of silence away from the whiny woman who just stormed out.

"I'm okay with it if you are," he says, looking up at me from his seated position. I throw away my empty hot chocolate cup before turning back to the sleigh.

"What the hell?" I shrug.

As I climb into the sleigh, he reaches out to help me in, and I feel a jolt as our hands touch. He looks at me at the same time I look at him, hands still clasped. Yeah. We both just felt that. They've provided us with a blanket to share and he lets go of my hand and lifts the other side of it so I can climb in next to him under its warmth. I smile at him as I sit down, and he reaches across me to tuck the blanket around my legs.

"Thank you," I say. I'm not even sure what we'll possibly have to talk about since we've never even met.

He holds his hand out to me. "Hi, I'm Mason, and though I have no doubts everyone within earshot heard that spectacular display my girlfriend just put on, I'd really rather we pretend you didn't just hear that."

Laughing, I reply, "I'm Callie, and I'm not sure what display you're talking about. I didn't see a display." Then I wink at him and shake his hand, and of course, there goes that jolt again.

The sleigh moves while we're still shaking hands and we both quickly let go and settle in for the ride. While we move along, the snow starts to fall, and I tilt my face to the sky, enjoying the beauty of the falling snowflakes, the feel of the cold flakes melting on my face. I stick my tongue out to catch some on my tongue. This is one of my favorite things to do when it snows.

Finally, I face forward and watch downtown Jackson go by slowly. Now we sit in what I feel is an incredibly awkward silence. We listen to the sleigh bells as the horses move throughout town, pulling us behind them.

We jump when we hear, "so where are you folks from?" from the driver.

I clear my throat before responding, "I'm from here originally, but moved to Laramie for college and got a job close to UW after graduating. I'm back here visiting my parents for Thanksgiving." I glance at Mason, and he's staring at me with a smile on his face. "What?"

His smile drops before he turns to face the driver and answers, "I live just north of here in Beaver Creek."

"Oh! I love the trails up there. It's a beautiful area," I say.

We settle back into a comfortable silence. I'm enjoying the sleigh ride, glad I didn't have to go around the square on my own. The town goes by, and I watch all the Christmas decorations they have displayed for us to enjoy on this wonderful, snowy day. My cheeks grow icy cold and they're probably red in the winter chill.

I'm startled when I feel Mason take my hand under the blanket. He doesn't say anything, just holds it and continues to look around at the decorations. His hand is warm and comforting, but I pull mine away from him.

"Everything okay?" he asks, turning to me.

"I am not the type of woman to hold the hand of someone already in a relationship."

"I'm sorry to have made you uncomfortable. It just felt right."

"And your girlfriend?"

"That won't be a problem for much longer. I really should have broken it off as soon as I found out about her and John."

That might be the case, but I'm not willing to fall for some "I'm leaving her, I swear" line.

Too soon, we're back to where we started, and Mason is helping me down from the sleigh.

"It was nice to meet you, Callie. Maybe I'll see you around?" His brown eyes bore into mine, and I can't tear my gaze away.

"Are you sure your girlfriend would be okay with that?" I respond, finally glancing away from him. Because really, the guy has a girlfriend. And I am not a homewrecker, or relationship stealer, whatever you want to call it.

"I hope to see you again sometime. This may be weird to say, but I feel it's something you should know: It's important to remember looks can be deceiving."

His last words made a shiver run down my spine. Briefly, I wonder who this Mason is, and what kind of supernatural shit was that?

"If it's meant to be, it will happen," I say, then I see my parents standing off to the side. I wave goodbye to Mason as I walk toward my parents.

"Who was that, sweetie?" my mom asks. She's weaving her head back and forth, trying to get a look at Mason over my shoulder.

"Apparently, the sleigh rides were two people at a time only. That was Mason, my extra person."

"Oh, honey, one of us could have gone with you if you'd have told us," Dad adds.

"I didn't want to take you guys away from your shopping time together." I wink at my mom, who bites her lip to hold back a laugh. We both know my dad would rather be at home watching some football game than out here shopping.

We stay and do a little more shopping together, and I grab a coffee, then we head back to the house for some dinner. As soon as I can, I slip back into my room to read more of the journal, pulling it out from under the mattress.

This time, I got ready for bed and brought my tea in here *before* I got settled on the bed. My slippers are still on my feet. Before I open the book up, I grab my phone from the nightstand to update the girls.

ME

Sleigh ride was fun. Rode with a hot stranger right after his very public fight with his girlfriend.

JEN

Did you get his number?

STACY

He has a girlfriend but rode with you?

ME

She stormed off. Ride was two at a time.

STACY

Awkward.

HUXLEE

Describe Hottie McStranger.

ME

Mason. His name is Mason.

JEN
Did we go to school with a Mason?

ME
He said he lives in Beaver Creek.

HUXLEE
Have his name and town but no number...
typical.

ME
He currently has a girlfriend! Headed to bed.
hugs

I set my phone on the nightstand and open the journal up to where I placed my bookmark last night and start reading the next entry.

Now for my story:

My father died before I was born, then when I was born, my mother threw herself into raising me and making sure I got a good education. She had the help of a benefactress, who helped her to watch me and make sure I did not get injured growing up and going through all the clumsy stages.

Benefactress? That's the second time the author has mentioned one. What kind of fancy people lunacy was this? Maybe it *is* actually a storybook? I remember reading through fairytales when I was a kid. Maybe my mom has some weird hand-written first edition copies? But everything is worded like a first-hand account of someone's life, someone's present life and now their past. I continue reading.

There was one concern my mother had about this

benefactress. She didn't have the best reputation. She was known to give terrible gifts to the people who made her mad. So my mother did the best she could to keep the woman happy, leaving me in her care more than my mother wanted to. I was the last remaining piece of my father that she had. She didn't want to give me up. But the woman insisted, and my mother did not want her doing something that my mother would come to regret.

It was around this time that a suitor decided he would marry my mother. He had heard of my father's passing and decided he was going to do everything in his power to marry her and gain access to my father's fortune. My mother had to leave me in the benefactress's care in order to spend some time with the suitor. She refused to let him meet me before she had decided he was an option for her to marry.

However, it took longer than she thought it would. I would find out later that he had locked her in his home, and I was left with the benefactress, who requested I call her by her name, Remilia, longer than my mother had intended.

My mother was forced to continue to spend time with the man, trying to figure out a way to get away from him. She wanted to make sure he would never return, and make sure he knew that there was no way she would marry him. She finally made a deal with this man and was on her way home when she got word that the suitor was on his way to Remilia's home in order to kidnap me and force her to marry him. This meant he was immediately breaking the deal my mother had worked so hard to attain.

She was forced to go back, and she stayed with the suitor to ensure I was safe from his clutches. For fifteen years she stayed, never bringing me to her to make sure that I, her first-born and only son of her true love, remained safe. She knew as long as the benefactress was happy with me, I would be safe as well.

The story captivates me and as I continue to read. I am further drawn into the story.

While my mother was fighting with her new husband, Remilia was educating me in all the ways of being a man. How to behave properly, the arts, and she brought in men to train me in swordplay and other noble activities.

But one day, she left on a trip. She never told me where she was going, but she left me for a couple of years in the care of the servants.

When she returned, I was now eighteen, and she began to act strangely toward me. This woman, who I had considered as a mother figure for most *of my life, was now being odd. I later learned that she was desperate to marry me and gain access to my family's fortune. But I apologize I'm getting ahead of myself.*

What the actual fuck? This is some crazy story. I can't believe what I'm reading. Benefactresses, attempted kidnappings, and now creepy advances from mother figures. Whoever made up this story had some twisted shit floating around in their head, or their life was just really fucked up. On the other hand, I've also read some twisted stuff in my twenty-four years.

Later, she told me she had every intention of becoming my wife. This woman had somehow twisted my behavior towards her in her head to believe I was in love with her. I was shocked by her proposal when she finally told me that I needed to marry her immediately.

Over the course of my time with the benefactress, she had told me many times I could not have an answer for this or that because my mother needed to make that decision. But no matter how many times I asked, she never allowed me to go to her. This time was no different. No matter how many times I insisted I needed to speak to my mother about this, Remilia would remind me that my mother was currently with her new family and that her job was to keep me safe. She also reminded me that sending me off to my evil step-father would not be keeping me safe.

But one day, she suddenly insisted that I speak with my mother, that I get approval to marry her immediately. It was later that day that we received a letter from my mother. She insisted I come to her. She needed me to protect her against my step-father, who she had been with for many years. He was trying to gain access to our family fortune, which, now that I was eighteen, belonged to me.

Remilia was terrified of me going into a potentially dangerous situation, but also wanted very much for me to get my mother's approval in our match. I wanted nothing more than to be rid of the benefactress and her daily proposals. So I packed my things, and Remilia arranged for me to go to my step-father's home, with her by my side.

Yawning, I put my bookmark in the book and tuck it back under the mattress. I reflect on my day and how comfortable I was in Mason's presence. I fall asleep with a smile on my face and hope in my heart that I bump into him somewhere else. Hopefully, after he's had a chance to break things off with his girlfriend.

Who am I kidding? I'll probably never see him again, I think, before drifting off to sleep.

CHAPTER 4

Over the River

The first thing I notice when I start to awake is the cold. I'm shivering and lying in what feels like ice. Underneath me, the mattress is exceptionally hard. It's when I open my eyes I realize this must be a dream. I'm looking up and all I can see is the sky and tree branches above me, and there is most definitely not a mattress underneath me.

While sitting up, my hand sinks into the cold snow beneath me. I look around and see a large rock and hear moving water in the distance. It comes as no surprise to me my imagination has conjured up a location similar to what I was reading in the journal. There aren't any beautiful flowers or smells, it appears to be winter here now; the ground is covered in snow. Inhaling deeply, my throat feels the effects of the freezing air, which smells like winter. I wonder how my mind transformed the world from the journal into this winter wonderland? Even without the flowers, I can see the beauty of this place. Trees stretch overhead, reaching toward the sky, their branches free of leaves.

Gingerly, I get to my feet and spin in a circle, the ground squishing beneath my slippers as I turn. Using my hands to dust off my butt, I feel my pajamas are slightly damp from lying in the snow for who knows how long. I reach up and feel my long blonde hair, slightly damp from laying in the snow.

It appears to be morning in my dream. I see the sun rising in what must be the east. Which direction should I go in this dream world? I decide to head over to what must be the large rock the writer sat atop while writing the first part of the journal. It's covered in snow and it takes some effort to get up it, my fingers aching as I claw my way up, but eventually, I can stand on it and look around.

All I see are trees, most without their leaves. In the distance, I see trees that are still green. They remind me of the Christmas tree I just helped to decorate at my parents' house.

Getting down is tricky as well, as I try not to slip on the wet surface. The snow on the rock and the smooth soles of my slippers don't help give me any grip to keep from falling. Eventually, I'm able to make it down and decide to walk along the river. *Maybe I'll come to a town or something else interesting.*

I've covered some distance when I notice how dry my throat is. I desperately need a drink. The stream is the only source of water I've seen besides the snow. Remembering reading somewhere you shouldn't try to eat or drink snow directly, I decide the river is probably my best bet. Thankfully, my pajamas have dried in the time I've been walking, so at least I can dry my hands off afterward, maybe warm them in my armpits. I'm not sure what the cold temperature will do to my hands, but I don't see another source of water nearby either.

Thankfully, I fell asleep with my slippers on, otherwise my feet would probably have frostbite by now. Who am I kidding? This is a dream. In the dream world, anything can happen, right? But I couldn't have dreamed up any better clothes than what I went to bed in?

I use my foot to clear the snow away from a spot close to the river. I don't want to end up with my knees freezing and more wet than they will be sinking down onto the slightly muddy ground to drink.

I take a minute to gather my long hair and pull it around my shoulder. Carefully, I bend down, using my hands to scoop up water and try to keep as much in my hands as possible when I bring them to my mouth. The water is freezing, as I expected with the melting snow. But it glides down my throat and quenches my thirst. I repeat the process a few more times before feeling sated and ready to continue my walk.

When I go to stand, I hear a branch snap nearby. Quickly, I stand up and look around, trying to find the reason for the noise. I'm almost back to where I started in my rotation when I spot it. There is a set of angry-looking eyes on a very large gray wolf.

I take a sharp breath, my lungs protesting against the cold air. The wolf comes closer to me, slowly stalking me, its prey. My heart feels like it's pounding out of my chest.

Slowly, I back away, keeping my eye on the wolf as I carefully make my way, following the river in the direction I was heading. I do my best to keep my breaths calm and steady. When the wolf snaps its jaws, licks his lips, and gets close enough to where I can hear a low growl emanating from him, I take off at a run.

Running in my slippers is difficult and I stumble a few times because of their bulk. Thankfully, they stay on my feet. The adrenaline from my fright and now my run have warmed me substantially.

I haven't gone far when I see a small cottage off in the distance. My arms pump and my feet pound the ground. I run faster than I ever have to make it to the house. Praying that someone is there to let me in, I slam into the door and start pounding and yelling, "Help! Someone, please! There's a wolf out here! Please help me!"

The wolf is getting closer. I can hear his growling getting louder, closer. Reaching for the doorknob, I realize I should have tried to open the door before alerting all the predators in the forest. My hand clasps around the cold knob, I quickly turn it, and the door opens. I run inside and slam the door closed behind me, locking it. I hear the wolf gnashing his teeth and growling outside.

Taking deep breaths, I turn and examine my surroundings. It's a small, two-room cottage. I see the area where the meals are prepared, a small table, probably for a couple or a very small family, and a sitting area. Across from me is what I assume must be the bedroom. The door is closed.

"Hello? Who's there?" An elderly female voice coming from what I believe to be the bedroom calls. "Amber, is that you?"

Slowly, I creep to the door and press my ear to the wood, trying to listen for anyone else on the other side. My heart is beating out of my chest. Scratching at the front door and a howl make me turn my head to look back.

"Amber, honey, have you finally come? I've been waiting ages for you," the elderly voice says.

I gently grasp the doorknob and turn it as I reply, "I'm so sorry to intrude. My name is Callie."

The elderly woman stares at me from her bed when I enter the room. "You're not my Amber. What are you doing in my house?" She's frightened, and rightfully so. I'm a stranger and I've just blasted my way into her home.

"My name is Call—"

"You already said that," she states. "Now tell me what you're doing in my house?" One, two, three breaths I take before I answer her. I can imagine how startled I would be if some stranger just barged into my house while I was sleeping soundly in my bed. I would be terrified.

"I'm not sure." Another howl from the wolf and I can visibly see her shudder in her bed. "I woke up in the middle of the woods. I was walking along a stream, or is it a river? I can never remember what makes it one or the other." I'm nervous, rambling. Clearing my throat, I continue slower, "A wolf started chasing me. I saw your house and ran as fast as I could to outrun the wolf. I'm so sorry to have disturbed you. I'll get out of here as soon as the wolf is gone."

"The wolf is never far away," she states ominously and turns back over, pulling her blankets over her head. I turn and go back into the other room.

I draw back the curtain and peer through the window. From here, I can see the wolf still stands at the door. He turns toward me and I quickly drop the curtain, backing away.

I hope she doesn't mind but, I don't want to go anywhere until the wolf leaves. There is a large bookcase in one corner, so I pick a book at random and take a seat on the couch. I hope the woman from the bed won't mind me reading one of her books. Engrossed in the story, I don't notice the scratching at the door and the howling has stopped.

Sometime later, I hear the woman in the other room get out of bed and go to what must be the bathroom. A few minutes after that, she slowly opens the door, looking around the small cottage. I remain seated, not wanting to startle her more than I did when I burst my way into her cottage.

"I didn't dream you up," she says before coming the rest of the way into the room. She moves over to the kitchen area and pulls out different food items, dishes, and the makings for tea. "Would you care for a drink?"

"Yes please," I stand and return the book I borrowed to the shelf. "I hope you don't mind that I borrowed one of your books."

"No, dear, help yourself."

As I sit at the table in front of the place she has set for me, she gives me a small smile.

"Why don't you tell me about yourself, dear?" Her tone has shifted dramatically from the snappy way she spoke earlier. I finally get a good look at her. She's shorter than me, overweight in that wonderful huggable grandmotherly way, and her curly gray hair is tucked behind her ears, round glasses perched low on her nose.

"I am so sorry I intruded into your home. I didn't know where else to run."

"Where are you from, dear?" she inquires as she pours my tea.

"Wyoming." Her eyes, which had been focused on pouring the tea, quickly rise to mine.

"W-w-wy-oming?" she stutters.

"Yes, ma'am, born and raised." In my mind, I'm trying to make sense of her odd behavior. Really, in this dream world, in my head, I know the names of the states. Especially the one I grew up in. And I wonder why this woman in my dreams doesn't know them as well.

"You need to go," she says, a panicked tone edging into her voice. "*Now!*"

Quickly I stand, looking around the room, frightened she is going to come at me with one of the knives on the counter nearby.

"I'm sorry I intruded." I slowly back my way toward the door, keeping my eye on her. This woman went from nice grandma to serial killer creepy really quickly.

Both of us jerk our heads toward the door at the sound of sleigh bells.

"Merde," she breaths.

CHAPTER 5

You're a Mean One, Mr. Beast

Without warning, the door is kicked in and two men walk in, swords drawn. One is tall, thin, and his arms are covered in some kind of raised designs. The other is short, fat, and balding. When he smiles, he is missing teeth. Since this is such a small cottage, there are no places to hide. They gave us no warning before busting into the house. It's not like I could say "Excuse me, sir, can you please look the other way while I hide?"

The tall man glares at the elderly woman, who looks as frightened as I feel. "Please, sir, I have done nothing wrong. This woman just burst into my house a few hours ago. I didn't know where she came from until seconds before you arrived." Her voice is frantic.

He crosses the room to her.

"Please no, don't do this, I swear I didn't know," she pleads. He takes her arm, just above the elbow, forcing her to stand.

Rising from my chair I say, "It's not her fault, she's telling the truth. I just arrived. Don't punish her for my presence."

The fat man comes to my side, grabbing my arm and jerking me toward the open door as he says, "You can save your honeyed words for the king, for it is him who determines who's lying and who's telling the truth."

They force both of us into the back of the sleigh they arrived on. The depth of the snow doesn't allow for passage of much else. They leave our feet free but bind our wrists, thankfully, leaving our heads uncovered.

Hours later, we're still bumping along in the sleigh. The men who captured us talk amongst themselves. I've been trying to get the elderly woman to talk. She's clearly mad at me, avoiding my glance the best she can. I keep my voice low, not wanting the men to hear our conversation.

"I'm sorry, I don't know why they're after me." I don't know how I can convince her. This may be my dream, but I'm terrified of what may come next.

Before this, I've had some really vivid dreams, but I don't recall ever feeling the bumps of traveling along a snow-covered path, the pain of a rope digging into my wrists, or the biting cold of a snowy day.

"Thank fuck that wolf alerted us to her presence. I knew giving him our scraps would pay off some day," the tall one states.

"You really think this broad is the one? She looks smaller than I imagined," his buddy replies. "Course, since a wolf gave us her description, I guess everything would be giant to him." He snickers.

The first one sees me watching them and says, "Hush, Ralph, the cargo has ears." He gestures to me and the old woman, who is still watching the scenery pass by. If I wasn't so scared, I'd be paying more attention to how beautiful the surrounding land-scape is, all covered in snow.

The old woman and I have been looking around us as we've been traveling. But as soon as the mountain comes into focus, it's all I can look at. The closer we get, the bigger it grows, until the sleigh stops at its base.

Both men come around the side of the sleigh and the woman struggles with her captor. I don't see the point, as both men are larger than me. They're going to wrestle us where they want us to go, regardless of what I want.

When the old woman looks at me, shocked at my acquiescence, I gently shake my head. Her eyes grow wide, then appear indignant before she seems to accept our fate.

"Really, Ralph, what do you think the king is going to do with her?"

"That's really none of our business, now is it, Joe?" He glances at me before cackling and saying, "We're just the muscle."

We're both dragged toward the base of the mountain. I don't see an entrance, and each of us has a thug grabbing our upper arms tighter than necessary. The old woman will not stop arguing with the men as they walk us up to the stone base. One of them reaches out and presses his hand on the rock, the surface slightly sinking in at his touch. A moment later, a door pops open and they force us through it, torches along the walls light our way.

"Just wait until they meet the king." The tall one chuckles. It really should be illegal to be a bad guy with a sinister chuckle. How more cliché can you be? We continue to make our way down the dimly lit hallway.

Finally, we stop in front of a short man with white hair and spectacles. He reminds me of the Cogsworth character in Disney's cartoon *Beauty and the Beast* I watched growing up. "Please state your name and purpose." He patiently waits, looking at our captors, waiting for them to give a response as to why they have come here with two women bound at the wrists.

"We've come back with the woman the wolf told the king about, the one he demanded we find and bring back immediately," the fat one responds, pushing me toward the man.

"And how do you intend to prove she is the one the wolf told us about?" Cogsworth asks. "Seems to me you could have just brought anyone and claim she's the one to collect the reward." They're offering a reward for me? I just got here. This dream just keeps getting weirder and weirder.

The tall one coughs twice before answering, "That's why we've got the old woman. Everyone knows the wolf is always hanging around the old woman's house." Apparently, I'm just the unlucky fool who ended up in the wrong place at the wrong time. If the wolf is always near the cottage, I guess it was inevitable that I would meet him moving in that direction in my travels along the stream.

"I see... Just wait here while I confirm with His Majesty where he would like you to deposit... our new visitors."

Neither me nor the old woman say anything during this exchange. My nostrils flare with anger, but I have a feeling I need to hold my tongue until we're able to meet with this supposed king.

He leaves the four of us in the hallway before returning sometime later with additional men. After handing our captors a single leather pouch that jingles when it exchanges hands, he sends away the two men who brought us.

They immediately untie our hands when the thugs' backs are turned. "I truly am sorry for how you were treated, miss. Unfortunately, not everyone who answers to the king has manners," he says. My wrists now free of the rough rope, I rub them to bring feeling back to the area.

Eventually, they take me to a room that is way more heavily ornamented than the dungeon I expected. It's ornately furnished, and has a washstand, I think it's called, so I take the opportunity to clean the dirt and other debris off my face and hands. I didn't get the chance to do so at the cottage.

It feels like hours have passed, but has probably been less than an hour, when a man comes to my room. He is nicely dressed, but not in what I would expect a king to wear. "I'm surprised they have stooped to sending spies into our land." Spy? They? Who is *they*? What the hell kind of crazy kingdom have I dreamed up? God, I hope they don't decide to go all "off with her head" on me. "But really, I'm more surprised that I didn't think of them doing this sooner. I really am very proud our network of spies is so loyal to *our* king.

"And really? Sending someone as inconspicuous as you is what I would expect." The strange man continues to drone on for who knows how long. I'm so far in my head trying to figure a way out of this that I've tuned him out. I tune back in when he asks, "Well, what do you have to say for yourself?"

Pausing, I consider my options. If I immediately deny I'm a spy, they won't believe me. If I don't answer at all, they will probably *also* not believe me. In the meantime, he's staring at me with his arms crossed and tapping his foot impatiently.

"Are you in the habit of giving your prisoners their own bedchambers? Should I expect a maid to come in and help me dress?" I ask instead of anything smart I should have answered. And really, who brings a prisoner to a room that looks like this?

He surprises me when he chokes back a laugh. I can tell he was going to laugh because he makes an odd snorting sound and his eyes are crinkled at the corners in mirth. Also, he's biting both lips to hold it in. "Spy indeed," he says as he turns to leave the room.

"Excuse me," I start, and he turns back around to face me. "What did you do with the older woman I was brought here with?"

His answering smile sets me slightly at ease. "Why, sent her back home, of course." He pulls the door shut behind him when he exits.

I'm left wondering how long I'm to be left in this room, when minutes later, a woman enters carrying one of the most beautiful gowns I've ever seen. The dress is yellow, with gold threads throughout, which accent the flowers embroidered on the surface. "Hello, miss, I'm here to help you get changed to meet His Highness." Her eyes are downcast the entire time she speaks. Is she terrified of me?

Taking a step closer to her, I dip down to catch her eyes and smile. "Hi, my name is Callie. What's yours?"

She moves to the wardrobe, opens one of the doors, and carefully hangs the dress from the top, leaving the door open before crossing the room to me. "If you could, please hold your arms up," she says, demonstrating by moving her arms above her head.

"Why do I need to change clothes?"

She slowly appraises my pajamas and I feel my cheeks flush. "Your clothes aren't proper attire," she says slowly, quietly.

I decide to humor her and do what she asks. She carefully pulls my pajama top over my head, and I am immediately grateful I fell asleep with my bra on. Even in this dream world, I'd hate for my breasts to be bouncing around in front of this stranger.

She drops my top on the floor at her feet before placing her hands on the waistband of my pants. She looks up at me, a questioning look on her face. It takes me a second to understand what she's asking me with her gaze. I nod and she carefully helps me out of my pants. "What are these?" she fingers my bra strap, then the waistband of my panties.

"My bra and panties?"

"Bra and panties," she repeats slowly. "Yes... Where did you get these? I've seen nothing like this. Is it some kind of corset?" Confused, I just nod my head.

She moves over to the wardrobe, opens the door that isn't holding the dress up, and digs through before coming back to me with things I recognize only from movies. She pokes and prods me into position as she gets me situated with the old-fashioned undergarments.

Then she walks back to the wardrobe, fingers the fabric of the dress, and carefully takes it down, brings it over to me and adds, "Up," with a jerk of her chin, indicating my arms.

Immediately, I lift both arms, carefully bending forward to help her get the dress over my head. She is considerably shorter than I am and my height with my arms in the air makes the motion difficult for her. I have to awkwardly bend forward to get my upper body through the dress.

It becomes difficult to breathe as she laces up the stays in the back of the dress. Then she helps me into some very uncomfortable shoes. When she's finished, she has me sit in a chair near the vanity and starts messing with my hair.

"What are you doing?" I ask.

"Why, getting you ready for dinner with His Highness, ma'am," she gives me a funny questioning look. "You have such beautiful blonde hair," she replies as she brushes through it.

"Thank you." I smile at her in the mirror's reflection. "What's he like?" As long as I'm here in this strange dream world, I might as well get some details for what to expect.

"The king?"

"No, the doorman," I quip. She hasn't said more than a few words to me since I've been here and it's grating on my nerves to be left to my own thoughts for so long in this strange place. When she finishes with my hair, she applies makeup to my face.

"Whatever happens, do whatever he says. It will not go well for you if you disobey the king's orders." She finishes my makeup and puts the things away. She quickly moves toward the door, opens it, and starts to leave.

"Wait! I never got your name." It seems trivial now, but I just want to know this small woman's name.

"Someone will be up to get you shortly. Don't wrinkle your dress." She closes the door behind her.

I stand and run my hands carefully over the dress. Looking at myself in the mirror, I think I look beautiful in these old-fashioned clothes. What confuses me is why I would dream up such clothes. Swooshing the skirt back and forth, I'm startled when someone else opens the door and peeks their head into the room.

"Are you ready, miss?" he asks.

Nodding my head, I make my way over to the door. I turn back to look around so I can remember every part of the beautiful room I got ready for dinner in. He closes the door behind me before holding his arm out for me to hold on to his elbow as we make our way through the strange palace in the mountain.

Magnificent. That's the only word I can think of to describe the ornate furnishings in the rest of the palace. As we walk, I look around at the beautiful carvings, paintings, furniture, and everything surrounding me. As all good things must come to an end, we eventually stop at a set of double doors.

He removes my hand from the crook of his arm before opening one of the doors. Inside, I see we've arrived at the dining room. The table is set for only two and my stomach does a somersault when I remember I am supposed to be having dinner with the king I was warned about a short time ago.

The man turns to me. "His Majesty will be here shortly. Please take a seat." He pulls out a chair and motions for me to sit. It feels odd to have someone push in my chair for me, but he does and then leaves the room, closing the door behind him.

Subconsciously, I bite my fingernails, nervously waiting for the king to get here. When the door slams open, I jump in my seat. Immediately trying to stand and turn around, instead I trip over my long skirt and start to fall. The newcomer steps forward and catches me around the waist from behind before I'm able to hit the ground.

Warmth. Warmth is what I feel while the arm remains around me. The warmth makes me squirm, uncomfortable that the arm is still there. I feel warm breath on the back of my neck, and *did whoever this is just smell me?*

"Excuse me," I say, getting my feet under me and straightening into a standing position. My back directly presses into this person's front, and I feel the same warmth on my back now surrounding me. The arm grips my waist tighter before releasing me.

Slowly, I turn around and look up, up, up to his face, which is half covered in scars. They cover his cheek and wrap around his eye and up to his forehead. There is also a scar on his forehead that looks like he was cut with a blade at some time.

While he's not wearing a crown, his presence oozes power and strength. His hair is long and reminds me of images I've seen of Vikings. When he smiles down at me, the dimples that appear make the butterflies in my stomach go crazy. He motions to my chair and again I sit and he pushes me back in.

Dinner is quiet and awkward. I stare down at my plate to avoid saying something stupid, to avoid staring at his scars. From the corner of my eye, I see he does the same thing, but he has a scowl on his face. I'm not sure what I could have done in the short time I've been in this dream world to make him so angry. Maybe it's not me, maybe it's the pressure of running this country? This world? I don't want to ask how large his domain is. I don't dare ask how he got his scars.

When we've finished our dinner, he stands and storms out of the dining hall.

"Well, hello to you, too, Mr. Beast," I mutter, inhaling the deepest breath I can with this damn corset and letting it out slowly. Well, that was both the quietest and most uncomfortable dinner I've ever had in my life.

Standing, I decide to attempt making my way back to the room I was in before dinner. When I get to the door, the same man who brought me down here opens it and extends his arm to me in the same way as earlier. I smile at him and take his proffered arm, walking with him back to my room.

The same woman from earlier comes in but this time, she doesn't speak, only motions with her eyes and body to get me back into my pajamas, which have been washed and dried in the time we've been at dinner. After she leaves, I climb into the large bed and fall blissfully asleep.

PART TWO

Week After Thanksgiving

CHAPTER 6

Santa Tell Me

I open my eyes to my room, the room at my parents' house I fell asleep in what feels like ages ago. Underneath me, I feel the comfortable mattress of a well-used bed. Touching my pajamas and pulling them out from me, I look down and they appear how they did when I went to sleep.

Standing, I'm not sure what to do with myself. The sun is just coming through the window. The curtains have separated a little and I open them more, tying them back so I can sit on the bed and watch the sunrise. My parents rarely wake quite this early, so I stay quiet and watch the sun come over the horizon before standing and getting ready for the day.

By the time I'm in the kitchen starting the coffee, my mom comes out and says, "Good morning, Callie. How did you sleep?" Her hair is tousled from sleep, and she wears her pajamas and fuzzy slippers.

"You ask the same thing every time I'm here." I smile at the cabinet in front of me. Moving to sit at the table, I decide to wait for the pot to completely finish brewing before getting my coffee.

"That's because I know how it can be sleeping in a strange bed..." She trails off in thought. "Don't mind me. What's on the schedule for today?" she asks as she pours herself a cup of coffee and prepares it just the way she likes it.

"I was thinking about going back into town and spending more time looking through the booths at Holiday in the Park since I didn't get to do much shopping yesterday." Usually, the vendors are only here for a couple of days. Today is the last day, so I need to get an early start before they pack up early this afternoon.

"That sounds like fun. Do you mind going by yourself? I think your father wanted to do something together today." My parents are so cute. They've been married forever but still enjoy their time together. They even have date night once a week. When we were kids, they would hire a sitter every Friday night. As soon as Jake was old enough, he was forced to stay with me and Andy when they left. My parents weren't crazy enough to leave us completely unattended. The neighbor would also watch us out of her window and report any shenanigans to my parents the next morning.

"Of course, Mom, you two kids have fun today."

My dad walks in, wraps his arms around my mom from behind, and kisses her on the temple.

"Who you calling kids?" he asks with a big smile on his face. His arm still wrapped around my mom, he continues to smile down at her.

"Oh, you know, just my sickeningly in love parents."

"Will you be okay today on your own, kiddo?" Even though I'm twenty-four, my dad will probably always call me kiddo. He usually adds something like "Just because you're grown up doesn't mean you're not still my kid."

"Of course, Dad, you guys have fun today. I'll see you for dinner?"

"We'll pick something up on the way home," Mom says.

I stand and move to the coffeepot that has now finished brewing. My favorite cup to use when I'm here is an oversized flowered mug. I finish making my coffee and sit at the table enjoying talking with my parents before getting up and grabbing my stuff for the day, including the journal, which I shove into the bottom of my purse.

Walking around looking at all the booths in town for Holiday in the Park, I'm browsing through some pretty scarves when I see Mason out of the corner of my eye. He's perusing the booth next to me, which has homemade knives and other metalwork. I select one that reminds me of the dream world with different colored flowers all over it, and pay the woman behind the table, thanking her for the beautiful scarf and decide to head to get some coffee.

As I walk away, I remember my strange dream and pull out my phone to send off a text to Huxlee.

ME

Had the weirdest dream. Will give you all the details when I get back.

HUXLEE

Hurry back before the store is a crime scene.

Chuckling quietly to myself, I'm startled when I hear, "Hey, long time no see," from behind me. Turning, I see it's Mason with a big smile on his face.

Slipping my phone back into my pocket, I reply, "Hey, what are you up to?" There is no whiny girlfriend with him today. *Good riddance*, I think.

"I rushed out of here so quick after our ride yesterday, I thought I would come back and look around, you know, help the local crafters and all. What do you think?" He holds out a beautifully handcrafted knife. The artist has used metal to create beautiful designs on both the handle and blade. It is definitely a show piece.

"That's beautiful. Is it a gift for your girlfriend?" I know I'm being a bit of a bitch by bringing her up, but it was only just yesterday this man was dating someone. Albeit a whiny someone, in a nails-on-a-chalkboard way, but a girlfriend nonetheless.

"Yeah, we're no longer together. I tried calling her right after I left here yesterday and she was with the other guy, so I told her we were through." Well, that sucks for them, but my stomach does a little flip-flop at the smile he gives me.

"I'm sorry to hear that."

Totally not sorry.

"I'm not. I knew from the first time I saw her with him they had something going on. I didn't know the true extent of it until her tantrum yesterday." I think people in relationships usually know something is wrong, even if they can't figure out what it is. Secret texts, whispered phone calls, and God forbid if you stumble across sexts on their phone that aren't to you.

"Well, I'm sorry all the same. It's a terrible thing to find out you've been cheated on by the one who is supposed to be loyal to you." Been there, done that. It hurt my heart like a son of a bitch.

"I was just about to get some coffee. Would you like to join?" He holds his hand out to me, a smile on his face, dimples showing on his clean-shaven face.

"I was just about to get some myself. I'd love to," I take his hand, it's warm. I feel tingles up and down my arm with the contact.

We walk to the café with the best coffee, and we talk about our lives and growing up here. When we were on the sleigh, he said he was from Beaver Creek, just north of where my parents live in Jackson. He tells me more about it while I talk about my favorite places around where I live in Laramie.

"How do you enjoy living in such a big city?" The entirety of his focus is on me. I stare into his brown eyes and can't help but think I've never felt so paid attention to with any guy I've been out with. Not that this is a date. It's just coffee, with someone who was dating someone else just yesterday.

Dammit, Callie, stop it.

"When I first got there, I thought I was some bigshot, living life on my own going to the University of Wyoming. But I still feel nostalgic every time the holidays come around. I come back here every year for Thanksgiving to help my parents get everything ready for Christmas." I don't tell him that Christmastime has always been my favorite and I don't know what I'd do with myself if I didn't get to spend these few days with them every year.

"So it's kind of like you are still on the college break schedule?"

"Well, I've never thought of it like that but, yeah, I guess so."

The barista takes our order, and he pays for both of us, despite my protests. *This is not a date, this is not a date, this is not a— oh, who cares?*

I start to walk toward the door when I feel his hand on my lower back, guiding me toward one of the tables in the café. "Why don't we stay here and finish our coffee?" I'm not going to complain. I'm enjoying his company, and it's much warmer in here than outside in the snow.

Looking out the window, I realize a lot of time has passed; the sun is now setting. We've been laughing and talking for hours, and I lost track of time.

Standing, I smile at him and say, "I am so sorry. I didn't realize what time it was. I really have to get home. My parents are probably worried about me, and they're bringing dinner home." I gather my things as I talk, putting my coat and scarf back on before pulling my purse over my head, the long strap easily settling across my body.

He watches me as he stands, holds out his hand. "It was wonderful getting to know you today. I hope we can do this again soon."

Reaching out my hand, I'm again amazed at the warmth of his hand as it engulfs mine. His large hand dwarfs my small, feminine one.

"Callie, it's important to remember looks can be deceiving."

I pull my hand back. "Maybe we'll run into each other again." I pull my gloves on as I walk away from the table, pull the door open, and step into the cold air.

My parents' house has never looked so welcoming. I don't know what it is about Mason, but he makes the butterflies in my stomach take flight. It's nice to take a breath that's not full of his scent, with his brown eyes watching me over his coffee.

And yet, I really hope we get to do that again soon. I can't help wondering how long he and his ex were in a relationship, and if dating him so soon after their public breakup would be a mistake. Can it really be considered public when only a few people were nearby? How many people have to witness it for it to carry that classification?

Who am I to make that judgment call? Also, I live a few hours from here, so it's not like a long-distance relationship is on the immediate horizon. At least, I've never wanted to be far away from the person I am dating. Especially not in the early stages. Early stages are for butterflies in the tummy and stolen kisses, not wondering where they are or what they're doing on the other side of the state.

I don't think I've ever clicked with someone as immediately as I have with him, though. It really made up for the awkwardness of our mostly silent sleigh ride when we first met, which was hardly his fault.

As I walk to my car, I pull out my phone and shoot off a text to my dad.

ME

Lost track of time. Can I bring anything home?

DAD

Just you safe and sound.

Then, because I can't leave my girls hanging, I open up the group chat.

ME

OMG Saw Mason, had coffee. It was not a date.

JEN

Who paid?

ME

He did.

STACY

It's a date.

HUXLEE

Hottie McStranger? Oh, it was sooo a date.

JEN

Did you give him your number?

ME

Ummmm... no. He just broke up with a real bitch.

HUXLEE

AND? He bought you coffee. 10 points for McStranger.

STACY

Callie, you need to give him your number when you see him again.

ME

LOL ok... ok... I doubt I see him again.

Reaching my car, I get in and stick my phone under my thigh for the trip back to my parents' house.

After dinner with my parents, I finish packing my bags and shoot off a quick text to Huxlee before pulling out of their driveway.

ME

Headed home. Will text when I set my purse down.

HUXLEE

Thanks for letting me know.

I tuck the phone away and drive the couple of hours back home. Tomorrow morning, I'm supposed to be back at work, and really, I miss Huxlee. I can't wait to give her a big hug.

As always, I'm careful while I'm driving on the snow-swept streets, but I can't help my mind drifting, wondering more about the journal world. I can't wait to read some more throughout the week. Briefly, I wonder if I'll dream more of the world from the journal.

It's still tucked in the bottom of my purse, but I can't be disappointed that I didn't get a chance to read this afternoon. I immensely enjoyed my time with Mason, and I wonder how we'll bump into each other when we live hours apart.

As soon as I get home, I unpack my bags, get ready for bed, and snuggle under the covers. Then I snag my phone from beside me and shoot off a couple of texts to make sure everyone knows I've made it home. First, I send one to my mom.

ME

Here safe.

MOM

Okay. See you in a few weeks. Dad sends his love too.

Then I open the Besties Group Chat, seeing they've been chatting back and forth, speculating on Mason and what he looks like. I roll my eyes and text:

ME

Home and headed to bed. I am beat.

HUXLEE

Sweet dreams of Hottie McStranger.

JEN

Thanks for telling me. Love you.

STACY

Glad you made it. Night.

Fumbling around, trying to find my charger on the floor, I finally snag it and plug my phone in. Then, I fall quickly to sleep.

CHAPTER 7

Good to be Bad

Sunlight streaming through curtains is what I open my eyes to. The bed feels different. The blankets covering me are softer and silkier than the cotton ensemble on my own bed. The canopy over my head tells me I'm back in the world from the journal.

A light knock sounds at the door and I quickly pull the covers to my chin, as if I can somehow hide myself with their soft protection. When the door opens, it's the same woman who helped me get ready the night before. She's carrying a tray with what looks like a teacup. There must be some kind of food on the tray as well, because I can see the steam rising up from my pathetic hiding place.

She comes to the bed and jerks her chin, motioning for me to move over on the bed. When I do, she sets the tray down on the side I have vacated and removes the covers on all the dishes. The smells coming from the breakfast tray have my stomach growling, and I think back to the dinner I shared in this world with a very grumpy beast.

As she turns to leave, I reach out and grab her wrist. "Stay," I plead with a rasp, my voice not quite awake with my parched throat, "eat breakfast with me."

"I can't. It wouldn't be proper."

Unsure of what she could be talking about, I respond, "There is way too much food here for just me, I would hate to waste it. Please join me for breakfast. I won't tell anyone, I promise." I release her wrist, allowing her to leave if she does feel it's absolutely necessary.

She glances back to the door, looks at me, and nods her head once. Then she moves to the door and pushes it all the way closed.

While we eat, I attempt to get her to speak. But she seems content to sit in silence.

Once we're finished with breakfast, she helps me get ready for my day. When I'm in this world, I feel like I've gone back in time. I've now learned how to use a chamberpot, something I had previously only seen in movies. Let me tell you, it's just as hard as it looks and I wish for something even *slightly* more modern. Hell, I'd settle for an outhouse. Then again, an outhouse inside a mountain would be a little gross.

There is also the washstand to wash my face and hands. Really, the cleanliness of the journal world makes me cringe when I consider the creature comforts of my world. At least they have some kind of homemade soap to use.

She deems me presentable after getting me all layered and strapped into a much more casual dress than she had me in the previous night. Then she leaves me alone in the room, waving goodbye as she closes the door behind her.

It isn't long before someone is knocking loudly on my door. Assuming it must be the butler man from before, I say, "Come in." I regret my chipper tone as soon as I see the frowning face of my dinner companion from last night.

He doesn't speak, a frown tugging at his eyebrows. The

gesture is evidently common for him, judging by the frown lines that dominate his forehead.

"You really shouldn't do that."

He grunts in return, then holds out his arm the same way the butler man did for me.

I hesitate, not sure if spending more time with the angry king is the best use of my time in the strange world. He motions me to him with his hand, pointing to the floor next to him and holding out his arm again for me to take. The scowl on his face stays in place, *totally* not making me hesitate to move towards him.

Right, left, I move my feet forward. I repeat it in my head as I walk toward my grumpy companion. His eyes follow me on my slow trek across the floor of the room.

Right, left, in the time I've been here, he's never spoken to me. The only sounds I've heard from him are grunts. The only look I've seen on his face is those grumpy facial expressions, but there was that one spectacular smile. I wonder how long he's been here. How long must he have been in this castle to be so jaded?

Left, right, I remind myself this is a dream world. I can change the people around me, if only I knew how. *Smile, just a little smile,* I repeat over and over again, willing him to do anything more than frown at me. Can he read my mind in my dream world?

Left, right, the expanse between me and the grump seems to grow and grow. Probably because of the dread I feel in spending another meal with his grunts and frowns.

Right, left, after what seems like an eternity, I finally make it to him. I smile obscenely, hoping to crack his rough exterior *to see his dimples again.* His long brown hair is braided back today, his beard appears freshly trimmed. I look into his eyes, one brown and one what looks like an ice blue. I've never seen two different colored eyes in person before.

He extends his arm to me again, bent, awaiting my hand so we can go on whatever walk through the corridors he has planned for me today. Tentatively, as I look into his eyes, I start to raise my hand to rest in the crook of his arm. I gasp when I feel an immediate spark on contact. His intake of breath tells me that he felt it, too. He leads me through the doorway, closing the door behind us, and away we go.

I can't help but keep up a constant stream of chatter. The tingles up and down my arm, stemming from the contact my hand has to the crook of his elbow, makes me even more nervous as we continue walking.

I ask all the questions that have run through my head since I woke up in this place what was last night in my world. Except the one question I want answered the most, *how did he get those scars?* So long in last night's dream I spent traveling, waiting, not really getting to explore anything, that now that I have time with an actual human who can answer questions, I can't stop them from flowing from my mouth.

I've asked several questions before realizing that he hasn't answered a single one of them. Holding my tongue, I admire the artwork on the walls as we pass by. Along with portraits, there are also many scenes of the outdoors.

Finally, we've made it to the end of a long hallway with a door at the end. Two doormen nod to my escort before each taking their respective doors and opening them wide so we can make our way through. I nod as I pass by, not sure if saying "thank you" is appropriate in this dream world. Although, I can't imagine it would be considered rude. It's polite, right?

As soon as we step through the door, I notice the colors: red, pink, blue, yellow, and many others. The air is cool and my long blonde hair whips around the both of us. He releases my arm before gently taking my shoulders and moving me so I am standing in front of him, facing away from him.

Back and forth, my eyes dart as I take in the beautiful garden he's brought us to. It's still winter, but there's a large clear dome over our heads. Some kind of fans are moving the air back and forth for circulation. This is some kind of large greenhouse, with every kind of flower I read about in the journal and so many more. Some I recognize from my world, and so many others I've never seen before.

I jerk away when I feel his hands in my hair. Turning around, I see he's holding a leather cord. He gestures to my hair and then grabs my shoulders again, forcing me back into the position I was in a moment ago.

It's weird to feel someone's hands in my hair. Shivers run throughout my body at the feel of the strange king's hands in my hair. But I recognize the feeling of his movements. My mother used to braid my hair when I was a child, anytime we were somewhere and it was windy. He makes quick work down the braid, clearly practiced in the art. It makes me wonder if he did his own hair today. When he finishes the braid, he secures it with the leather cord.

His fingers graze my neck. I gasp at the contact, warm, with that damn spark again. Goosebumps spring up on my arms, I move my hands up and down them, trying to get them to go away.

I slowly turn back around to face him. His face has relaxed, his hands are in his pockets, and he looks like a regular guy.

He turns and walks down an aisle of flowers, and I follow him. There is so much to see here, so many colors, so many flowers, so much beauty in the middle of winter. I am in awe of the entire garden.

Aisle after aisle, we walk side by side. He occasionally stops to pick a flower and he motions for me to turn as he places the flower in my braid. Neither of us speaks. It's when we're finally back at the entrance I say, "Thank you."

He tilts his head to the side, a puzzled look on his face. I decide to answer the unspoken question.

"Thank you for bringing me here. Your garden is beautiful."

There's that smile, those dimples, and his eyes light up like I haven't seen before. It takes years off his face and I decide to do what I can to keep the smile on his face.

He walks away from me, holding his pointer finger up, indicating to me he'll be back in a moment. He grabs a pair of garden shears off a cart of other gardening supplies and moves toward a rose bush. The roses are a deep, beautiful red color. He cuts one, puts the scissors back on the cart, and hands me the rose with a flourish.

Tentatively, I reach out and grasp the stem of the rose. I bring it to my face and inhale the wonderful scent. It's been a long time since someone has bought me flowers, let alone trimmed one off the bush themselves.

"Ouch," I hiss, looking at the palm of my right hand, beads of blood already forming along the small cut on my hand. Automatically, I clench my hand into a fist, trying to hide the scratch. Something I used to do as a kid to keep my mom from finding out I was hurt.

His hand comes up and grazes the back of my injured one. Carefully, he grasps my wrist, and with his other hand, gently pries my fingers apart. Then he brings my hand up to his face to examine the wound, a frown marring his brow again.

He holds out his arm again for me to take and we make our way back inside the mountain. I'm not sure how he doesn't get lost in this place, tunnels branch off in all directions. Finally, we come to what looks like a small medical facility. He leads me to a table and turns to me, placing his hands on my waist and lifting me to sit on the surface.

I watch his back and wide shoulders as he walks away and moves toward a cabinet, opening the door and looking through its contents. He returns to me with supplies to bandage my hand and sets them on the table next to me.

His eyes meet mine, and he holds out his hand, palm up. I

place my injured hand in his and again unfurl my fingers so he can examine my hand once more.

The goosebumps appear again on both my arms and legs as he carefully tends to my wound. Cleansing the area with a wet cloth, he washes the area before drying it. Then, he carefully wraps it in gauze he ties off snugly, but not so tight as to cut off the circulation.

When he stands, turning to dispose of the used medical supplies, I jump down from the table. My good hand grasps the flat surface to steady myself after the slight drop. He spins around at the noise and moves back to my side.

We both look down as my stomach growls, loudly. "I guess we should make our way towards some lunch?" I suggest.

Taking my uninjured hand, he places it in the crook of his elbow again and we make our way out of the medical facility. I glance back and try to piece together the grouchy man I had dinner with before with this kind, gentle version.

We take so many turns and stairs I don't know where we even started from, before we arrive at what appears to be a study.

I gasp when I see what's inside. Floor-to-ceiling bookcases, filled with more books than I've seen in anyone's home, or any place really, except maybe a bookstore or library. I walk to one of the shelves and read the titles when I'm startled by a bell ringing. Turning, I see he is holding the bell, and shortly, one of the staff comes in with a tray of food.

They leave quickly and I move over to the tray, grabbing the first thing I can and shoving it in my mouth. The sound of a shocked laugh pulls me from my food-consuming distraction, and I look up to see him staring at me, a big smile on his face, and those dimples.

Carefully, I set down the food. "I'm so sorry. Is it improper for me to eat before you?"

He motions for me to go ahead, coming around to pull out my chair for me, and slowly pushing me in. He sits in a chair beside the table and grabs a plate from the tray to fill with his own lunch.

It's now that I notice there are plates for us to use. Here I was eating like I was raised in a barn. My mom would shake her head at me if she were here. He places the second plate in front of me, already filled with an assortment from the platter.

"Thank you." I wait for him to start eating his food before picking something up and taking a bite. "You don't talk much, do you?"

He shakes his head slowly, chewing the food in his mouth.

When we've finished eating, he stands and comes around to help me to my feet. His hand lingers on mine before he moves toward a desk in the corner of the room. He grabs an old pen, the style of which I've only ever seen in the movies. I take the opportunity to look at more of the books, eventually snagging a worn copy of a book I don't recognize the name of.

There is a soft-looking couch nearby and I stretch my legs out in front of me on the cushion. I cross my legs and prop the volume up on the top knee, carefully turning the pages and getting lost in the story.

When I finally glance up from the book, I realize hours must have passed. I stand and stretch my arms above my head, my back and ribs really feeling the fact I've been hunched over a book while wearing a corset for hours.

Movement out of the corner of my eye startles me. I glance over to see him walking toward me.

He smiles and again holds his arm out for me to take. I should find it odd that I've never heard this man speak, but something about him seems calm and composed. His demeanor has changed entirely from our first dinner together. It's like he knows what he wants and he's not afraid to take it. Right now, I think he might want to take me.

I place my hand in the crook of his elbow again, and he leads me out into the hall and back to the room where we had dinner last night.

Remembering my startled fall from last night, I chuckle at my clumsiness. I sneak a glance at him and see the corner of his mouth turned up, and mirth in his eyes. He must be remembering the same thing, my ridiculous tumble.

Unlike last night, once we're finished eating, he is the one who walks me to my room. His entire demeanor has transformed from the frown he had on his face this morning. He looks almost calm, content. He follows all of my movements with his eyes as we climb the stairs to my room.

I've enjoyed the day I've had with this quiet, brooding man.

When we reach my door again, I turn to him to say good-night. Before the words can escape my lips, he brushes the backs of his fingers across my cheek. A warm flush immediately comes to my cheeks. He moves both of his hands to gently grasp my face, fingers wound in my hair. My hands move to his elbows, gently holding him in place. Anticipation looms in my belly, those butterflies going crazy again.

I hold my breath, looking into his different colored eyes, thinking he'll kiss me, not sure if I want him to or not. But some-times doesn't it just feel good to be bad? Not that kissing him would be bad. I hold my breath in anticipation. He begins to move toward me, then he just releases me, quickly turning and making his way down the hall. I watch after him, not sure what just happened, and also not sure why I feel like I've just been abandoned. My hand comes up to my chest as I watch him disap-pear around the corner.

Opening the door, I realize I'm on my own to get ready for bed tonight, and I struggle to unlace the strings behind my back. For the first time today, I'm able to fully expand my lungs. It takes me a while longer to pull all the flowers out of my braid and untie the leather strap he used to secure my hair. But when I finally do, I climb into the bed, briefly wondering what kissing the beast would have felt like, before falling blissfully asleep.

CHAPTER 8

Star On Top

Cotton sheets, and my normal nightgown, remind me that the dream world is just that, a dream. Although I can't help but wish it was real this time. The beastly man who led me around his palace under the mountain makes me wish I had a man of my own to lead me around beautiful gardens somewhere.

I enjoy the time I get to spend at my parents' house, but it's really nice to be back in my kitchen with my fancy coffeemaker. This morning I really need to make a trip to the grocery store to stock up on food for the week.

Once I've finished breakfast, I head out on a short run and then it's time for me to get ready for the store. I call Huxlee to let her know I won't be at work today to have time to get myself set up for the week. She tells me to have fun and she'll see me back at work.

Maybe I'll stop by the bookstore and snag myself something to read. My dream last night reminded me I haven't read a good book in a while, maybe one of my favorite authors has released something new recently.

I'm washing my hands when I realize I have a cut on my hand. It's in the exact same place as the one I got from the rose in my dream last night. I probably just scraped it on something and don't remember. I'm constantly finding bruises and scrapes I don't remember getting.

My phone rings and makes me jump. I walk into my room to grab it from my nightstand where I left it last night. The number on the caller ID isn't one I recognize. "Hello?"

"Callie? It's Mason. I hope you don't mind. I ran into your mom today and asked for your number."

That little scheming mother of mine is going to get a piece of my mind, or not. I know she loves me and that's why she's interfering. "Oh, hey, how are you?" Considering I just saw him yesterday, I'd assume about the same as the last time I left him. But hey, who knows?

"I'm good. Thanks for asking. You?"

"Same," I respond, because really, we did just see each other yesterday afternoon.

"Well, look, I was calling because I just so happen to have some business in your neck of the woods today, and I thought I'd stop by. Since your mom said you'd gone back home last night, I thought I might see if you wanted to go grab lunch?"

"Lunch? I eat lunch." I smack my forehead at my stupidity. Of course I eat lunch, what kind of idiot doesn't eat lunch? I've certainly never been one to miss a meal.

"Great, meet you at twelve at The Grill downtown?"

"Absolutely, I love that place! Their burgers are amazing!"

We say our "See you laters" and I rush to finish getting ready. I have plenty of time to make it to the store and home before I need to meet him for lunch, but I don't want to look rushed when I get there, either.

My phone rings again and it's my mom calling. "Hey, Mom." I keep a neutral tone in my voice. While I'm slightly irritated she just handed my number out to some guy she had never truly met before, I do love her.

"Hey, honey, I wanted to let you know I gave that cute guy from the sleigh ride your number today. He seemed pretty bummed you'd left last night." At least she recognized him and didn't just give it to a *complete* stranger.

"I know, he already called. He's gonna be in town today. We're grabbing lunch."

"You didn't tell us you'd run into him again yesterday." Maybe because I didn't want to have this exact conversation.

"Must have slipped my mind when I was packing up my car." Yeah, let's go with that one.

"Give this one a chance, will you, Callie? I'm not getting any younger and I need some more grandbabies!" Not the grandbaby guilt trip again, good grief. My brothers are like fucking rabbits and yet, I still get guilt-tripped.

"Mom, I just met him. In fact, he just got out of a relationship." *In front of the entire town*, I don't add.

"Callie, clearly it wasn't serious, or he wouldn't be asking for your number a couple of days later."

"Mom..."

"Callie," she lowers her voice, like she's admonishing me. I'm immediately five years old again and getting caught with my hand in the cookie jar. "Just remember to give him a chance. Remember, I met your dad right after he broke up with a girlfriend and look how that turned out!"

I can't help but laugh at the reminder. But I'm also tired of her pressuring me to get married. Some people just aren't supposed to be with someone. And really, what are the odds that I would end up married under the same circumstances my parents did?

I've dreamed of my husband, wedding, and kids since *I* was a kid. At one point, I even made a scrapbook with pictures I cut out of my mom's magazines. My brothers made fun of me endlessly for it.

As I got older, though, it felt like a distant dream. Then more like an impossibility. Throughout high school and college I would date but, no one was ever the right guy. No one ever clicked with me. I could absolutely never see myself long term with any of the boys I grew up with, or met in college.

Once I started working, it just felt like I didn't have the time or opportunity to meet anyone. I am 100% against dating apps—gross. Seems like a better way to meet a serial killer than a future spouse.

"If it's meant to be, it will be, Mom. I don't think either of us wants me marrying the wrong guy. Marriage is forever, right?" Immediately, I roll my eyes. Isn't the divorce rate like fifty percent?

"Of course, honey. You'll let me know how it goes, right?" I roll my eyes at her eagerness.

"I'll call you later," I say, intentionally not promising her every detail. Some things I'd rather just keep to myself.

I'm rushing through the grocery store since my mom took more of my time than I would have liked. Once I've reached the checkout, I feel like I finally have a chance to breathe. It's not until this moment I realize I've left my purse at home.

"Oh, my God, I'm so sorry. I just realized I left my purse at home," I tell the cashier. She looks at me with a pitying look. I hate that look.

"We can keep your stuff for you in the walk-in until tomorrow morning, honey. Do you think you can get back by then?"

"I've got it," I hear from over my shoulder. Immediately, I recognize the voice and hang my head in shame. Of course, I would run into him here before our lunch date.

"No, Mason," I turn and respond to him. "I'll be back in about twenty minutes," I say to the cashier as I walk out the front door.

Footsteps and the sound of a cart's wheels behind me a moment later make me turn around again. Mason smiles at me, pushing my cart of food. I am beyond embarrassed at the turn of events. How the fuck did I leave my purse at home? This has never happened to me before, and it sure as shit won't be happening to me again.

"Please don't be mad at me." His eyes and smile have an apology written all over them.

"I'm not mad, Mason. This has never happened to me before and I am beyond embarrassed it happened in front of you." Seriously, I can feel the heat in my cheeks, which means they are probably blazing red right now.

"It's no big deal, really. More selfish on my part. I was hoping I could hang out with you more before lunch?"

The sly smile he gives me makes my heart flip over in my chest. It's been a long time since I've been out with someone so damn charming. The last guy I dated was nothing to write home about, that's for sure.

He helps me load my groceries into the back of my car, then gets in his own to follow me home.

When we get to my house, he helps me unload the groceries from my car and put them away in the cabinets. I have to point him to where everything goes, but he does his best and thankfully is well mannered enough to not just open every single one of my cabinets in his search. We talk the entire time, and I've never found conversation so easy with anyone before.

"So, Callie, what do you do for work?" he asks. And really, I think it's funny we haven't talked about things like that and yet we haven't lacked for conversation.

"I work in a bookstore, stocking shelves, helping with customers, and spending my days reading and enjoying stories." I have liked it more than pretty much every job I've ever had. Every time I talk about my job, I talk faster, more excited, my hands gesticulating as I do. I love what I do.

"Really? Sounds like you're pretty passionate about it."

"I've always loved books, getting lost in a story, getting to spend one day as a servant who falls in love with the master of the house, the next day riding on the back of a dragon and learning magic."

"So, a little romance, a little fantasy?"

"And a little of everything else, too. I'm an equal opportunity reader." I wink at him and start giggling.

He smiles the biggest smile I've seen from him. His dimples are especially prominent on his clean-shaven face. I'm a sucker for a man with dimples.

"What do you say we have food delivered instead? I'm enjoying the company and I would hate to have to fight to be heard over the sounds in the restaurant."

"Sounds like a plan to me. I think SpeedyDelivery delivers The Grill here."

Quickly, we place our order using the app on my phone. When I'm exiting out of the app, I decide to shoot off a quick text to the Besties Group Chat while I continue talking to Mason while we wait for the food.

ME

Mason is at my house. We are having dinner. Just letting everyone know because True Crime podcasts.

STACY

Really? That is great!

JEN

Do everything I would do.

HUXLEE

Do not do anything Jen would do. Should I come by?

I look up when Mason clears his throat and quickly tuck my phone back into my pocket. "You know, I've heard people around Jackson say that your parents' house is the talk of the town when it comes to Christmas decorations. Why does your house look so..." He trails off.

I can't help but laugh. "Well, if you must know, I helped my parents decorate while I was in town. I haven't had a chance to get my tree yet." Glancing around, I realize how few personal items I have in my house. I really need to remedy that.

"I could help, if you want?" He looks at me like he really wants to.

"Sure, if you don't mind following me around the Christmas tree lot for hours while I find the perfect tree." Because really, I am *very picky* when it comes to picking out my tree.

"How perfect are we talking?" He leans in closer to me in interest, then his brown eyes move to my lips and I hold my breath. It's been a while since I've kissed anyone, or wanted to kiss anyone, in real life at least. My mind wanders back to the warmth of the beast as his arm wrapped around me from behind. The feel of his fingers in my hair while I wished he would kiss me just last night.

Slowly, I lean forward. He brings his hand up to rest on the side of my neck, and I feel a jolt. Butterflies start to go crazy in my stomach and I glance away. My eyes move around the room. How is it I've never felt a jolt until the last couple of days and now it's happened with two different men, one in real life, the other in my dreams?

"Everything okay?"

"I... don't know." A knock on the door saves me from my

thoughts. I pull away from him, stand, and make my way to the door, greeting the delivery driver and grabbing cash from my wallet for a tip. "Thank you," I say as he leaves.

We divide the food between us. Mason ordered a spicy burger and French fries. I got a mushroom burger and sweet potato fries, my favorite. Biting into the juicy burger, a moan escapes me and Mason glances over at me before quickly taking a bite of his burger.

When we've finished lunch, I shoot off a quick text to the Besties.

ME

Venue change. He has volunteered to help me find a tree. Headed to the lot.

JEN

How sweet. Keep this one.

STACY

So romantic! Sounds like he is worth a real shot.

HUXLEE

Sus, text when you get home.

ME

LOL. I promise.

I shove my phone into the front pocket of my purse before we bundle into our winter gear to head to the tree lot. I've been using my fake tree for a couple of years now. It will be nice to have the scent of a real Christmas tree in here again. It is a bit of a pain to dispose of it by myself at the end of the season, though.

It takes a couple of hours to look, but I find the perfect tree for my house. I let Mason have the pleasure of chopping it down. This is my favorite kind of Christmas tree lot, the ones where you get to pick and chop down your own tree. That way, you know it's extra fresh.

Once we're done at the tree lot, we strap the tree to the top of my car and drive back to my house. We wrestle the tree inside and I drag him back out for one more important Christmas tradition.

"We just need to stop at the store for a minute," I say.

He looks at me like I've grown a second head. "Weren't you just at the store?"

"Well, yes, but not this store." I grin and I walk back out to my car, waiting for him to climb into the passenger seat.

We enter the store and see every decoration, wrapping tools, and supplies one could need or want for Christmas. I make my way to the ornament section and think back on my year. What is something I want to remember from this year for years to come?

I've looked through most of the aisle when I see it, a tiny wooden chest. I also grab a second one that looks like a tiny journal. It feels like some weird kind of fate.

"These are perfect." I beam up at him, and we make our way to the register.

"I'm glad you found them. What are they for, exactly?"

"Putting on the tree, silly." He gives me an expression that could only mean *duh*. I decide to throw him a bone and explain, "In my family, we have a tradition every Christmas. We pick a special ornament that represents something monumental that happened to us during the year."

"A chest and a book?"

"It's personal." I'm not ready to share this new part of my life with anyone yet, let alone someone I've barely known for a few days.

Back at the house, as soon as I've removed my coat and gloves, I pull my phone out to let the Besties know I'm safe.

ME

Home safe, tree is perfect. Even found the perfect ornaments for this year.

JEN

See, perfect.

STACY

I still need to find our ornaments.

HUXLEE

Where did you find a B.O.B. ornament?

JEN

Ha!

HUXLEE

Jen's should be a pregnancy test this year.

JEN

Oh, it's on!

Setting my phone on an end table, he helps me pull all my boxes of decorations down from the attic. It's nice to have a second person to help me this time. I usually do all of this by myself, sliding the boxes down the attic stairs and hoping they don't break at the bottom. It's so much easier with a second person to catch—and less destructive.

I always start my tree decorating with lights and any garlands I plan to use this year. A different colored strand of lights in each hand, I turn and let Mason choose the color scheme for this year.

Once the lights and garland have been hung, I carefully pull out each of my specially chosen annual ornaments. I place them on the tree at perfectly-spaced intervals. I'm a bit of a perfectionist when it comes to decorating for Christmas. A few years ago, I picked up some colored and sparkly ornaments to fill in my tree the rest of the way, since my ornament collection does not quite rival the one my parents have.

Standing back, I check around the tree to make sure I have left no large ornament free gaps in the foliage. Satisfied, I take a step back and look at the tree from further back.

The last ornaments I place on the tree are the ones to represent this year. These I place right at the front so I can see them and remember this year's weird special moment.

Finally, I pull out my star tree-topper. Since I don't want to pull out the stepladder, I try to hand it to Mason. "Would you like to do the honors?"

He looks at me shocked. "You'd give me the honor of topping your tree? You just met me."

"It's that or go grab the stool." I shrug.

"Come here," he motions with his hand for me to come to him.

Still holding the star in my hand, I move to him, unsure of what's coming.

"Turn around," he gently grasps my shoulders and turns me around to face the tree. "I'm going to count to three and I want you to jump."

"What?" I turn and look at him, pretty sure he's lost his damn mind.

"Will you just do it?"

I turn around and wait for him to count.

"One, two"—he places his hands on either side of my waist—"jump." As I do, he helps to lift me up to place the star on top of the tree. He carefully lowers me down, my back gliding down his body. I hold my breath as I feel him against me. Those damn butterflies in my stomach fly all around and my spine tingles everywhere we make contact. Safely back on the ground, he wraps his arms around my waist and rests his chin on my shoulder. "Why don't we turn it on?" he whispers in my ear, his breath warm against my cheek at the close proximity.

I move away from him toward the plug, illuminating the tree and brightening up the room. My body returns to normal at the loss of contact. I don't know if I should feel relieved or disappointed.

"Wow! Do you go all out every year?" He spins in a circle, observing the room we've been decorating for the last couple of hours.

"Christmas is my favorite holiday." I shrug. "I can't help but decorate my house every year, just like I grew up with. It helps me get into the Christmas spirit. And I love watching the lights as they flicker and glow when I sit on the couch at night with my tea and a good book."

"That's nice," he has a wistful tone in his voice.

"What traditions does your family have?"

"I don't remember my family." He looks away, seemingly ashamed of this.

"I'm sorry to hear that." I don't want to pry but, his response makes me want to ask so many questions. Questions I have no right to have answers to. I've only known this man for a few days.

After several moments, he finally speaks. "Do you ever feel you've lived entire lifetimes in the span of moments? Or maybe you feel you've met someone before, in another lifetime? Or maybe it feels like déjà vu."

This feels deep for our third day knowing each other. But somehow, I know exactly what he's talking about. "I know what you mean. I've been having these baffling dreams lately that feel so real. In fact, I woke up this morning with a cut on my hand exactly like I got in the dream. I'm such a klutz, though. I must have injured myself before bed and just don't remember it."

"I have to go," he abruptly says, moving away from me. I'm so startled by his sudden need to leave, I feel like I've said something wrong.

"I'm sorry to have offended you." I can't keep the disappointed tone out of my voice.

"What are you talking about?"

"I feel like you're leaving because of something I said…" I look down at my feet, dejected and wondering what I could have possibly said to make him leave, at the same time feeling I don't have the right to feel this way. It's stupid how quickly I've started to fall for this guy.

"I'll talk to you soon." He pauses. "I want you to remember, looks can be deceiving."

"What does that even mean?" I cross my arms, huffing in agitation.

He stands at the door, holding it open, one foot outside my house already. "Goodbye, Callie."

Well, that was ominous and confusing. "Bye, Mason."

In an attempt to clear my head, I send off a text to Jen.

ME

Mason left. I feel like I offended him. He says I didn't. IDK.

JEN

Oh, sweetie. It is going to be okay. Did he run out or did he leave with an actual goodbye?

ME

He said bye, and this weird "remember looks can be deceiving" line. It is the third time he has said it.

JEN

Okay… that is weird. Is he warning you off or…?

ME

No idea.

JEN

Does he scare you?

ME

Not at all. It is oddly comfortable when he is around.

JEN

Hmmm…

CHAPTER 9

Once Upon a December

It takes me a while to feel up to doing much of anything after Mason's exit. I never do figure out what I could have possibly said to have scared him away. Maybe he has a problem with klutzy girls? But he said he would talk to me later. And what is up with him always repeating that damn phrase, *"It's important to remember looks can be deceiving."*

Finally, I decide to order in again. I don't feel up to cooking dinner. I watch the lights on my tree change colors as I wait for the food to get here. Every year, I randomly select which lights I'm going to use. Mason chose the ones that change colors. They're my favorite. It makes me feel like I don't have to settle for one color all season long.

After I've eaten the BLT and kettle chips I ordered, I decide to lie in bed and read more of the journal.

I spent days wandering around the forest, trying to find more permanent shelter. Finally, I decided to head in the same direction for a while, hoping to find someone, anyone, who might tell me where I could find a comfortable bed to sleep in.

In the distance, I saw what looked like the top of a mountain. I decided to aim for that point in the distance. At least it would keep me traveling in a straight line.

After I'd walked for hours more, I finally reached the base of the mountain. The closer I got, I started to see a small entrance. I walked up to the door and used the knocker to alert the occupants of my presence.

I waited and waited and waited. No one came to the door. I knocked again and waited some more. After another extended wait, I finally decided to try to open the door. It swung easily. Peering inside, I noticed a coating of dust on all the surfaces. "Hello," I said, not wanting to scare anyone more than a stranger in their home would.

No one responded. I spent the rest of the day wandering around the halls. The place seems to be fully furnished. I can't imagine someone just leaving all of their things here, but there are no signs of anyone having been here for some time.

Unfortunately, when I found the kitchen, I also discovered there was no food to eat.

I chose a room from the wing of this place that seemed to house all the sleeping quarters, and I sat there settled in to sleep for the night. I'll worry about food tomorrow. Right now, I needed a bed, and a good night's rest.

I decide now is as good a time to put a bookmark in my place as any. Even though I hadn't gotten to this part before my journey into the journal world, I somehow still dreamed of the castle in the mountain. I'm beginning to wonder if it's not a dream at all. The feeling of running from the wolf through the woods was so real. The terror of being captured and transported miles away felt real. The scratch on my hand. There's no way all of those things can be coincidences. They all happened over only a couple of nights.

Placing the journal on my side table, I pull my blanket over myself and curl into its warmth.

I'm shocked and disappointed to wake up in my own bed. I wanted to explore the castle under the mountain, find out what other secrets it contains besides the beautiful flower garden.

My phone ringing in the other room makes me get out of bed quickly, tripping over my slippers, trying to get them on my feet. Unfortunately, I get to the phone too late and wait to see if whoever it was leaves a voicemail.

Might as well go to the bathroom while I wait. While I'm sitting on the toilet, I hear knocking on my door. Quickly, I finish what I'm doing and make my way to open it. Looking through the peephole, I see my parents standing there.

Opening the door, I greet, "Hey, what are you guys doing here?" I open the door wider to allow them into my warm house.

"I tried to call, but you didn't answer your phone," my mom says as she removes her gloves, shoving them in her pockets, followed by her scarf and coat.

"You just called two seconds ago, Mom." I hang her coat in my front closet, wrapping her scarf around the upper part of the hanger.

"Honey, I've been calling all morning." She gives me a disapproving look. God forbid I sleep in for once.

"What time is it? I just woke up."

My dad gives me a hug and kisses the top of my head. "Oh, Callie, you always could sleep through anything."

"It's eleven, dear," Mom adds. Wow, that's really, really late. I wonder briefly if super vivid dreams can affect your sleep?

I grab my phone and mutter distractedly, "Wow, I must have really needed the sleep. What are you guys doing in town, anyway?"

"I had an appointment for my ankle this morning. They freed me from my bandaged prison today!" I look down and see that indeed, her foot is in a normal shoe for the first time in a while.

She's so excited to finally get her wrappings off. I can't help but chuckle. "Good for you."

Quickly I shoot off a text to Huxlee.

ME

Hey, forgot to set an alarm and the parents just showed up. See you tomorrow?

HUXLEE

You better! Love you!

"The tree looks beautiful this year, sweetie," Mom walks around and checks out how I placed all the ornaments this year. She freezes at the front of the tree. "Are these new?"

"Which ones?" She points to the chest and journal ornaments I picked out yesterday with Mason. "Oh yeah, I got those yesterday, like them?"

She stays quiet, and I move closer to her. "Mom?" I say tentatively.

"What *exactly* made you pick *those* ornaments?" she hisses.

I bite my lip, my fingers tug at the hem of my top, and I flinch back when her gaze turns towards me.

"You just couldn't leave it alone!" She shocks me with her

sudden outburst. My heart jumps in my chest, beating a frantic rhythm.

"Caroline, your blood pressure," my dad speaks calmly. I take a few deep breaths as he rubs his hand up and down her back.

"No, Jerry, she asked about that damned chest and I told her to just leave it alone. And here she's gone and opened it, before her time, too!" I've never seen my mom come unglued so quickly. Okay, maybe when we used to fight with each other as kids, but it's been many years since that has happened.

"Before my time? What are you talking about?" My gaze moves from my mom to my dad and back again, wondering which of them is going to tell me what's going on.

My dad leads my mom to my couch to sit. I follow behind, taking a seat in my favorite chair.

"It's never been done before. I don't know what happens now. It's never happened before. How could I let this happen? I should have hidden that chest years ago. What happens now? My mother never prepared me for this. What do I do now?"

My dad and I look at each other as my mom continues to mumble. I reach out my hand and place it on her knee. "Mom, could you tell me what's going on?"

"I told you not to open the chest!"

"What do you mean, 'what happens now?'" I figure this is the easiest and most broad of the questions I can ask right now.

"You're not supposed to know until your birthday." Well, that sounds odd, but okay.

"My birthday is in just a couple of weeks. Maybe it'll be okay."

She takes a deep breath and turns to my dad, "Can you get me a glass of bourbon, Jerry? I need a drink."

I look up at my dad, who appears as shocked as I do. My mom rarely drinks, and definitely not bourbon.

"Over there." I jerk my chin toward my TV cabinet, with my liquor in the bottom section.

When he comes back and she downs the first glass, she holds

the glass out to him for another. Only when she has the second glass in her hand does she speak.

"The firstborn women in my family have a gift, Callie." She takes another sip of the brown liquid. "But as I said, you're not supposed to know about it until your birthday.

"Those journals are histories... histories of the people who have been banished from our world, leaving their life behind only as the fairytales we tell to our children as they grow up." I'm starting to wonder if we need to take Mom for some kind of mental health evaluation.

"No one in my family has ever been told, as far back as I know, why these people have been banished, or who is doing the banishing. But we are the keepers of the world they are banished to, a gateway, if you will." Like prison wardens? I definitely don't want to be a prison warden.

"Also, no one in our family has ever seen this world. We only know what we've been able to learn through the journals." At my sharp intake of breath, both of my parents turn to face me, eyes focused on my face.

"How do you get the journals?" I can feel the heat creeping up my face.

"The earliest known recorded journal appeared when our family was on a ship to America from France. An additional chest somehow made its way into their part of the cargo in the ship's hold. The same chest you saw in our attic the other day.

"The chest has been preserved with magic all these years, and every few years, a new journal shows up in the chest. One day, many years ago, my many times great-grandmother took the chest and journals to a witch. The witch told her that the firstborn females in our family are a sort of key or gateway to a prison world.

"But we have never been able to figure out who is banishing these people to this world, or what the world looks like beyond the journal. While we are the gateway, we have never been allowed to see into the world." She takes a large gulp, finishing off the remaining bourbon in her glass and holding it out for my dad to fill again.

"So we just... what? Get these journals and hope in a couple of years there isn't another one? Have we ever been able to track down family members for one of these people who have disappeared?" Why the hell has my family been so okay with this over the years?

"I don't know, Callie, I've told you almost everything I know. I was supposed to tell you on your twenty-fifth birthday when it was your turn to take over the keeping of the chest. But you just couldn't keep it to yourself! You never listen!" Her volume seems to have been turned up as a result of the alcohol running through her veins.

"I'm sorry Mom, I didn't know it would cause such a problem for the family secret. I didn't even know there *was* a family secret." I keep my voice calm. We don't need two of us yelling at each other, even though I'm sure Dad is planning how to diffuse the situation.

"Well, Caroline, I think it's about time we head back home. It's a long drive back to the house." He carefully takes the glass from her and sets it on my coffee table. Then places a hand on her back in a calming gesture.

"Yes, dear," she says, standing. "I love you, Callie. I hope you know that."

"Yes, Mom, I love you, too."

I hug them before they leave to head back home. As soon as the door closes behind them, I take a deep breath in and slowly out, trying to calm my racing heart. I go to the coffee table and down the rest of the contents of mom's cup before washing it in the sink. I return the cup and the remaining bourbon to their places in my liquor cabinet.

Even though it's late, I make myself another cup of coffee. What I really want is another stiff drink but, I fear it would make me unable to puzzle through what my mom just told me.

If no one is supposed to be able to travel to the journal world, why can I? And how do I find out why I can?

An incoming text pulls me from my thoughts.

After spending the rest of the night spinning the wheels in my head, with no way of knowing the answer to this question, I finally fall asleep on my couch.

CHAPTER 10

Prayers for this World

Bright light, and the beautiful room at the castle under the mountain greet me when I open my eyes. After what my mom shared last night, the only place I want to be is here right now. Maybe they will have some of the answers my mom can't give me.

I climb out of bed, and shortly after, hear a knock on the door. The woman I've seen before comes in empty-handed.

"Good morning, miss, I hope you've slept well." I'm surprised by her speech since she's usually so quiet, at least until I make her talk to me.

"I slept well, thank you." I smile at her, hoping she'll warm up to me.

"The king would like you to join him for breakfast this morning."

I walk toward the vanity where she usually helps me get ready. Lifting my arms, I help her get my modern clothes off of me. Truly, I never appreciated my normal panties and bra before being here. Corsets are so uncomfortable.

First she helps me into my undergarments, then the rest of my clothes. I hold on to one of the posts on the bed as she tugs the laces and ties them closed, binding me into the corset for the day.

Shallow breaths are all I can take once I am strapped into this thing.

She has selected a nicer gown for the day; I imagine, because I will be dining with the king.

Upon reflection, I realize I have met very few people in the palace. While I find it slightly odd, I haven't really been to many of the rooms since I've been here.

She spends a lot of time pinning and tucking my long blonde hair. My long blonde locks are beautiful under her ministrations. Somehow, I know it would take hurricane-force winds, or very adept hands to bring my hair back to its natural state.

I look at myself in the vanity's mirror. Admire the red tint she gave my lips. My pale face she has powdered to perfection. *Why is she putting in all this effort just for breakfast?* I wonder.

"He'll be here to get you soon, miss."

"Who?" My words fall on deaf ears as she closes the door behind her before acknowledging my question.

It doesn't take long before there's a knock on the door. Really, I could probably make my way to the dining room by now, but I'm terrible at directions. And with the long dress, I'm likely to trip down the stairs on the way.

"Come in," I fully expect the butler to open the door and greet me.

Instead, I am greeted by the king. He opens the door, and he's glancing down at the ground. When he looks up at me, I swear I see him stumble in his gait.

"You look..." He trails off. It's the first time I've heard him make coherent words.

"You can talk." I slap my hand over my mouth, horrified at the words that fell out. It's times like these I wish I had a filter on my mouth.

He laughs, and the sound is so infectious, I can't help but join in the merriment. "Did you really think I couldn't talk?"

I don't answer, instead choosing to smile and move toward him to take his arm. "Where to this morning?" I ask instead.

He stands up straight, all business again. "We have had some messengers come in from the outer reaches of my domain. I figured your presence might bring a calming atmosphere to the meeting. It calms me, at least." He closes his mouth, jaw clenching beneath his beard. I don't think he meant to say that last part.

"Is there actually going to be breakfast at this meeting? I seem to be rather hungry this morning." Turning my face to him, I smile, trying to be reassuring.

I stare into his different colored eyes for a moment before we make our way down the hall. At the bottom of the stairs, he grabs my hand and pulls me into an open door. My back is up against the wall, him in front of me, facing me, *pressed against me*. The room is dark, no windows to the outside visible in the blackness.

"What are you—" The backs of his fingers graze over my right cheek. I quickly take in and hold my breath, both wanting and not wanting him to kiss me in this moment.

"It's been a long time since someone new has come here." He holds the sides of my face in his palms, attempting to weave his fingers into my hair. He grows increasingly frustrated at my carefully constructed maze of an up-do. "What the hell did she put into this thing?"

I can't help but laugh at the look on his scarred face, made visible by the small amount of light coming in from the open doorway. "I couldn't even begin to tell you."

He huffs before saying, "We really must be getting to our guests." He steps back, straightening his clothes and offering me his elbow once again.

"You really should stop changing the subject at all the good parts," I mumble. He glances at me out of the corner of his eye.

Looking both ways at the door, he makes sure no one sees us exit, then we leave the room and head into the dining room.

Thankfully, I see there is a full buffet set up, so many foods laid out, I can't fathom how many people they could feed with this amount.

I grab a plate from the edge of the buffet table and pile it with pastries and other breakfast foods. The delicious smells have my stomach growling. When I look down, I realize I have piled my plate higher than I can reasonably finish. I move to take the same seat I've occupied previously at the table.

Before taking a bite, I watch him pile his plate full and sit in the same seat he sat in last time, next to me. It's only now I look up and notice the messengers. Each of them has a plate piled equally high in front of them, eating their breakfast with their eyes focused on us.

"Did you really think I couldn't talk?" he whispers, asking me for the second time, amusement dancing in his eyes.

"Can you *really* blame me? At our first dinner, all you did was grunt and frown. At least I got some decent smiles out of you on our garden adventure," I whisper back, glancing over at the two men, who are pretending to be focused on their plates.

"It's been a long time since someone has been here that hasn't been a..." He stops, glancing down and picking up one of the pastries he has on his plate, taking a large bite.

I decide to let him keep his thoughts to himself, for now. It's time I try to figure out how I can come here when the rest of my family has never been able to.

"How do people get here?" I ask quietly, instead of the dozens of questions running around my head.

His eyes meet mine, a frown marring his brow again. "No one knows."

"What do you mean, no one knows?" My voice rises slightly, disbelief evident in my tone.

"How do you get here?"

It's my turn to look at my plate, select a pastry, and take a large bite.

We spend a few minutes in silence, eating our food, before he takes his napkin and wipes at his mouth, eyes on me. I follow suit, ready to get this meeting started.

"Gentleman, how can I help you?" His forearms rest on the table, his body leaned forward in interest.

"Your Majesty, we were hoping to speak with you in private," the one on the left speaks, pointedly staring at me.

"She stays," the beast replies. They glance at each other, seemingly speaking to each other telepathically. "I don't have all day, gentleman."

The one on the right begins hesitantly, "Your Majesty, we received word from our sources that there has been a movement of the troops across the water. They haven't done that in centuries. We fear they may be preparing for an attack." Even though he's seated, I can tell he's tall. He also holds himself well, poised, trained in the art of how to properly present yourself in front of royalty.

"What makes you think they are preparing for an attack?" I ask. "Couldn't they just be mov—" I stop talking when I feel a warm hand slightly squeeze my thigh. When I look into his face, he appears unfazed, but he clearly wanted me to stop my line of questioning.

The one on the left continues to stare at me, and his beady eyes creep me out.

"Thank you for letting us know. Please let me know if anything changes," the beast replies.

"But, sire, aren't you going to prepare?" left asks.

"Prepare for what? The lady is right. We don't know that they are going to attack, and we certainly don't want to provoke one by moving for no reason. As I said, let me know if there are any changes."

He stands, effectively ending the conversation, and helps me up, escorting me out of the room.

I can't help but think about how weird that entire conversation was. Shouldn't a king be preparing for battle?

"So you aren't concerned about a possible war?" I ask.

"I didn't say that. I just don't think it's any of our business." He shrugs.

"Aren't you the king? I'm pretty sure it's in the job description."

He stops and glances over at me. "Do you say everything that comes to your mind?"

I stop talking, focusing on my steps, putting one foot in front of the other. He leads me to another part of the palace. This one has thousands of paintings spanning from floor to ceiling in a sort of chamber.

I drop his arm, amazed at the surrounding artwork. Walking around, looking at all the paintings, I lose track of the time.

"They're beautiful, aren't they?"

"Yes," I breathe.

I'm standing in front of a painting of a meadow. The grasses are tall, flowers of all colors interspersed throughout the entire place. In the distance is a waterfall, which flows down into a stream. It looks identical to the place I stopped to get a drink before being chased by the wolf, except this scene is not covered in snow, like it is today.

I reach out and run my hand over the raised paint, amazed at both the scene and the talent of the artist.

A few paintings down, I find a more terrifying sight. This painting is of the wolf in front of the cottage I ran to. This time, the cottage is covered in vines and flowers, in full springtime bloom. The wolf's face is captured in a snarl. I wrap my arms around myself, remembering the terror of being chased by the massive creature.

"I believe you had a run-in with the wolf?" I feel his gaze on me as I continue to stare at the painting.

"I've never been more terrified in my life." A shiver runs down my spine and I turn away from the painting, moving on to the next.

"I've known Zev a long time." He jerks his chin toward the painting and I realize he's referring to the wolf. "He's been working for me almost as long." He follows me as I proceed to make my way around the room.

"Working for you?"

"A king needs spies in many places."

"You don't act kingly," I reply, and truly I mean it. He seems just like a regular guy. Except I guess regular guys don't have servants waiting on them hand and foot. Or giant castles under mountains.

"You know many kings where you're from?" He smirks at me.

"Of course not." I reach out my hand and gently shove him.

He grasps my hand softly under his much larger one, holding it against him. "Tell me about the world now, Callie. It's been so long since I've seen it."

I don't even question how he knows my name. I'm sure the woman who's been helping me get ready gives him a full report of our conversations. And I can't believe I didn't even think that was a possibility until now. Something about this man makes me want to trust him, but I don't even know him.

"What do you remember?"

"Open skies, beautiful, open lands, and possibility as far as the eye could see."

"I think you'd be disappointed in it now." I take my hand back and move to look at another painting.

Several minutes later, I look at him, and he looks concerned. "What, not what you expected? People are inherently selfish creatures."

"I remember the world being full of hope, so many traveling to the New World for a new, better life."

"What has it been like being here?"

"Lonely." He turns and walks away from me my eyes trace the length of his brown braid which falls down his back. He sits on a couch against the wall. I give him his space, allowing him to gather his thoughts.

Finally, I move to him, sitting down, "I'm sorry it didn't turn out how you thought."

"Nothing to be done for it now. Why don't we have some food and turn in early? I feel suddenly exhausted." He stands and reaches out his hand for me. I take it and let him help me stand.

Instead of going back to the dining room, he takes us to the library where the book I was reading before is waiting for me just where I left it.

After several hours of reading, we eat dinner together again.

When we finish, he walks me back to my room and says goodnight. Again, I manage to get myself changed into my own pajamas, and stand at the vanity, carefully taking my long hair down.

The bed swallows me when I snuggle under the blankets, and I slowly drift to sleep.

CHAPTER 11

I Just Called to Say I Love You

Unsurprised, that's what I am when I wake up in my own bed. Today I really have to get back to work. I've called in the last two mornings, Monday, to get everything ready for real life again, and yesterday while my parents were here. My boss-slash-best friend is pretty amazing and believes family is super important, so she didn't have any problems with me taking the time off. But it's getting into our busy season with Christmas around the corner. I really can't leave her alone for another day.

After a short run, I get ready to spend the day with Huxlee at work.

"Good morning, Huxlee, holding down the fort?" She's sitting on the floor setting up a new book display. Her face lights up when she turns around and sees me.

"Callie! So good to see you. You look like you've had a good long weekend. How are your parents?" she asks. Huxlee is short and petite, her swing bob is a constantly changing variety of colors, right now a rainbow. She's also sporting one of her many pairs of reading glasses. I do not know where she finds such an enormous selection of colors and styles.

"They're doing well. Mom got her ankle trap off yesterday."

"She must be excited to get to race around on two feet again." She laughs.

"Let me just put my purse and coat in the breakroom. I'll be back to help you out in a minute," I say over my shoulder as I make my way to the back.

"Take your time. I've got company."

Both of us have taken to referring to the books as if they're our friends. Because really, who doesn't feel the love, pain, and sheer terror along with the main character when they get lost in a good story?

We spend the morning rearranging the display shelves. Every year, Huxlee orders in lots of special bookish merch and as many signed books as she can get ahold of for the holiday crowd. This year, she's also set up some book signings with some local authors in our area.

Huxlee inherited money from her grandparents when they passed away. Her grandma encouraged her love of books growing up.

I will be forever grateful to Huxlee for giving me a job. It was inevitable we would become best friends as we bonded over our love of books.

When the chime above the front door goes off, I stand up and wipe my hands down my jeans, making my way to the front. "Welcome to Enchantments and Fancies. Can I help you find anything?"

I freeze in place when I see him standing at the front door. "Are you some kind of stalker?"

"I swear, this was a happy accident. I needed to kill some time between appointments and thought I'd check out the local small bookstore. I can leave if you'd prefer?" Mason suggests.

He looks good, jeans and a cream-colored sweater hugging his upper body. For the first time, I see some scruff on his face. Suddenly, I can't help but think he looks really familiar. I just can't place who else he reminds me of.

"Anything in particular you were looking for?" I still haven't forgotten how he abruptly left me the other day. Having been burned in the past, I honestly didn't expect to see him again. But then again, he didn't come here to see me, he just randomly stumbled into the bookstore where I work.

Really, though, he must have subconsciously been looking for me since I told him I work at a bookstore in town.

"What would you recommend?"

"What kind of books do you like?"

"It's been a while since I've sat down and read a good book. Probably since school."

"You haven't read a book since high school?" My jaw drops. I can't imagine not reading. In contrast, I have read almost every day *since* high school.

"How's your hand?"

"What?" He nods at my right hand, the one I injured the other night in the fantasy world. He must have seen the scratch, because I don't remember telling him which hand I injured.

He reaches his left hand out and I place my hand in his, palm up. He carefully traces the lines of the scratch. Goosebumps erupt up and down my arms.

"Callie, did you hel—" Huxlee stops abruptly. "Oh, hello. Who's this?" She faces me with a big grin on her face. I quickly pull my hand out of his and hide it behind my back.

"This is Mason. I met him when I was visiting my parents. Mason, this is Huxlee, the amazing and expressive owner of this place, and my best friend."

"Nice to meet you. I like the hair." He motions around his own short brown hair in some weird kind of move to show where hair is. I cover my smile with my hand.

"Thank you! It's my way of sticking it to the man." She bursts out into giggles. "Just kidding, I figure why not do what I like? I don't have a boss to answer to." She shrugs, then picks up a random book nearby.

"Do you mind if I steal Callie away for lunch?"

"Mason! I just got here. It's my first day back. I can't just leave

Huxlee to get everything ready for the Christmas rush on her own!"

Huxlee is so entertained by the conversation, I may as well get her some popcorn so she can enjoy the show.

He turns to her for her approval. "You two kids have fun."

Traitor.

I stomp my way to the back to grab my purse, knowing Huxlee will refuse to let me help with anything until I come back from lunch.

"I'll bring you something back," I promise.

"You know what I like," she replies, wiggling her fingers in a goofy wave goodbye. I blow her a kiss as I close the door on my way out. My phone chimes with Huxlee's ringtone and I pull it out while walking.

HUXLEE

OMG! He really is Hottie McStranger! Take your time. I want all the details!

There's a little café just down from the bookstore where we go for lunch. Huxlee picked a place right on a busy strip to give her store the best chance of success. She gave me a job at her store while I was finishing up college, and I loved the place, and her, so much I just couldn't bear the thought of leaving.

We order sandwiches and some flavored lemonades before sitting at a table and waiting for our food.

"Sorry to have intruded on your day again," Mason says.

"You didn't intrude. I enjoy your company, truly I do. It's just..."

"We've only known each other a few days?" he guesses.

"*And* you just broke up with your girlfriend."

"Annette was many things..." He pauses, clearly thinking

about the words he wants to use before continuing. "We've been together only a short while, but I wouldn't even say it had been in any kind of romantic capacity for most of it. I had a suspicion she had been cheating on me pretty much since the beginning, but even having it confirmed, I'm not angry about it. I just feel... relieved."

"Is it horrible of me to say *I'm* glad?" I sneak a peek at him under my eyelashes.

His brown eyes meet my own blue ones as he reaches across the table and grabs my hand. "I just told you I feel relieved. I think anything you could say after that would be definitely okay." He smiles at me, flashing those dimples I like so much.

When we finish lunch, he walks me back to the bookstore with a promise to meet me for dinner tonight.

"Hot damn, girl, I need you to spill *all* the tea," Huxlee says as soon as he's gone.

I move to one of the displays and start to organize it according to the chart Huxlee has printed out. "I met him when I was at my parents'. We were waiting in line for a sleigh ride. He was with his girlfriend. Apparently, she was a royal bitch, and they broke up shortly after. But we ended up on the sleigh together and for the first time, I felt a spark when I touched someone's hand."

"Wait, wait, wait, you held hands right after he had a fight with his girlfriend on a romantic as fuck sleigh ride?"

"Well, when you put it that way, I'm surprised we're not married and pregnant yet." I chuckle and roll my eyes. "No, Huxlee, he helped me *into* the sleigh, hence hand contact and spark."

"Marriage and babies. Damn girl, you move fast."

"Oh hush, you. Do you want me to tell you about what else happened at my parents' house or not?"

She holds her thumb and pointer finger together and mock zips her lips.

"When I was helping my mom pull down the Christmas stuff, I found somethi—"

"Yeah, I'm sure a dust bunny or two. Really, Callie, did the dust monster give you a scare?"

"I thought you said you were going to stay quiet. Fine, I guess I'll keep my super special family secret all to myself." Turning, I start to walk toward the back when I feel her pull on my shoulder.

"Wait! I'm sorry! I've just been too damn lonely here by myself. What did you find in the dusty attic of Christmas ornaments?" She's literally bouncing on the balls of her feet.

"I found an old chest. When I asked my mom about it, she told me not to mess with it and seemed real shady."

"But you didn't listen, right?"

"Girl, it was basically a dare at that point. So when I was cleaning the house getting ready to put up all the decorations, I searched for the key."

"Please tell me you found it!"

"Of course I found it. The chest was full of all these journals, some dating back several hundred years. So I snagged the oldest one I could see and hid it for later."

"Please don't tell me you found some weird family love letter chest?"

I bark out a laugh at this. "Really, Huxlee?"

"What?" She tries to look innocent, but fails miserably when we both burst into giggles. "Why don't we grab some cocoa and take a seat? Looks like today is going to be a slow one."

When we're both settled in our favorite reading chairs, I continue, "So that night I finally got a chance to look at the journal. At first, I thought it was someone's attempt at a novel—a pretty good one, too. But as I kept reading about this person's life, and the world they found themselves in, I found it easy to imagine the world. I was so immersed in the journal, I even dreamed about it that night."

I love Huxlee like a sister, but I don't know if I want her to know that I'm pretty sure I actually travel to a different world at night. She might petition my parents to have me committed. Also,

I don't want my parents to know that little tidbit until I can find out *why* this is happening to me.

"So are these some kind of ancestor journals? What's so secret about them?"

I decide to go with a modified version of the truth. "My mom said a few hundred years ago, my family started collecting these journals from different places they travelled to. So they're some kind of collection of all these strangers' lives and dreams."

"That is pretty cool. Think you could bring one by someday?"

"Yeah, I'll bring it by sometime."

Right after I find a witch to tell me what is so special about me.

We spend the rest of the day getting the store ready for Christmas shopping, which really started right after Thanksgiving. Thankfully for Huxlee, the store is usually pretty quiet the week right after Thanksgiving and picks up at the very beginning of December. Probably because that's when she runs all her Christmas specials and brings in the special authors.

I make my way home and curl up on the couch with the journal to read a little more right before Mason calls to ask if it's okay for him to bring over dinner and a movie.

"Of course that's okay. Do you remember how to get here?"

"Yeah, I should be there in about ten minutes. Pizza okay?"

"Pizza is always okay."

He shows up, and the food smells amazing. I grab some paper plates and set them on the coffee table. When I see he's brought one of my favorite movies, I say, "I love this movie!"

"Yeah?"

"Definitely! Me and my friends would watch it over and over, quoting lines from the movie all the time. It has kind of a cult following."

"Oh, I'm well aware. My friends and I would do the same thing."

"Have you ever read the book?"

"No. Is it any good?"

"Let me put it this way, it's so well done, I actually believed the book was some retelling of the history of the land. Had to Google it to be sure it wasn't." That probably says more about my gullibility than the author's writing, but hey, it's true.

"I'll have to check it out sometime. It's important to remember looks can be deceiving."

"If you promise to bring it back, you can borrow my copy."

Once we finish watching *The Princess Bride*, Mason stands at my door with the book tucked under his arm.

"I had a good time tonight," I say.

Mason raises his hand to rest on my cheek. He runs his thumb back and forth along my cheek, and I close my eyes, leaning in to his touch. Shivers run down my spine. "I had a good time, too. Goodnight, Callie."

In the same movement, he pulls his hand from my face and grabs the doorknob, turning it and leaving quickly.

The next morning, I'm the first to get to the store. I unlock the door, turn off the alarm, and turn all the lights on.

The store is so quiet in the morning. I run my hand along the spines of the books on the shelves as I pass on the way to the back room.

Huxlee has a list of things to get done each day to get the store ready for Christmas, and I immediately get started on today's tasks.

First up, dusting all the books to kick off a deep clean of the store.

As I pull each book out to make sure it's completely clear of dust, I mentally make a list of books to add to my increasing to-be-read pile. I could probably finish a book every day for the rest of my life and still never finish the entire list.

"Oh, Callie," Huxlee sing-songs, "where are you hidden away?"

"Over here in the dust cloud."

When she comes around the corner, she's holding two to-go cups from the coffee shop. "I grabbed your basic bitch pumpkin drink." She holds out the cup, a mischievous glint in her eye.

"What are you up to?" I take the drink from her. Sipping cautiously, I know it's not the drink she's tampered with.

"Oh... nothing." She turns and waltzes off, way too chipper for this early in the morning.

It's only a few minutes before I know exactly what her meddling ass has gotten me into for the day. When the bell above the door chimes and Huxlee is nowhere to be seen, I move from between the shelves and see Mason leaning against the counter.

"Mind if I help?" he asks, taking a sip from a takeaway cup.

"It seems I have been left out of some meddling," I say loud enough for Huxlee to hear in the back. Her answering cackle makes me shake my head. "Come on, let's get you a rag to wipe down the shelves with."

He follows me to the back, where he takes his jacket off and lays it on top of where I've set my purse.

"Just tell me what you need me to do."

"I've been pulling the books out and dusting them. You can follow behind me and wipe the shelves down. You need to wipe it first with this towel." I hold up the one I've sprayed with the cleaning stuff. "Then wipe it back off with this one." I hold up the clean rag. "That way I can put the books back on the shelf quicker without them getting gooed with chemicals."

He takes both rags from me and nods his head. "I think I can handle that."

I move back to the shelf I was working on before Huxlee came in and he stays right behind me.

"So, do you guys do this every year?" he asks as he wipes a shelf I've cleared of books.

"Yep! While we're rearranging the store for Christmas anyway, might as well clean everything too. We do the same thing at the beginning of the year when we rearrange things again."

We talk back and forth while I pull books from the shelf and set them on the cart I pull around so the books don't have to be set on the floor. Then I wait for Mason to clean the shelf and dry it off before dusting each book and placing it back on the shelf.

When my stomach growls loudly around lunchtime, we take the cleaning supplies to the back before making our way to the counter where Huxlee has been straightening all the wrapping supplies.

"Hey, we're gonna go grab lunch. Do you want me to bring something back for you, or do you want to head out after we get back?"

"Just bring me something back. You two have fun!"

When we sit down at the café, he reaches across and takes my hand in his. "Thank you for letting me spend time with you today."

"I thought you were in town for some work stuff?"

"I might have lied..." He trails off, staring at our entwined hands.

"About?" I probe when he doesn't continue.

"I don't know how to explain it. But when I met you at the sleigh ride, something about you. Your smile, the easy conversation, perhaps just the spark I felt when I held your hand, that I *still* feel every time I hold your hand. I wanted to get to know you better, and I knew that long distance would not be the best way to do that."

"So you are some kind of stalker," I joke, and he chuckles.

"Perhaps, but you're the first woman I've ever wanted to spend time with this much. It's like I just can't get you out of my thoughts... or dreams." He looks up at me with an odd expression I can't place.

"Well, I won't lie to you and say it might have worked long distance because I loathe long-distance relationships."

We order our food; I opted for a club salad and we continue to talk about everything and nothing before I order Huxlee's favorite panini to go and we walk back to the store.

At five, we close up and head our separate ways, Huxlee heading home and Mason coming back to my house with me. We order dinner in and while we wait, we start watching the newest Marvel movie while we snuggle on my couch.

I'm nestled in the crook of his arm, settled between Mason and the back of the couch, and he runs his fingers up and down my back, causing goosebumps all over my body.

When the delivery guy gets here, Mason gets up and answers the door. I head to the kitchen to grab some chopsticks before settling down on the couch and divvying up our food.

Tonight we ordered Chinese food. I got my favorite, orange chicken, and Mason ordered some chow mein.

"Hey, do you have a fork I can use?" He holds up the chopsticks.

"What, don't know how to use chopsticks?"

"Not really," he answers.

I head into the kitchen to grab him a fork before returning to the couch.

We finish our dinner and the movie. Mason gets up to leave and pulls his coat on, then wraps a scarf around his neck before pulling me to him and pressing me against the door. I expect a kiss but, rather than that, he just rests his palm against my cheek again, and looks down at me with a smile on his face.

"I've enjoyed spending time with you today, Callie. I hope you won't kick me out if I show up tomorrow?"

I shake my head in response.

He comes in close before whispering in my ear, "It's important to remember looks can be deceiving." Then pulls back as his hand trails down my arm and he takes my hand in his. Gently, he pulls me away from the door before he opens it and leaves.

I curl up on the couch with the journal and open to where my bookmark is before deciding I'd like some tea and quickly make a cup. Settling back on the couch, I open back to the page I left off.

This morning when I awoke, I looked through various rooms and every cabinet I could find to locate something I could use to set traps for food.

Finally, I was able to find some thick rope and other thinner string I could use to set snares.

In one bedroom, I found some brightly-colored buttons in a drawer that must have belonged to a seamstress at one time. I took those to use as markers to find my way back to the entrance.

In another room, I located brightly-colored fabric, and I tore it into strips to use to mark where I would leave the snares to make it easier to find my catches.

The last room I stopped in was the kitchen so I could grab a basket to hold all the items. Also to hopefully collect something for me to eat today, knowing I would need to let the snares sit overnight to allow time for creatures to be caught.

It took me a while to locate the passage that led to the door I entered through but I was finally able to find where I thought I came in. Instead, I found another entrance. This one was hidden from the outside.

When I exited and looked back, the door was invisible and I felt around the door looking for some kind of knob. The only sign a door existed was a very thin line around the perimeter of the door.

Finally, I found where to press to get the door to swing open and I dropped the buttons at intervals along my path.

Once I entered the woods, I set several snares and marked their locations with the torn fabric. Then I looked around me for some edible berries or other plants I could eat today.

Nearby, I found some wild berries, and I collected them in the now-empty basket and followed my button trail back to the entrance.

As I now sit writing in the journal and snacking on the berries, I pray I find some small creature so I can enjoy something of more substance tomorrow.

At the end of the entry, I place my bookmark back in the journal and get ready for bed. I hope to wake up in the prison world. While I am enjoying my time with Mason, I miss the beast.

Every morning I wake up in this world, I grow more and more anxious about what might be going on in the dream world. What is happening to the king under the mountain? Have I missed the war? I wonder if something is wrong with me. Why can't I get back there? This anxiety seems to be worst when I am by myself, like right now.

There is a part of me that is holding back with Mason. I enjoy his company. I enjoy watching movies, talking, and laughing with him. But there is some part of me holding back from kissing him, doing *more* than kissing him. I just can't seem to get the beast king out of my mind.

Sitting up and stretching my arms over my head, I groan when my spine cracks as I carefully lean right, then left. When I see the clock, I realize I must have forgotten to set my alarm last night. I won't have time to stop by the coffee shop this morning. Pre-coffee Callie moves much slower than properly caffeinated Callie, so my first stop after climbing out of bed is to get the coffee started.

I make my way back to my room and pull out some clothes before heading into the bathroom to take a shower and get ready for the day. The last thing I do is apply mascara to my long eyelashes and step back to make sure I haven't forgotten something in my normal routine.

I dab some Vaseline across my lips before making my way back to the kitchen. My mugs are in the cabinet above my coffeemaker and I pull out a travel mug, filling it almost to the rim before adding some sugar and creamer and putting the lid on.

My purse is right beside the door and I snag it on my way out, locking the door behind me before getting in my car and heading to the bookstore.

Huxlee is already here when I arrive, and I greet her on my way to the back.

"Hey, girl, no coffee for me this morning?" she asks from between two of the shelves.

The bell above the door dings as I reply, "Sorry! I woke up late and didn't have time to stop in for coffee."

"Did someone mention coffee?" Mason holds a drink carrier with three cups in one hand and a bag in the other hand.

"Callie, you're not allowed to get rid of this one, ever,"

Huxlee moves to Mason, bouncing on the balls of her feet as he hands her a drink and pulls a warm breakfast sandwich out, handing it to her as well.

He moves to me, and then he notices the cup already in my hands. "Oh sorry. I guess I should have asked."

I look down at my cup and shrug. "I can guarantee you my homemade coffee does not taste better than whatever you've brought. I'll just pour it out or drink it later." He follows me to the back and I place my mug in the fridge before turning around and accepting the drink and food from him. "Thank you."

"You're welcome, Callie." He throws away the drink holder after pulling his cup out of it. Then he wraps his free arm around me and pulls me to him, kissing the top of my head. "Mmm, you smell good." He inhales the flowery scent of my shampoo.

"Does that mean I usually smell bad?" I poke fun at him.

"Of... of course not," he stutters, and I chuckle as he's caught off-guard.

"Don't worry, I'm just poking fun at you." I bump him with my hip and head back out into the store. Huxlee has hopped up on the front counter and I join her as we eat our food and drink our coffee.

Mason stands across from us and eats his breakfast. "So what's on the cleaning agenda for today?"

"More of what we were doing yesterday," I reply. "There are a lot of shelves in here."

"Sounds good to me."

"I'll just be manning the counter while you two canoodle in the stacks."

I elbow Huxlee and she breaks off into giggles. She's laughing so hard it's infectious, and Mason and I laugh right along with her.

"Canoodle, really? Where do you come up with this stuff?"

"I've probably been watching too many movies lately." She gets up and throws her trash away. "But really, you two let me know if you need me. I'm going to step out and grab our lunch today, if that's okay with you."

"Sounds good to me." I jump down and throw my trash away before grabbing Mason's hand and pulling him with me to the back to get our cleaning supplies.

I don't ask when Mason has to go back home. I don't want to stop spending time with him. We enjoy our time together as we continue to work our way through the store.

At lunchtime, Huxlee comes to let us know where she's heading and Mason gives her his order. She already knows what I always get from the restaurant. I tend to stick to the same few menu items wherever we go, only sometimes branching out if there's a new item offered. Why mess with what you already know you like, right?

When she gets back, we all sit around the breakroom table, in view of the screen showing the security camera feed. The door stays propped open so we can hear if someone enters the store.

Mason scoots his chair closer to me, and while we talk to Huxlee, he rests his hand on my knee, occasionally running his fingers in little circles slowly edging up along my thigh. The motion does not go unnoticed by Huxlee, who smirks each time she catches my eye.

Another side effect of his movements. My hormones are going crazy, and I have to clench my thighs together to relieve some of the gloriously torturous flutters running through my core.

As I wiggle in my chair for probably the tenth time, Huxlee finally excuses herself and heads to the front of her store. "Don't do anything I wouldn't do," she says over her shoulder as she closes the door behind her.

I stand and throw away my trash, Mason following my movements. Before I'm able to make it out the door, he grasps my hand and pulls me to him. My hands rest on his tall shoulders, while his rest on my waist.

"Callie, I... don't want things to move too fast. But I've never felt this way with anyone before." His hands dip just beneath the edge of my shirt and butterflies fly around in my stomach as I look up at him.

Slowly, I move my hands to his neck. I use my fingernails to graze lightly along his scalp. He closes his eyes and moans in pleasure as I continue the movement. "Mason, despite what Huxlee said, I will not jump your bones or whatever in the backroom of my place of work." I pull back and open the door, heading straight for where we left off our cleaning.

At the end of the day, we head back to my place, order dinner in again, and start a movie. As we're again lying on the couch, Mason on his back and me pressed gloriously between his side and the back of the couch, my head rests on his shoulder and I tip my face up to his. Sometime during the day, I decided there was no good reason to hold back with Mason and decided if he was willing to go for it, so was I.

But rather than being a grown up and telling him that I've changed my mind, I lay here hoping he can somehow *read* my mind. After a few minutes of acting like an idiot, the delivery guy knocks at the door and I propel myself up, rolling over Mason and head to the door.

By the time I get back to the couch, Mason is sitting up, holding silverware in his hands and ready to eat.

I pull out my chicken alfredo and hand Mason his lasagna. We place the breadsticks in between us on the table, and I snag one immediately, taking a bite of the garlic buttery goodness before taking my fork from Mason and twirling my pasta around it.

After dinner, we move back into our horizontal positions on the couch. I decide to settle in and watch the end of the movie.

Too soon, it's time for him to leave again. He presses me against the wall by the door, and immediately his fingers tangle in my hair. He gently pulls my head back by tugging on the strands. Looking down at me, he observes my reactions to the movements. I gasp and he continues to hold my hair, keeping my head from being able to move. Too slowly, he descends. His breath skates along the column of my throat and I feel tingles all the way from my head to my curling toes.

His lips gently graze the sensitive skin just below my ear before he quickly pulls back. He opens the door. "It's important to remember looks can be deceiving." Then he leaves me reeling with his sudden absence.

In a daze, I get ready for bed, climbing under my covers and falling quickly to sleep.

I am startled out of sleep when my phone rings.

"Hello?" I answer groggily.

"Hey, Callie, it's Mom." We haven't talked since she got so mad about the ornaments. "I just called to say I was thinking about you and I love you."

"Mom, I'm so sorry. If I would have known about the secr—"

"Callie, I was a kid once, too. I know what curiosity is like. I should have hidden the chest better many years ago."

"I'm still really sorry."

"It's not like anything bad happened, right?"

"Right," I say. Knowing I should probably tell her about the traveling, but unsure how she would handle it.

"Well, I can't wait to see you for Christmas. I hope you have a wonderful day. Love you."

I sit up in bed and I can feel some of the anxiety lift with just those simple words. Sometimes I think my mom has some extreme version of mind-reading capabilities. I swear she always calls just when I need her.

"I love you, too, Mom. I can't wait for Christmas either. How are you guys?"

She spends the next several minutes telling me all about what she's been doing now that she has been cleared to walk again. Her excitement is palpable and I'm so glad she wasn't forced to sit for any longer. She might have driven my dad crazy with much more time in a chair.

My mom is what I would call a busybody. Any amount of time where she can't be out doing what she wants with the people she wants makes her upset. And an unhappy mama makes for an unhappy everyone else. Dad always says, "Happy wife, happy life." I've never understood that simple statement until mom's stint off her feet for a few weeks.

We say our goodbyes and I take a deep, cleansing breath, trying to get the rest of my anxiety to leave. I feel like I can breathe better knowing that she's not still mad at me.

When Mason gets to my house, I'm waiting for him at the door, opening it before he has a chance to knock. "Hey, want to go somewhere with me today?"

"We're not going to have to cut down Christmas trees again, right?"

"No, I thought maybe you'd like to go horseback riding with me."

"Lead the way." He helps me into my coat before walking in front of me so I can lock my door.

On the drive to the stables, our conversation comes easily. "I'm hoping you know how to ride?" I ask when we're almost there.

"I learned how to ride when I was a kid. You?"

"When I was a kid, I begged my parents for lessons. When I moved out here, I found a stable that would let me come in and ride the boarded horses for free. They use volunteers to help exercise the horses, with owners' permission, of course."

When we pull up, I see they already have two horses tacked and ready to go for us. "Looks like we'll be riding Thunder and Daisy today." I run my hand along Daisy's neck and she nickers in response. "This beautiful girl is Daisy. She'll treat you real good today."

"And who's this strapping man?" Mason pats Thunder's hindquarters.

"That is Thunder. He's a little particular about who he lets ride him," I say.

He nods at me before moving to Daisy and mounting in one fluid motion.

I get on Thunder and lead us down the nearest trail, this one wide enough to accommodate us riding side by side.

We spend the afternoon riding back and forth through the trails near the stables. Sometimes we talk but, for most of the ride, we enjoy the surrounding scenery, the sound of the horses' hooves against the well-worn paths.

When we finally make our way back to the stables, I am hungry and suggest we grab some burgers on the way home. The Grill is on our way back to my place and we order the same delicious burgers we had the last time.

While we sit and watch some random show on television, he ignites all my hormones with his caresses. The few times his lips graze along my skin, my hair, anywhere but my lips, leave me breathless and wanting more.

When I walk him to the door, I'm again left wondering if something's wrong with me. I wrap my arms around myself as he leaves.

As I get ready for bed. I pray I can make it back to the fantasy world tonight. I need to know how the people there are, whether war has broken out. Whether they've survived.

PART THREE

Christmas

CHAPTER 12

Let it Go

Birds singing wakes me this morning. As soon as I open my eyes, I am thrilled to be in the dream world. Immediately, I jump out of bed and start to get myself ready.

Soon, though, the maid comes in, her eyes growing wide when she observes my state of undress.

"You're back, miss," she says. It's the first time anyone has acknowledged me occasionally being missing from this world. I wonder if Huxlee will notice back home if I don't show up to work tomorrow?

"I didn't mean to scare you, I just wanted to find out what's going on here as soon as I can."

"If you'd like, I can take your breakfast back down so you can eat with the king this morning. He can fill you in on what's been happening around here."

"That would be lovely, thank you."

She curtsies and exits the room, my tray in her hands. I find it sweet they've been sending food to my room, even when I've been missing for several days.

I look down at my legs, trying to get them into the massive quantity of skirts and other underthings I must wear in this world. When a few minutes later my door opens abruptly, making me jump, and trip over the skirts wrapped around my knees. I look up and see the beast standing in my doorway, breathing heavily.

"You're back," he pants. Clearly exerted from running from wherever he was in the castle.

"I'm back." I smile from my spot on the floor.

It only takes him a few strides to make it to me where I'm sprawled across the floor. He extends his hand down and helps me up, motioning for me to turn around.

I'm frozen in place as he bends. I hold my breath as he grazes his hand down my leg to bring my skirts up to their proper place. He then ties them securely around my waist and reaches to grab my corset.

"I thought... it doesn't matter what I thought. I'm glad you're back," he says.

"I don't control what world I wake up in. I've been worried about you here. Has there been any further movement?" The words tumble out of my mouth so fast I wonder if he can even understand me.

"I don't want to talk about that now. It doesn't matter."

He brushes my hair out of the way, bringing it around to my shoulder, out of the way of my corset strings, as he carefully laces me up the back. Thankfully, not as tightly as the maid does, so I can still breathe today.

"Will you join me for breakfast?" he asks.

"I believe I was told breakfast would be available soon." I grin as he reaches out his arm for me to place my hand in the crook of his elbow. We walk out the door and down the stairs, but he moves in the opposite direction of the dining room I am used to eating in.

"I thought we might eat out in the garden this morning."

"That sounds lovely." I mentally kick myself, *lovely? What the heck is happening to me?*

When we get into the garden he brought me to before, I notice things are rearranged. Someone has been busy planting new flowers since I was last in here. The arrangement of colors, smells, and various flowers is beautiful.

But rather than making my way over to the flowers, my stomach demands food first.

"You sure have a demanding appetite," he says, chuckling.

"You've noticed?" I reply, a corner of my lips lifting.

He pulls out my chair for me, pushing me in so we can eat.

"Are kings supposed to push in chairs for commoners?"

"You are anything but common, Callie." My eyes raise to his ice blue and brown ones. He stares back at me. "You have the most beautiful blue eyes." He briefly grazes my cheek before taking his own seat.

"What do you mean?" I ask slowly, skeptically, wondering if this king possibly knows more about my being here than I do.

"Because you're the one from the prophecy," he says dismissively, shrugging. Then looks down at the trays covering the table and loads his breakfast plate.

I don't have any words. Prophecy? My mom mentioned nothing about a prophecy. It makes me wonder if any of the journals might mention this "prophecy." It would take me a long time to read my way through every journal in the chest. There were at least a few dozen in its depths.

"What prophecy?" I finally ask, lamely.

"A woman will come differently from the rest. And she will save us from this world, this prison."

"How do you know *I'm* the woman?"

He looks up at me, and his next words chill me to the bone. "You're the only one who has left this place in hundreds—no, thousands of years."

Thousands of years? Some of these people have been trapped here for *thousands* of years?

"This place is some kind of prison world, right?"

"That's exactly what this place is, a prison for those of us who dared to cross the person who banished us here."

If they've all been banished here, why would they wage war

against each other? Why would they want to destroy the other people who have been sent here against their will?

"If that's true... If all of you have been banished here for crossing some person who has the power to create a prison world and send you here, then why are you attacking each other? Why is there a potential war on the horizon? Why does it matter that the people across the water are moving their location?"

"There are bad people everywhere, Callie. Each of us has been banished here for a different reason. And everyone I've talked to has no memories of what exactly happened, or who sent us here. All we know is that we remember being sent here for crossing *someone*, and were all left with a journal, the clothes on our back, and the words of the prophecy ingrained in our brains."

If I am this "prophecy" woman, what am I supposed to do to save them? I just learned this is a prison world for sure, like two seconds ago. My mom didn't seem to know much either, or I'm sure she would have told me. And according to her, I'm the first person who's been able to come here.

That begs the question, how *am* I able to get here? All I know is I disobeyed my mom, stole a journal, read it, and *bam!* I'm in this world every night when I go to sleep. Or *almost* every night.

Was it me finding the journal that triggered me coming here? Mom said I wasn't supposed to know about the world yet. She said I was supposed to find out on my birthday. Is that what messed this all up? Is that why I'm here today?

"Penny for your thoughts?" His voice breaks into my speculations.

"There's an immense problem with this whole prophecy. I don't know how I get here, nor do I know what triggers it."

"Why don't you tell me what you remember?"

I take a moment to gather my thoughts before starting, "I was at my parents' house helping decorate for Christmas. I found a chest in my mom's attic and asked her about it. She told me to stay away, but I found the key and opened the chest. It was full of journals. I searched to find the one that looked the oldest, at least of the ones I could see, and hid it away to read later—"

"What was in this journal?"

I tell him what I can remember of the journal. I've read most of it at this point. When I look up at his face, he's gone pale. "Are you okay?"

"You... you... found... my journal."

"What?"

"The words you just spoke, the contents of the journal you found, that is *exactly* what I wrote in my journal when I arrived here."

"That's impossible. That journal was from over 300 years ago..." I trail off, an odd expression taking over his face.

"What year is it now, Callie?"

I spout the answer off automatically.

"I arrived in this world in the year of our Lord 1740."

My jaw drops open. He looks damn good for someone over 300 years old. Maybe this world also freezes them in time? "But you don't look that old," I say stupidly, my mouth and brain working at two different paces.

He chuckles. "All of us who have been banished here have been frozen in time. And I have been here a long time. I'm ready to continue living my life back in the real world. I think you just might be the one to save us all."

"Or the one that fucks everything up..." I say under my breath.

He reaches out, gently lifting my chin with his fingers, forcing me to look into his eyes. "Even if you do 'fuck everything up,' I still believe you will save us all."

"Yeah, right after we fight a damn war!"

"Callie, just let it go. Wars have been going on for centuries. I, for one, am not going to worry about a war in a prison world."

"Are you messing with me? How can you not be concerned about your people here? Aren't you concerned they might die? Aren't you worried about what might happen if you don't help?"

"Callie, I said *let. It. Go!*"

He shoves back from the table so forcefully he knocks it and everything on it over. Food, drinks and dishes fly across the floor and shatter. I flinch at the sudden outburst, turning away in fright from the king.

He immediately reaches out for me. Flinching away, I get up from my chair and move to the other side of the garden. I need to be alone with my thoughts. I need to think about what I can do to help save this world. And I certainly don't want to think about it in front of a king who loses his temper like a toddler.

I hear the doors into the castle slam closed. When I glance back, I'm alone in the garden with the servants left behind to clean up his mess. I move over to them in an attempt to help them clean up, since I'm somewhat responsible for the outburst. They quickly shoo me away, not wanting the king mad at them for letting me help.

I walk every inch of the garden, smelling every kind of flower on my trek. Unfortunately, I don't get any closer to a solution for the possibly impending war than before. I don't know enough about this world to make an educated decision.

Also, if this is a prison, what happens if someone dies here?

When I decide to go inside, I notice some of the artwork in the entryway to get to the garden has been removed. He must have carried his tantrum inside.

Since I have awhile before it's time for bed, I decide to wander the castle. Fortunately, I don't run into the beast, but I make my way down some dark passages that look like they've been abandoned for some time.

It all makes me wonder how the castle got carved into the mountain. It looks like it would take years and many more people than I've seen in this place. Also, in his journal he said the place was empty, no people. So when did the rest of the people who live here get here? Maybe the answer lies in the part of the journal I haven't read yet.

My luck was bound to run out at some point. In one of the dark passages, I carefully push open a door and finally find the beast. He's sitting on a couch, elbows on his knees, head in his hands. I can barely make out the look on his face, but what I can see looks pained. Holding my breath, I stand in the doorway, watching him.

Taking another step into the room, my foot hits something and it rolls across the floor, making an incredible racket in the quiet room. He raises his head to look at me, and I've never wished I could disappear until this moment.

"What are you doing in here? You shouldn't be here."

I have no excuse for why I'm here other than I was just exploring. "I didn't know what to do with my sudden time alone. I was unaware there were places down here off-limits."

"So rather than ask someone, you just started snooping around someone else's home?" he snaps.

"And who exactly was I supposed to ask? The person I'm usually with threw a tantrum like a damn toddler and left me alone."

He laughs so hard, I think something must be seriously wrong with him. "A toddler? Really?"

"How would you describe that display out in the garden? Are you even aware it took your people an hour to clean up that mess?"

He stands and walks to a window off to the side. Since we're under a mountain, there aren't many of them I've seen and I wonder what this one looks out onto.

I don't dare move from my position, afraid my stay here may hang in the balance. What happens if you anger a king beyond reasonable means?

Gently, he says, "Come, I want to show you something." Slowly I make my way over to his side, looking at the side of his face as he looks out. The window is so small we can't help but touch. His heat emanates up my arm as it grazes him. "Do you see the houses down there?"

I look out the window, and what I see surprises me. There are many small cottages down below, filling the entire valley of the mountain range, along with farmland and farmhouses as far as I can see. Children playing, dogs running around, parents talking to each other. We must be on the other side of the mountain from where I came in from. The scene below looks nothing like I remember from my approach to the mountain, however many days ago.

"These people are who I am trying to protect. They are the reason I don't just 'get ready for war.' Everyone who has been sent here—everyone who has settled in my part of the world, I have sworn to protect. One does not run blindly into a fight that may not happen, or they may indeed make that fight happen. All we know now is that another part of the world is moving. It may be something, but it could be nothing. My citizens are moms and dads, farmers, and children. We do not have armies on standby to wait for war to come. My people just live their lives here. I will not send them to their deaths unnecessarily."

Down below, I watch the children run back and forth with their friends, laughing and playing. They don't have a care in the world; they are content here. "Don't they deserve the chance to make that decision? What if it comes, and it's too late to decide or to get ready?"

He lets out a loud breath, turning and walking back to his couch. This time when he sits, he's more relaxed, leaning back against the cushions, laying his arm across the back of it. "Therein lies the eternal plight of a king. You have to know when to strike, and when to hold back, and pray you're not wrong."

"It sounds terrifying." I come to sit next to him on the couch, taking hold of the hand in his lap and weave my fingers between his. "And lonely."

"You have no idea," he says with a sigh.

We sit in silence for some time, me wondering where I'm going to wake up this time. When I get back home, I really need to find a witch to help me figure some things out.

"Does the other side have a king?" I ask.

"I guess you could call him that," he replies.

"What do you call him?"

"A pain in my ass." I bark out a laugh at his candor. "I'm not sure when he got here in relation to when I did. We may have gotten here at the same time. It could have been a hundred years apart, or more. I did little exploring when I got here after I found a place to live."

"I remember reading about that in your journal. Did you find it strange when you found a fully furnished castle?"

"No more weird than showing up in some prison world."

We continue to talk in this manner, even through dinner. When it is time for bed, he again walks me to my door. "I hope to see you in the morning." His palms hold either side of my face, thumbs rubbing side to side on my cheeks. I run my eyes across his bearded face, doing my best to keep my glance away from his scars. When he moves his thumb to run along my bottom lip, I hold my breath. "Goodnight, beautiful Callie."

"Goodnight," I breathe as he opens my door, and I go inside.

CHAPTER 13

I'll Be Home for Christmas

The ringtone on my cell phone wakes me from the fantasy world and my heart sinks. I wanted some more time to spend with the beast. "Hello?" I answer.

"Good morning, beautiful, I wanted to let you know I have to go back home this morning. Where are you planning to spend Christmas?" I smile at Mason's voice, and his thoughtfulness to ask about my plans.

"I'll be home for Christmas," I pause and rethink my answer. "What I mean is, I'll be at my parents' home for Christmas." I sit up in bed, trying to clear the sleep from my head.

"Perfect, I'm sure I'll talk to you between now and then but, let me know when you plan to be there and I'll come spend some time with you."

"Of course." I can't wait. The smile on my face grows thinking about spending more time with him.

"Sorry to call and then run so quick, but I really have to go. I'm about to drive out, I just wanted to make sure you knew as soon as possible. I'll talk to you later, Callie."

"Okay, bye, Mason."

"It's important to remember looks can be deceiving." That. Damn. Phrase. Why does he say it almost every time I talk to him?

"What does that even mean?" I ask, since he didn't answer me the last time. The phone goes silent in my hand when he hangs up.

I get out of bed and run to the bathroom to get ready for my day. My running clothes hang on the back of my bathroom door and I briefly think about how much I've been slacking off. Huxlee and I have a store to finish getting ready and hopefully some Christmas shopping customers to help, so I get dressed in normal clothes, deciding I'll make more of an effort to get back outside soon.

"Good morning, my favorite boss ever," I say as I walk into the store.

"Morning, Callie! What's that you've got there?" Her eyes focus in on the large coffee I'm holding in my hand.

"I knew you could use some extra energy today. I'm sorry I've kinda ditched you this year."

"Where is your boy-toy this morning?" She waggles her eyebrows at me.

"He had to go back home." My voice gives away my disappointment. But really, how long could I have expected him to be here? At least he seems to want to see me when I'm at my parents'.

"Oh, hun, I'm sorry." She gestures for me to hand over her coffee.

"Are you sorry, or did you just want the treat I brought you?" I laugh.

"Well, if you truly knew me, you would have brought—" She stops when I reach into my purse and pull out her favorite, pumpkin bread. "You do love me!" she squeals.

I laugh when she snatches it out of my hand, immediately taking a bite and moaning. Really, who doesn't love some good pumpkin bread at the holidays?

Huxlee and I usually take turns bringing in coffee and breakfast for each other. Because it's been a while since I've been here consistently, and with Mason recently thrown into the mix, I figured it was my turn.

"You are my favorite employee. I was thinking employee of the month? I might be willing to push that to employee of the year if you keep bringing this deliciousness for me. And if you keep bringing Mason around to get some extra cleaning done, I might splurge for employee of the decade."

"I'm your only employee." I chuckle. And really, I feel incredibly fortunate to have Huxlee as a boss. Even if she is a pain in my ass sometimes.

"Well then, it's a good thing you've gotten on my good side, huh?"

"What's on the agenda for today?"

"There's a list over there of what I'd like to get done. We're almost finished with getting all the displays changed over for the holidays. We just need to get the decorations up, too."

"I can definitely handle that today." And really, after decorating two houses for the holidays, what's one more bookstore? "Did you want me to do some window-painting as well?"

"You are the best at it, my art skills are limited to shitty stick figures, and even shittier Christmas trees."

"Admitting your faults *is* the first step." She smacks me playfully before we both burst out laughing.

"What would I do without your smartass mouth?"

"Hopefully, you never have to find out. I love this place."

Huxlee and I spend the rest of the day getting the store completely decorated for Christmas. I hang garlands across the now-clean shelves and paint the front window with a Christmas scene. The only images that came to mind were of the view I had when I approached the river in the prison world. So I drew the vision in its snow-covered glory.

"Damn, girl, I knew I kept you around for a reason." Huxlee looks at the front window.

"You like it?"

"Like it? I love it! You're hired to do all the window-decorating, forever."

"How generous," I deadpan, before breaking into giggles.

"I'm gonna go grab some lunch, bring you something back?"

"Of course, you know what I like."

I go inside and stand behind the counter while waiting for her to come back. A couple of customers come in and I help them wrap the books they select for Christmas presents. Huxlee started offering complementary gift-wrapping a couple of years ago and the customers seem to appreciate the effort.

My favorite part of this job, though, is helping people find the perfect book for their loved one. I can usually pick out a good match based on their personality and other things they're able to tell me about the person they're buying for.

Today's lineup of recommendations include some fantasy, romance, and dark romance, my personal secret obsession. My life has been boring until recently, but I love me some good, dark storylines to remember that not everyone has it as easy as I have.

Huxlee comes back with lunch and we talk back and forth about what we should get each member of our family for Christmas. We've known each other long enough, we've met most of each other's family.

"Are those brothers of yours bringing their families for Christmas this year?" she asks.

"Last I heard, the whole gang is going to be there for the week."

"Are you going to bring Mason?"

"He called me this morning and wants me to let him know when I'm back in town. I'm nervous, though. My feelings are growing for him but, something is holding me back."

"Is it maybe all those dark romances you've been reading? You know guys aren't like that in real life, right? At least not any guy I've ever met."

"You mean you haven't dated any crazy stalkers?" I joke.

"At least none that I know of. Of course, they wouldn't be a very good stalker if I knew they were stalking, now would they?"

"True." I laugh.

We get back to work after lunch and finish up the last of the Christmas decorating. Huxlee takes some pictures of the store to post on our social media.

At the end of the day, I head back to my house alone. After a dinner consisting of a sandwich and some chips, I make myself a cup of cocoa and sit down with the journal to read until bedtime.

> This morning, I awoke and got ready to check my snares. When I approached the first one, the snare had been triggered, but nothing was caught in the loop.
>
> Slowly, I followed the same line I had set the snares along yesterday and continued to encounter more of the same. When I arrived at the last snare, I found the reason for my discovery. Lying on the ground, consuming my food was a dark grey wolf.
>
> As I approached, he watched me, continuing to pull apart the dinner I was looking forward to. It seems in my efforts to feed myself I had made it easy for other predators to catch their own prey.
>
> Carefully, I backed away from the creature,

turning around only when I felt I had travelled a safe enough distance away from the wolf.

From behind me I heard a man say, "Hey, wait."

I spun on my heel, reaching for a sword I didn't have. Facing me was a man, completely naked in appearance. The wolf was nowhere to be seen. "Where did you come from?" I asked.

"I'm sorry. I didn't know someone else inhabited this area. I have seen no one in this part of the world in a long time. I suppose I should have known when there were suddenly snares set up. But you see, the wolf doesn't always think rationally, and the wolf was hungry," he said.

I stared at him, unsure what he could be talking about. The wolf must have run away before this man came up to me.

"The wolf?" I questioned, my body's state of hunger completely taking over any further rational thought I could have had at that moment.

It was after I spoke he did something so unbelievable. Right before my eyes, the man shifted into the wolf. The sheer surprise overwhelmed me, and I fainted. I was told it was several minutes before I came to again. The man sitting on the ground next to me inquired about where I was staying.

Skeptically, I told him of the place I had

found under the mountain. He knew the area I referred to, being so near where we currently sat.

He helped me to my feet and walked with me back to the hidden door. Before leaving, he introduced himself as Zev and told me he was banished here eight hundred years prior. He told me of the many other people who have come through these parts during his time here.

He also told me of the elderly woman who was banished here with him and he vowed to take me to her cottage at a later time. Although, he did warn me that she is not exactly fond of him since it's his fault she was banished here. He vowed to leave my snares alone, but told me he could not guarantee the wolf would comply with his promises.

Wow, so Zev is a werewolf! I wondered how he could have been working for the king since, well, wolves don't talk. I wonder how the woman got sent there with him?

Yawning, I decide it's time to stop reading for the night. I put my bookmark between the pages and set the journal on the side table. Before going to my room, I make one last trip to the bathroom and then climb into bed, pulling my blankets over myself.

CHAPTER 14

Imagine

My heart jumps in my chest when I wake up in the prison world. I quickly remove my pajamas and redress into the clothes of this world before opening the door to my room and traipsing down the stairs.

At the bottom of the stairs, I run into the woman who usually helps me get ready. She yelps when she looks up from her feet and sees me already dressed and downstairs.

"Miss, you're dressed already."

"I couldn't wait to get down here for breakfast," I lie.

"Of course, miss, breakfast is waiting in the dining room." She jerks her chin toward the familiar doors.

"Thank you. I realize I don't even know your name. What can I call you?"

"My name is Kenna, miss." She smiles.

"Thank you, Kenna." I reach my hand out to her shoulder and squeeze in appreciation. "You've always been kind to me."

"It's my job, miss. But thank you for noticing." She curtsies and her smile grows even wider.

She continues on her way up the stairs, and I move to the dining room. I'm disappointed that it's empty. The beast is nowhere to be seen and my heart drops to my stomach at the realization that I've developed feelings for him. I haven't had feelings for anyone in a while, but give me two interesting guys at the same time and here I go falling for both of them.

Before wandering around the castle, I know I need to eat something. There's no telling how long it will take me to locate the beast, or how far I'll have to walk through the castle to find him.

I grab a reasonable amount of food and pile it on my plate. Slowly, I eat and plan out which direction I'm going to go first. I've seen such a small part of the castle, I figure I'll try the places I have been first before traveling to unknown areas.

When I leave the dining room, I immediately head to the study. He's not there, so I head to the room I found him in the last time I was here. Also empty. On a whim, I decide to look out the window at the village below. I smile when I see him talking to a group of people.

Unsure where any of the exits to get out of this place are, I change tactics and decide to search out Kenna. Hopefully, she can point me in the right direction. I haven't even seen the door I entered through when I was brought to the castle, since the day I arrived.

Kenna is in the kitchen when I finally find her in my search. "Miss, what are you doing in here? You shouldn't be here."

"I was trying to find His Majesty. I found him but, he's down in the village. Can you help me get out to him?"

She looks at me skeptically before responding, "Miss, we're not supposed to let you leave the castle."

"What? Why? I'll be with the king. I saw him out there."

"How exactly did you see him out there?" She seems to not believe me. I remember now that I wasn't supposed to be in the room I had found before. But, I haven't seen another window here so I don't have any other choice but to tell the truth.

"Yesterday when I was here," I start, "I was wandering the castle looking for the king when I found him in a room. That room had a window in it. He showed me the town down below." I take a breath before continuing. "I was looking for him again today when I looked in that room again and he wasn't there. But through the window I could see he was down in the town talking to some of the people. I don't know how to get out of here to get to him."

She watches me, then her eyes wander around the room. She sighs before relenting, "Fine, I'll show you the door. But you can't tell anyone who showed you."

"Deal."

Quickly, she leads me back out of the kitchen and down another dark passage. She glances both ways before pressing her palm to a place on the wall. The stone sinks in beneath her touch and a hidden door pops open. Immediately, I can see the daylight. "There's a stable just over there. Tell them Kenna sent you and to provide you a horse." When I turn around to thank her, she is already at the far end of the hallway, moving faster than I've ever seen her move.

I take a deep breath, hoping he doesn't get mad at me *again* for doing something I wasn't supposed to do. Then I step through the door, raising my face up to the sunlight. The first thing I notice is I do not feel warmth on my face. The sun is high in the sky. I should be able to feel its warmth, but instead, it just feels cold.

A few steps out of the door, I feel an icy breeze and remember that it's winter. I regret not looking for some kind of coat or something warm to wrap around my arms before coming out here.

Looking up the mountain face, I try to find the window in the rock. When I find it, I look out into the village, trying to figure out where he is. I wrap my arms around myself to stave off the chill as I walk through the dirt streets looking for the stable.

It's a small one, hidden among other businesses, and when I arrive, I repeat the words Kenna told me to say. It only takes him a moment to saddle the horse and carefully I climb onto the horse, pulling my skirts up so I can ride the way I am accustomed to. The man's eyes grow large, and I realize he was probably expecting me to ride sidesaddle.

There's a crowd surrounding one area of the village, and I assume that must be where the king is. I make my way over to them and I can see above everyone's heads from my place on the horse.

In the very center, I see his head above the tops of everyone else's. His eyes meet mine across the crowd and I climb down, securing the horse on a nearby fence before I make my way to the center. Carefully pushing my way through the crowd, repeating, "excuse me," each time I need to push past someone.

It only takes me a few minutes before I'm standing in front of him. Only now can I see he's surrounded by children, face animated, hands gesturing wildly as he tells the children a story. I realize I've never seen him this relaxed. A smile ghosts my lips as I watch him.

A few minutes later, he finishes his story to applause from the crowd. I clap along with them, my grin so large my cheeks start to hurt. He stands and makes his way over to me.

Leaning into me, he whispers, "Callie, what are you doing here?"

"I saw you through the window we were looking through yesterday and found my way out here," I whisper back.

His gaze says he doesn't believe me. Considering the door was hidden, he knows someone had to have shown me the way out. It wouldn't take a lot for him to track down *who* let me out.

"Why aren't you wearing a coat?" he asks.

I shrug before answering. "I didn't think to grab one before I came out."

Quickly, he removes his own, holding it open for me as I slide my arms into the sleeves before he holds his arm out to me. "Let me show you around." His wide smile makes those damn dimples appear.

"But what about—" I turn my head to glance at where I tied the horse.

"Someone will take the horse back to the stable. Don't worry."

I take his arm, and he introduces me to the surrounding people. He knows the names of everyone here, and they delight in that fact.

As we continue to walk around the village, I look around and notice that these houses have been kept up well. These people seem to take great pride in living here. Briefly, I wonder if perhaps the homes are magically repaired. But as we walk and the people go back to work, some people grab tools and do some minor repairs to a fence, a roof, and a chimney on a home.

One villager invites us for lunch. The beast declines, leading us back to the castle as my stomach growls. "Your stomach sure likes to make it known it's hungry, huh?"

"It's always been that way. Although, I never eat when I'm sleeping. But, I guess coming here, I'm not really sleeping, am I?" I've never thought of it that way. Besides the rare morning when I have woken up where I went to sleep, I have been constantly running.

"No, Callie, I don't think this counts as sleeping to your stomach since you're constantly moving when you're here."

"Yeah, or running," I say under my breath.

"I truly am sorry for how Zev behaved when you got here. He wasn't sure if you were another of us, or what you were. It had been a while since we've had a new person sentenced here." I remember the name from my recent journal reading and I nod my head in understanding.

Remembering my revelations last night about Zev being a werewolf, I think about how I thought those were just from stories. I mentally smack my forehead when I remember that *everyone* here is from a story. Their lives are remembered in the pages of the books we start enjoying as children, and the journals my family was cursed to protect.

He guides me through the entrance I exited through, another secret pressure point or some such makes the door appear, swinging open to allow us entrance. His large hand is warm on my back. As soon as we're inside, he gently grasps my hand and places it back in the crook of his arm.

After we've gotten some lunch, he stands and gestures for me to join him. "Would you care to see another area of the castle today?"

"Sure, why not?" Most of my time here has been spent with a guide or searching for him. I really haven't gotten a chance to look around at many of the passages. Most of them are blocked off or so dark, I wouldn't dare journey down them unattended.

"This is one of my favorite wings of the castle." He moves to a table in the hall and pulls a candle and candleholder out of a drawer. Using a match to light the candle, he holds his arm out again for me to take. He uses the candle to light our way down the dark passage. We finally stop at a large, ornately carved door. "I haven't brought anyone in here, ever."

I hold my breath as he pulls a necklace from around his neck, a skeleton key swinging from the end. He uses the key to unlock the door and leads me through. Inside is bright, lit by windows along one wall, letting in the bright sunshine. The walls are covered in various cages, holding all kinds of animals. Along one wall are all different kinds of birds, every color you could think of, and some I have never seen on a bird before.

Another wall has various kinds of snakes and other reptiles. The third wall has all different types of rodents. I imagine some are meant to feed the snakes. "What is this place?"

"This was here when I got here. It was the only sign of life when I arrived. I'm not sure how they got food before I got here, but they all appeared to have been taken care of."

"It's almost like whoever has been sending all of you here didn't want you to be here completely alone."

"Or they wanted to keep me busy. Do you know how long it takes to feed all of these?" He motions around the room. I walk over to the wall of birds. Some are looking at me, others seem completely oblivious to there being someone in the room.

"It's so strange." I'm baffled by the room of animals.

"You will never guess the next room either." He leads us out of the room and down the hall a little way to another room. This one is not locked. He turns the handle and holds the door for me to go inside.

I laugh at its absurdity. Inside is an elaborately carved hand-puppet stage. Around the walls of this room are all different kinds of hand-puppets. "What on earth?"

Behind me, he is chuckling as well. "Whoever created this place really took entertainment to the next level, right?"

"Did you ever use any of these?" He gets silent. I turn to glance at him and his face has turned a shade of pink I have not seen on him before. It appears he is embarrassed. I find it endearing. "No judgement from me, I would have put on the best puppet shows to an audience of more puppets."

He bursts out laughing, those dimples I like so much appearing on his bearded cheeks. "You know, that's exactly what I did!"

I can't help but laugh with him. We're both clutching our sides as we make our way back into the hall.

Sometime later, we sit in the study again, the same book poised in my lap while he works on something at the desk. "Can I ask you something?"

He looks up at me. "Of course you can, Callie."

"Why do you pretend as if nothing is happening?"

He clenches his jaw at my words. I refuse to back down this time. He stormed out the last time I tried to ask him about this. Deep in my gut, I have a feeling that something is going to happen and I would hate for the wonderful people I met in the village to be caught unprepared.

"Callie..." he grinds out, his tone angrier than anything I've heard from him before.

"No, you know what? No. I won't back down for your tantrum. You refusing to acknowledge there *might* be a problem will not make something not happen. What about those villagers? Do you want to explain to their families how you buried your head in the sand and avoided it, hoping it just wouldn't happen?

"Frankly, it's selfish, and I wouldn't want to waste any more of my time with someone who would do that to the people they rule."

He stands, comes over to me, and grabs my forearm, bringing me to my feet, the book in my lap falling to the floor. "You want to know what's happening, what I'm doing or not doing? Fine!"

My arm hurts as he continues to grip it while he drags me down another passage in the castle I haven't seen before. He stops in front of a set of double doors, releasing my arm to push open both doors at the same time. There's a loud bang when they hit the surface behind them. Inside are tables everywhere, all covered in different maps. I can't help but to immediately think of this as a war room. There are also several men, including the two messengers I met before. They stop talking when they see us enter.

"Please, don't let me stop you," he grinds out. "Continue with your report."

The one with the beady eyes speaks. "They've gathered into organized masses, sire. We continue to monitor them daily.

Unfortunately, we have been unable to implant our spies among the other side. They have positioned themselves to see us approaching across the water."

The beast grunts in acknowledgement.

The tall one gives his report next. "We have been able to observe the type of weapons they are gathering, crafting, and forging. It appears they are mostly preparing swords, maces, and cannons. We have not figured out how they plan to cross the water to get here. No ships have been spotted—"

"Come back when you have more useful information," he bites.

Their eyes grow wide, both of them shift uncomfortably. While the two messengers were talking, one of the other men had been placing things on one of the maps. The man has old-school glasses, the kind I've only seen in museums. Hunched over the table, it's hard to tell how tall he is, but I would guess about my height. His hair is tied back in a low ponytail. He also holds some kind of book he keeps looking down at. I move out of the beast's grasp to move closer to the table. When I get closer, I realize the book he's looking at has page after page of strings of numbers. I think they may be coordinates. I wonder how they measure these types of things in this world when I have not seen any modern tools for such a task.

Looking down at the map, immediately I recognize the circle of the mountain range, and the village in the center. The map covers a much larger area than I have seen before. But glancing around at the other tables, I realize this prison world is much larger than I had initially thought. It makes me wonder how many more people might be here.

"Are there other settlements? Other kingdoms?" I look up at the man who was placing the markers on the map. He looks at the king, a look passing between them.

"We are unaware of any other settlements, miss," he finally answers. It's only now that he's standing I recognize him. I've met this man before, when he was accusing me of being a spy. The room is quiet, the only sounds our breathing. As I glance around the room, I see them all looking at each other.

"Have you ever looked?" I ask after an uncomfortably long silence. Looking back to the king, he has a broad smile on his face, eyes focused on my face.

"Your Majesty, what is she even doing here?" Beady Eyes asks.

"I want her here," he answers. "Now, you heard the lady's question. I expect you to answer."

The tall one replies, "We have sent out scouts, but none of them have ever returned with news of other settlements. Other than the one across the water."

"How far did you travel?" When no one answers me immediately, I decide to rephrase my question. "How many days out did you send the scouts? How long did it take them to return? How many times have you tried to find more people?"

They again look to the king before Beady Eyes responds this time, "They were on horseback. They could only take a few days of provisions along with gear to survive the unknown elements."

"And how often did you do this? Every week? Every month? Annually? Or did you just do it once and give up, leaving your fellow man to possibly die alone?"

"Enough!" the king shouts. "You've proven your point, Callie. My men do not need a continued tongue-lashing." Turning to the messengers, he says, "Send out more scouts, have them take wagons if they need to."

"Yes, Your Majesty." They bow and exit the room. The rest of the men standing around the room continue to study the maps and the beast moves toward me. His penetrating gaze makes me shiver all the way down to my toes. I cannot tear my eyes away from him while he stalks toward me.

"You would make a wonderful queen," he observes when he reaches me. He gently reaches out and grasps my hand, bringing it to his lips to kiss the backs of my fingers. "Shall we?"

Lamely, I nod my head. Afraid to speak. Afraid to break the bubble of tingles currently running up and down my body. His hand on my upper arm helps to keep me moving forward, keeps me from stumbling over my own two feet. When he opens the door to exit back into the hallway, we hear a commotion further down the hall. I hear a twang sound, followed by the king stumbling backward into me, causing me to fall, his entire weight slamming into my body. All the air whooshes out of my lungs as we both hit the floor.

The men with us rush forward, one pulling the king off of me, dragging us both out of the way. Another pulls the door closed while a third man pushes several pieces of furniture in front of it. I don't realize what's happened until one of the men shouts, "Someone run for the healer, the king has been shot!"

Gaping at him, I see an arrow sticking out of his thigh. "Oh, my God!" I rush to his side, adding my hands to the other ones trying to stop the bleeding. It seems hours have passed before the man who ran for the healer returns with a petite woman. She has two more men behind her, a stretcher-type item carried between them.

The trio gets the king onto the stretcher. One of the other men holds me back, keeping me away from the king. His face is pale, the blood loss making him speak incoherently. When his eyes roll back in his head, I fall to my knees, arms wrapped around myself, but the tears won't come. Quickly, they carry him away.

"Miss," someone says gently. The man who was marking the map earlier kneels beside me. "They caught the people who did this. There's no need to be afraid anymore."

The rest of the men have left me alone, going back to studying their maps. Occasionally, I can feel their eyes on me.

"Will he be okay?" I ask.

"The healers have him now. I'm sure he'll be fine." He looks over at a nearby couch. "Would you like me to help you to sit over there? You might be more comfortable."

He helps me to the couch before one of the other men calls him to help them.

"Miss, miss, you need to eat something." I glance up and see

Kenna holding a tray of food and some tea. She sets it on a table next to the couch. "Can you eat something for me?"

Blindly, I reach out toward the tray, grabbing whatever my hand falls on and bringing it to my lips. Bite. Chew. Swallow. Bite. Chew. Swallow. I repeat over and over again until the item in my hand is gone. She hands me one of the cups and I take a sip. The liquid flowing down my throat warms my chilled insides.

One of the healers enters to let us know the beast would be okay, but there was so much blood loss, I wonder how he will ever recover from it.

Once I have finished everything in the cup, she helps me to stand and leads me out of the room. When we get to my room, I take the time to finally look at myself since it happened.

My hands are covered in dried blood. I rush to the washstand and frantically start scrubbing them. Kenna comes over to me and places her hands over mine, stilling me from the rough scrubbing that has left my skin raw and just shy of bleeding.

She helps me out of my clothes, taking care to keep the dried blood from touching my skin any further. She drops them just outside the door, closing it and blocking my view of what evidence remains from the horrifying ordeal.

It isn't until she's tucked me into bed and turns to leave that I react. Reaching out, I grasp her hand. "Don't leave," I croak. The anguish and lack of speech have left my throat raw. It hurts to speak and I grimace.

She removes her shoes and climbs into the large bed with me. "He'll be okay, miss, the healers are working on him now." She guides me to turn toward her and wraps her arms around me.

Finally, the tears fall.

CHAPTER 15

Merry Christmas, Happy Holidays

The cold is the first thing I notice when I stir. Before opening my eyes, I know it's one of two possibilities: either Kenna has left during the night, or I'm back in my world.

I open my eyes to my modern bedroom, and immediately I worry about the beast. When will I see him again? Will he be okay?

When I look in the mirror, my eyes are bloodshot, dark circles beneath them. Further evidence of the lack of sleep from tossing and turning. In my nightmares, the beast was killed in the attack, the arrow piercing his heart. I lost count of how many times I woke up screaming, Kenna's soothing words and hand running up and down my back, the only comfort during a bleak night.

Because of this, I expected to wake up in the prison world again. I'm not sure how I'll make it through the day, or however many days I'm stuck here without knowing if he really survived.

I struggle to go through the motions while I get ready for the day, and again on the drive to work. I park behind the bookstore, then walk to grab coffee for Huxlee and me. Before walking inside, I take a steadying breath and paste on the best smile I can.

As soon as I enter the store, Huxlee looks up from the book she's reading at the counter and quickly comes around and makes her way to me.

"What happened, Callie? Is it your parents?" She frantically searches up and down my body, making sure I'm not hurt.

"No..." I sob, the dam I've carefully constructed all morning finally breaking hearing the concern in my best friend's voice. Huxlee follows me to the back and guides me to sit on the couch against the wall after setting everything on the table. She rubs her hand up and down my back, soothing nonsense falls from her lips. It only makes me cry harder, and it's several minutes before I'm able to get it together.

"Whatever it is, we'll handle it. Is it Mason?"

I shake my head and take a deep breath before telling her the truth. "Do you remember the old journals I told you about a while ago?"

"The ones your family collects? Yeah, I remember. That reminds me, you never did bring one in for me to see."

"About that... I might not have exactly told you the truth." She stares at me, waiting for me to continue my admission. "Most of what I told you was true." I rush out, not wanting her mad at me.

"Okay, what part did you lie about, then?"

"I haven't even told my parents some of this, so I am trusting you to keep it quiet." She nods in confirmation before I continue. "The firstborn women in my family are a kind of gateway to a prison world. We're responsible for keeping the journals of the people who are banished there. And for hundreds of years, that's all we have been, journal keepers. But something is different about me, Huxlee."

I pause, knowing that the moment the next words are out of

my mouth, I can't take them back, and someone else in my world will know my secret. She reaches over and pats my knee. "You don't have to tell me if you don't want to. You know that, right?"

I nod my head and take a deep breath. "At night, not every night, mind you, sometimes I travel to the prison world." Huxlee's eyes grow wide and she reaches to grab her coffee from the table, taking a sip before setting it back down.

"Damn, that coffee isn't strong enough for this information." She's silent for a minute, processing the information. "Wait. So what's up with the crying?"

A tear glides down my cheek, and I swipe it away with my finger. "Each person who is banished to the prison world is sent there with the clothes on their back and a journal. The man who wrote..." I choke up and it takes me a minute to gather myself again. "The man who wrote the journal I took, I met him on my first trip to the world. I've spent time with him, I've grown to lo —" I stop myself just before the word leaves my lips. "I've grown to really care about him.

"Last night, I was with him. The world is experiencing unrest, and they have been preparing for a war. And right in front of me..." The tears flow down my face freely now as I remember what happened last night. "They shot him right in front of me," I choke out.

"Oh, sweetie," Huxlee wraps me in her arms. She holds me until I have cried all the tears. She hands me a tissue and I blow my nose loudly. "Can I ask a question?" At my nod she asks, "Are you *sure* the prison world is real?"

"My mom told me about our family's involvement in everything so, pretty sure, yeah. Plus, there have been other things that have confirmed it. Things that I read in the journal after I experienced them in the world. One day, I was scratched in the prison world and that same scratch was on me here."

"Wait, what?" she asks, mouth agape.

"Yeah, I was scratched on my palm by a rose's thorns and when I woke up back here, same scratch, same place."

"So if that's true, what would happen if you were to die in the prison world during this war? Would you be dead here too?"

I nod in response, "I think so."

She grips my hand in hers. "Well, I've never known you to spin such stories so, I believe you." That simple truth is enough to lift some of the weight from my shoulders.

Huxlee gives me a hug before we get up and head back out into the store, Huxlee to the front and me to the bathroom to clean up my face.

A few weeks later, it's the twenty-third and I'm packing to leave for my parents' house. My brothers are coming in with their families to spend the week.

Huxlee and I have been busy at the store, so many customers coming in and loving the customized wrapped gifts for their loved ones. I said goodbye to her yesterday until after New Year's. Her sister is in town to help her with the store while I'm gone.

Just having one other person know the truth has helped me tremendously over the last few weeks. She would listen to my worries, give me a hug when I needed it, and even came and stayed with me a couple of nights, wrapping her arms around me while I fell asleep. The one thing I could not bring myself to do over the last several weeks was to read the journal. I couldn't bear to read about him, not knowing if he's alive or not. But it was never far from me every night as I fell asleep.

I stay at my parents' until after New Year's every year, helping them take down all the Christmas decorations before coming back to my life until the next year.

Mason hasn't called since I last came back from the prison world. I really thought we had something, but I am never okay with someone ghosting me. Maybe he has some good excuse. He said he wanted to come see me when I was at my parents', so I'll reach out to him when I get there, but I'm doing my best to prepare myself for disappointment.

It's easy to admit to myself that seeing him when I am so concerned about the beast would probably have resulted in me not being much fun to be around, anyway.

I look around the house one last time before zipping up my suitcase. Anytime I leave to go anywhere, I do my best to make sure I forget nothing. Even though I can always make a stop at a store somewhere if I leave my deodorant at home. I open my bag again and make sure I remembered to pack it this time. Then I zip everything up, grab my suitcase off my bed, and roll it to the door. Before I get bundled up, I send Huxlee a text.

ME

Headed out. Don't miss me too much.

HUXLEE

Too late. Be safe.

I awkwardly hold my phone with my chin as I pull my coat on, shoving the phone into my purse before grabbing my suitcase, walking out the door, and locking it behind me.

My car is cold, the heater taking a while to kick in and warm it up in the freezing temperatures. I can still see my breath several minutes into the drive. When my car finally heats, I take my gloves off so I can grip the steering wheel easier.

My phone rings about halfway there and I dig it out of my purse, one hand on the steering wheel, the other hitting accept and bringing the phone to my ear. "Hello?"

"Hey, sweetie, I just wanted to make sure you were on your way?" Usually Mom doesn't call when she knows I'm driving, but I forgot to text her when I left my place. She likes to make sure, especially when the roads are in their winter state, that I am being careful.

"I'm about halfway there," I reply, then get silent. Through the floor of the car and the pedal, I can feel my car lose traction with the road. "Fuck, fuck, *fuck!*" My car spins on the frozen road, and the phone flies from my hand as I again grip the wheel with both hands. By the time I remember what my dad told me about driving on slippery roads, the car has stopped. Thankfully, there are no other drivers crazy enough to be out here today.

"Callie? Callie! *Callie!*" I hear from somewhere near my feet. Reaching down, I grab the phone and bring it to my ear again. One, two, three deep breaths I take, trying to calm my frantic heart. "*Are you okay?*" she yells in my ear.

"I'm okay, the car is okay, everyone is okay." Yet, my heart is still racing in my chest. "I'll see you in a little while, Mom. Love you."

"Drive carefully. Love you too, Callie."

I put the phone back in my purse and slowly press the gas pedal again, both hands firmly on the steering wheel this time.

I arrive in one piece and see my brothers have already gotten here. They both live further and probably drove in during the daylight. Never again will I be making this trip at night.

"You made it!" My dad wraps me in a bear hug, holding on a little longer than necessary. I snuggle into his embrace, taking a deep breath and enjoy being on solid ground once again. "What can I help with?"

He grabs my suitcase from the trunk, and we head into the house. "Mom said you tried to get out of Christmas this year," Jake claims as soon as I walk in the door.

"I said no such thing, you brat!" She swats his arm before wrapping me in her arms. She smells like Christmas cookies and pumpkin roll.

"You guys better have left me some pumpkin roll. I did almost die getting here," I joke. Jake hugs me next, patting my back before passing me off to the next family member.

All the kids are noticeably absent. "Where are the munchkins?"

"Mom got them all a game to play. They've been arguing over it ever since," Andy responds. While Jake is tall, freakishly muscular, and has dark hair and eyes, Andy is the complete opposite. He is of average height, lean muscles, with blond hair and blue eyes.

Dad puts my suitcase in my room, and I set my purse on the bed. "What's for dinner?" I ask. My stomach finally over the anxiety of the trip here.

"Your mom made chili and Stacy made cornbread to go with it." Stacy and Jake are the active couple in this family. They go hiking and camping with their kids often, preferring the outdoors to being stuck inside a house.

In the other room, I hear the kids yelling and laughing. "Keep it down in there," I hear Jen yell from the other room. With two older brothers, Jen was my best friend and partner in crime in high school. We would spend our days hanging out and making fun of them. When she and Andy started dating and finally got engaged, I was so excited that we would officially be sisters.

"Jennifer, get your sexy ass in here and give me a hug!" I yell down the hall. When I see her come out of the kitchen, large, obviously pregnant belly out front, I gasp. "You didn't tell us he knocked you up again." I carefully wrap her, belly and all, in the biggest bear hug I can.

"I wanted it to be a surprise?" She shrugs. "If only I could keep Andy off of me. I don't think he's figured out where babies come from yet."

Gross. I do not want to hear about my brother's sex life.

"Why are you blaming me? You're the one that struts out of the closet in sexy lingerie," he quips.

I fake gag and leave them in the hallway.

In the kitchen, I sit down next to Stacy, who is spooning chili into small bowls with cornbread for the kids. "Hey, Callie, would you mind grabbing some of these and following me in there? Your dad set up the folding table for the gremlins." She grabs half of the bowls and I grab the rest, both of us careful not to spill chili on the carpet. "Can you believe Jen didn't tell us she was pregnant again? Besties chat betrayal." She smiles as she says this, then sets her bowls down on the table.

"What a traitor." Once I've set my own bowls down, I link my arm with hers in camaraderie.

With the kiddos fed, we head into the dining room for some adult time. I shoot off a quick text to Mason to let him know I'm back in town. Then, I send off another text to Huxlee, letting her know I made it in one piece. I leave out the piece about Jen, knowing she'll want to announce it herself.

"Did Mom say we're going to meet your new boyfriend?" Jen asks.

"I haven't heard from him in a while, so I'm not sure if he's coming or not," I whisper, not wanting the entire table to hear. Or my brothers to be assholes.

The kids are allowed to stay up later than their normal bedtimes, but eventually, we all settle into our assigned rooms for the night. Each of the couples stay in the room my brothers grew up in, and the kids sleep in a tent in the middle of the media room.

The next morning, I realize that Mason never texted me back. It was so insane here with everyone under one roof, I didn't have time to look at my phone. I text him again.

ME

> Hey, wanted to see if you're still wanting to come meet my family?

My back pops when I stretch my arms above my head and get out of bed. As soon as I exit the relative quiet of my room, I smile. The boys are waiting in the hallway for their turn in the bathroom. A few of them look like they're doing the potty dance.

"Girls, you may want to let the boys have their turn soon or grandma is gonna make you clean up the puddles," I say through the door. Their responding giggles make the boys groan. "Why don't you guys go use the other bathroom?" I suggest, shooing them toward the other hallway.

"Why do girls have to take so long to get ready, Auntie Cals?" Tuck asks. The oldest of the brood at twelve years old, he looks exactly like Jake did at his age. Stacy was unknowingly pregnant with Tuck at their wedding. She laughed when she found out it wasn't bad shrimp after all.

"I don't know, little Tuck. When will you guys learn to beat them to the bathroom?"

"Hey! I'm not little anymore. I'm almost as tall as you." He scratches the top of his head before asking, "Why should we be punished for them needing so much time?"

"It seems you have a decision to make then, kiddo," I say over my shoulder as I make my way to the kitchen for some coffee. "Who made the coffee this morning?" There are *some* members of the family who should never be allowed to touch the coffeemaker. Why is it that the worst cooks are usually the ones adamant they be allowed to cook? Not that coffee is cooking, but how the fuck do you burn coffee?

I bring the cup to my nose and inhale the wonderful aroma. Jen brewed this batch. She always brings in the fancy stuff when they come. We both spent a summer working at the local coffee shop and both learned a thing or two about making a damn good cup of coffee.

"I knew I'd find you in here with the coffee," Mom says as she moves to pour herself a cup. She brings the cup to her nose and inhales the coffee before taking a sip. "Thank God Stacy didn't make it in here first."

"I heard that!" Stacy yells from the doorway, and we all burst out laughing. "I definitely did not inherit my mom's cooking abilities. Thankfully, Jake learned something from growing up in this house."

"Jake? My Jake?" Mom asks. "You'd never know that from how much he complained about helping me growing up."

"I think he just did that so he looked cool in front of his friends," I say. Looking down at my phone, I see that I have no missed calls or texts from Mason.

I see a couple of new texts over in the *Besties* chat and I open it up, seeing Stacy and Jen tattled on me and my near-miss on the way here.

HUXLEE

What do you mean "slid on ice"

JEN

Callie tried to get a new car for Christmas.

ME

I did not! I'm fine. Car is fine.

STACY

We need a girls' day before Jen pops.

ME

Agreed

JEN

Hey Hux… I have something to tell you.

HUXLEE

Well, that doesn't sound good. You finally decide to ditch Andy for someone better?

JEN

Well, that would leave me knocked up and single, so I'm gonna go with a big, fat, not anytime soon

HUXLEE

Wait, are you serious? We're gonna have another baby?! Congrats girl!

I sigh as I set my phone down on the table and my mom reaches over and pats my hand. "Maybe he's busy with his family, sweetie."

"Maybe, but he said he wanted to see me and I haven't heard from him in weeks. I feel like a crazy teenager with a crush on a cute boy."

"I know that feeling," Jen says, waddling into the kitchen, with a hand on her back. "I see you guys found the coffee."

"I don't think I've ever been so grateful you're an early riser." I wink at Stacy. We sit around the table drinking our coffee. "Are all the guys still sleeping?" I ask. So far, the only people of the male persuasion I have seen awake are the kids, and they never seem to sleep in when they're all under the same roof.

Right on cue, the kids come tearing through the kitchen, chasing each other in some game or other. "Kids, no running in the house," Jen tells them.

"Yes, Auntie Jen," Tucker says. He's the last one out of the room and I can hear him yelling at the other kids. Ever the one in charge of the group, he's twelve going on thirty.

We spend the day catching up and enjoying each other. Dad pulls out some of the board and card games from the closet. We are a competitive bunch and we enjoy this time of year, and spend the rest of the year gloating over who won what.

We decide to start out brutal this year with some Monopoly. The kids know better than to come in here when the "grown-ups" are mid-game. Someone is liable to get in trouble, or get blamed for someone losing if they're interrupted mid-turn.

Mom helps the kiddos make sugar cookies and they spend the afternoon decorating them. The rest of us vote on who did it best and then help them consume all the sugar.

We each open one gift on Christmas Eve—Christmas pajamas. The youngest of the brood also gets to open up a new Christmas story for us to read before everyone heads off to bed. I curl up in my bed with the journal, tucking it under the mattress before falling asleep.

CHAPTER 16

That's Christmas to Me

The smell of Mom's cinnamon rolls wakes me up. Someone has opened my door this morning to make sure I have as much of the delicious smell wafting in as possible.

The kids giggle outside my door. "You better run or Auntie Cal is going to get you!" Their little feet patter as they run barefoot down the hallway, giggling the whole way.

We always spend Christmas morning in our jammies, enjoying the company. The fire is burning in the fireplace and Mom or Dad stuffed the stockings and hung them along the mantle. With the family growing so much, their mantle had to be cleared of everything else to make room for so many stockings.

I make my way into the kitchen where someone has made coffee. I can smell some kind of Christmas spice in the air, probably cinnamon and nutmeg. Mom is pulling the cinnamon rolls out of the oven when I come in. I help her ice the top with cream cheese icing. "Morning, sweetie." She licks icing off the tip of her finger.

"Morning, How'd you sleep? *Did* you sleep?" I ask. My mother is notorious for staying up late and making sure all the presents are laid out and ready for the rest of us in the morning.

"Stacy and Jen stayed up helping get the gifts ready for the kiddos. We weren't up too much after you went to bed," she replies. Judging from the large ring of gifts around the tree, I'd say her timeframe is an exaggeration.

While our family has never believed in spoiling us, my parents made sure we always had something under the tree on Christmas. If they had the money, we would have something to wear, something to read, and then something that we had been really wanting under the tree. Usually some extras there as well. Dad liked to visit the candy store before Christmas, saying, "The kids need to have a treat in their stocking for Christmas." We all know he just went for himself, but none of us kids were going to say no to the yummy peppermint sticks and other Christmas treats he would bring home.

I help Mom dish cinnamon rolls onto disposable plates. We do not believe in doing all those dishes for the entire family on Christmas. "Kids, breakfast is ready," I yell into the other room. They come running in, cheeks pink from being outside in the snow.

"Do your mommas know you guys were outside in your jammies?" Mom asks. All the kids look at her, their eyes as big as saucers. Two of them grab her hands and beg her not to tell on them.

"Grab your breakfast and sit at the table. You know Grandma won't tell on you." I laugh. When they all vacate the kitchen, I grab a couple of plates and move them to the adult table. I have yet to see any adults except Mom this morning, but I know they'll be in soon. The call of breakfast is a universal sign it's about to get crazy up in here.

Right on cue, Andy and Jen come into the room, hand in hand. "Morning, Mom," Andy says, kissing her on the cheek as he passes to get to his seat.

"Morning, kids," she responds.

Dad walks in and spins her into a dip before giving her a kiss. "Merry Christmas, my love."

"Merry Christmas," she replies, a big smile on her face.

We take our seats and Jake and Stacy enter a few minutes later, whispering and smiling as they take their seats across the table from me.

"Anything from the boy-toy yet?" Jen asks.

I glare at her before answering, "No. And I'd appreciate if you'd stop asking."

She looks down at her cinnamon roll, cutting off a large bite with her fork and shoving it in. That ought to silence her for a minute. Around the table, I catch a few pitying looks and stare down at my cinnamon roll to avoid any more questions. I don't dare tell them that Mason isn't the only reason for the dark circles under my eyes.

The kids finish their breakfast first and immediately come in to beg us to eat faster. They know they aren't allowed to open presents until everyone is settled in the living room.

"Why don't you go use the bathroom and we'll be done by the time you guys are finished?" Stacy suggests. They run off and we're able to finish our breakfast in peace.

We're settled into the living room on the couches and various chairs Dad brought in just for the occasion. Some kids have to sit on the floor in front of the rest of us so we can see what's happening.

We like to open gifts one at a time so everyone can see what each other got. Starting with the youngest kiddo, Dad plays Santa, handing out gifts to the rest of us and opens all his gifts last.

The littlest ones get dolls, craft stuff, and other educational things along with clothes. The older ones get some kind of hand-held gaming systems. They remind me of the days we would play on our Nintendo DSs as kids. Adults get a wider variety of things, books, tools, kitchen appliances, to name a few.

The joy on the faces of the kids is my favorite part. It's also entertaining when you can tell it's not something they wanted. Tuck frowns when he opens a package with underwear. You'd think he'd have learned by now that Christmas is the time for new underthings, too.

Once all the presents are opened, and Jake has helped collect all the wrapping paper trash, the kids run off to play with their new toys. The girls head to the table to start on their craft kits.

I help get all the stockings back on the mantle, now empty of their delicious confections and other small goodies.

Around lunchtime, the kids want to go outside and play in the snow again. First, their parents have them get out of their pajamas and into their clothes for the day. Then all the adults help get the kiddos bundled up in their snow gear before the men get suited up to go out and watch the kids. The women stay inside for a little longer to help Mom make the cocoa and get it poured into insulated cups we can take outside and help keep us warm.

The kids come running when we get outside with the warm, chocolaty goodness. There are so many Christmas traditions we cram into the couple of days we're all together. My brothers and their families will head back to their own homes in the morning. We usually try to get together a few times a year.

My phone chimes with an incoming text.

HUXLEE

Last minute shoppers crack me up. I think I may have sold a copy of Haunting Adeline as a gift for their nana.

ME

LMAO! What is our return/exchange policy again?

HUXLEE

I will make an exception if a nana walks in with it.

I set my phone down on the table a moment before I hear, "How are you doing, Callie?" From Jen as she swipes the snow out of the chair beside me and sits down with her cocoa.

"I'm okay," I reply, both hands wrapped around my cup for warmth.

"I've seen you check your phone a few times this morning alone." She jerks her chin towards the phone sitting beside me. Really she's asking about Mason without *specifically* asking since I told her not to this morning.

I shake my head before responding, "I really thought he was different. We seem to have such great conversations. The last time I saw him was good, and I talked to him shortly after. I didn't think he'd just ghost me."

"It's definitely a shitty way to bring in the holidays. I'm sorry, hun." She reaches across the space between our chairs and wraps her arm around my shoulders.

"Thanks, Jen. I'm sure eventually I'll find someone who doesn't make my head spin." If only she knew.

"Definitely! You're a great catch. You just need to find the right guy who will appreciate you for who you are. If this guy isn't the one, you'll find him." Jen's positive attitude makes me feel both better and worst at the same time.

My mind drifts to the other man in my life. I wonder if he were here right now, would the beast be ghosting me as well?

When the kids all have rosy cheeks and noses Rudolph would be jealous of, we all go back inside, unbundle, and sit around the fire to warm up.

Dad grabs stuff for the kids to make s'mores in the fire and we watch as they get marshmallow and chocolate all over their faces, fingers, and the floor. The little ones just eat the chocolate and marshmallows cold. The bigger ones have learned the fine art of roasting a marshmallow to perfection, burnt on the outside, ooey and gooey on the inside.

When they've filled their tummies, they sweetly keep bringing finished s'mores to the rest of us. "Auntie Calth, I know theth are your favorite," Macie says. Her lisp more prominent with the stickiness of the s'mores in her mouth. Jen wanted to wait to have kids for a few years after they got married but, she ended up getting pregnant on their honeymoon. Macie is six, has blonde hair, blue eyes, and the biggest smile you've ever seen.

I gratefully take the s'more she offers me and lick off my fingers from the melted marshmallow that ends up all over them.

Mom makes a seafood bog for dinner: crab, shrimp, scallops, brats, corn, and potatoes covered in tons of butter. All of us gather around the large pots on the big dining room table. Christmas dinner is the one meal we all squeeze in around the same table.

Sometime during the day, dad has hung mistletoe over the entry to the dining room. He catches Mom around the waist on one of her trips back and forth from the kitchen and gives her a lingering kiss. Us kids start yelling, "Gross, get a room!" Before they finally break apart, Dad with a smirk on his face when he looks at us. Mom has a wistful look in her eye as she goes back to what she was doing.

After dinner, everyone leaving in the morning packs their things except what they'll need to get ready first thing. Then we all hug and say goodbye before going to bed. They'll leave before the rest of us are up to get home at a decent time tomorrow.

I crawl into my bed, turning off my alarm for tomorrow morning before pulling the covers over me and falling asleep.

PART FOUR

Week After Christmas

CHAPTER 17

Amazing Grace

I jolt awake, something inside of me alerting me to the change of location. Immediately recognizing the bed I'm in, I jump and run for the door. After grasping the handle, I throw it open and step into the hallway.

It's dark outside. The hall is lit only by candles at infrequent intervals down the hallway. My heart pounds in my chest as I look either way. Unsure where the king's room might be, I open each door and briefly look around, searching for any human outlines in the dark.

At the end of the hallway, I have not found his room. I turn back, heading the other direction, and start opening doors once I've passed my own again. As I make my way down the quiet hallway, my motions grow louder and louder, more frantic the longer I cannot find him.

The last door on this side has more ornate doors than the rest. Somehow I know in my heart this is the king's room.

My hands shake when I reach out. I hold my breath as I turn the handle, slowly pushing the door open. All the air leaves my lungs at the sight before me. The room is brighter than the rest I've entered. Candles sit on every surface, a fire burns in the fireplace. There are several people in the room moving back and forth with various things in their hands.

I step into the room, and all eyes turn toward me. No one stops me as I move closer to the bed. When I approach, I notice the sweat dripping down his face. His eyes are closed but his head tosses back and forth, his long brown hair sticks to his skin. He sleeps, but not restfully. My eyes follow the lines of his body and I can see they have covered him with a layer of ice. My heart clenches in my chest.

Gently, I reach out and feel his brow. He is burning up. Without a modern thermometer, there is no way to gauge how high his temperature is. If I had to guess, his fever is high enough for someone to be rushed to a hospital.

His injured leg is sticking out from under the covers, the bandages large around his thigh. I can see the red lines as they come above and below the bandages there. A strange smell emanates from the location. My hand flies to cover my mouth and I hold back a gag. Someone touches my shoulder and it startles me. I look up to see a man standing next to me, a questioning look on his face. "Are you Callie?"

I swallow the thick saliva that has accumulated, taking a few deep breaths through my mouth to rid myself of the smell. "Yes," I respond. I can clearly see he's in a bad place. I don't dare ask how bad the situation is.

"He's been asking for you." The man jerks his chin toward the bed, indicating the beast.

"How..." I pause, swallowing again. "How is he?" I finally ask. My mind struggles to remember anything I've read about wound care. Immediately regretting that my experience is limited to fiction adaptations and possible false descriptions, rather than having read some books that might have been helpful in this situation.

He takes a deep breath before answering, "We've been fighting the fever off and on since it happened. We cut out the infected area of his leg, but the limb is still inflamed."

I clench my jaw as he talks. I was stuck in my world. I had no way to get here, and yet I struggle with guilt over not being here for him.

We turn toward the bed at a single word croaked out from its occupant: "Callie." His hand stretches toward me. I immediately reach out and take it. "You came," he croaks, a small smile on his face. His eyes close again. My hand stays grasped in his. The grip is not as firm as the last time he held the same hand, however many days ago.

The doctor has the decency to walk away from us. Carefully, I climb up onto the bed, curling up against him. I rest my head on his chest, draping my arm across the ice they've placed there. Behind me, I hear the door opening and closing several times and the room progressively grows quieter.

The man from earlier appears on the other side of the bed where I can see him. "I'll be in the room just next door. Call out if you need anything," he tells me.

I nod in response.

I am not a praying person, but I call upon any god who will answer me, asking them to save his life. Heal his body from the infection. *Don't let him leave me, too.* It's selfish, I know, but it isn't until this moment I truly realize the depth of my feelings for the king in the prison world.

Sometime later, I wake up when an arm wraps around me, and then someone kisses the top of my head. My face is pressed against something warm, moving up and down in a steady rhythm. I turn my face up and see the beautiful, smiling face of the beast, his two toned eyes much more alert.

The doctor leans across the bed on the other side, clearing away the remaining ice. "The fever broke a little while ago. You seem to be his good luck charm," he states.

I snuggle deeper into him and his hand rubs up and down my spine, causing goosebumps all over my body. His even breathing calms me, and again I fall asleep settled against him.

When I wake up again, I can finally think clearly. It isn't until now, with a clear head, I realize how worried about him I have been over the last month, and how much sleep I've lost. I rub my cheek against his bare chest before looking up into his smiling face. "Although I would love to continue this, it seems Kenna has come to strip the sweaty sheets from the bed."

I turn carefully so as to not fall off and see Kenna standing at the foot of the bed, new linens in her arms.

No one else in the room seems to care that we're snuggled up in bed. I sit up and move my legs off the edge of the bed, and gravity makes me realize how much I need to pee. I glance down at myself and see I'm still wearing my pajamas from home.

Slowly, I slide off the side of the bed, and I wonder how I scrambled up here so fast by myself. He reaches out and grasps my hand before I have a chance to move away. "I just need to use the bathroom, and maybe change into some more presentable clothes," I say.

He nods and releases my hand. "Don't be long," he replies as I slide through the door.

I rub the sleep out of my eyes while I make my way back to my room. The door is standing open, Kenna has already set out my undergarments across the foot of the bed. A simple dress hangs from the door of the wardrobe.

First, I use the restroom, washing my hands at the washstand. Then I strip off my pajamas, which are soaked through from the melted ice and probably sweat from being pressed up against another person for hours.

Kenna comes through the door when I'm pulling the shift over my head. She helps me into the rest of my clothes, braiding my blonde hair simply down my back. She does not apply any makeup today, instead leaving my face plain. "We've missed you," she says as she ties the ribbon around the end of the braid.

I reach out, grabbing her hand and pulling her to me, enveloping her in a hug. "I've missed all of you, too."

When I walk back into his room, he is sitting up, leaning against the head of the bed. His chest is now covered in a shirt, blankets pulled up over his lap.

He pats his hand on the bed next to him and I move, struggling to pull myself onto the tall bed.

My stomach growls. Loudly. I think back to the last time I ate something. "Merry Christmas."

"Merry Christmas," he replies with a smile. He reaches down the other side of the bed and drags a tray of food up so we can both reach the breakfast someone has brought for us to share.

We spend the day in his bed, talking about our time apart. His recovery from the arrow wound was not a smooth one. He tells me that he's had a fever off and on the entire time. I don't tell him that the doctor already shared the information with me. He also tells me they had to cut away some of the flesh on his leg to get rid of the infection, but unlike the doctor, he grimaces at the reminder.

The healer tells both of us he believes he has finally come to the other side of the danger.

During the day, the beast seems to get some of his strength back. He tells me how much he's missed me being here. The healer, who did not know there was another person who sometimes came to the castle, thought he was just hallucinating every time he would ask for me. It wasn't until Kenna told him I had not been back one morning the healer realized I was an actual person.

"When I first woke up, I was terrified you had been injured as well. It wasn't until I saw Kenna that she assured me you had sustained no injuries during the brief attack." I reach out to intertwine my fingers with his.

Gently, I rest my head on his shoulder. "I was terrified not knowing how you were. How much damage had been done?" A tear glides down my cheek and falls to his shirt.

He gently grasps my chin and turns me to face him. Using his thumbs, he wipes the falling tears from my cheeks. "I'm okay. I'll recover."

I reach up and run my fingers gently along his scars. "How did you get these?"

"I don't remember. When I woke up in this world, my face was like this."

"You didn't mention it in the journal."

"I didn't want to write it in the journal in case whoever sent me here was able to read it. I didn't want them to know they'd won, that they'd caused me pain in those first weeks as it healed." He runs his hand down my braid, gently tugging on the end. "Your hair is nearly white, I've never seen anything like it."

Allowing his change of subject to end my line of questioning, I snuggle into him while he continues to play with my hair.

We fall asleep wrapped in each other's arms, my head again pillowed on his chest. We breathe as one, heartbeats in tune to each other.

CHAPTER 18

Hallelujah

His hands in my hair is what wakes me up the next morning. I glance up at his face and he's smiling down at me.

Briefly I look around and see that there is no one else is in the room. "Where did everyone go?"

"The fever has not returned. The healer said my leg looks better, so they left us alone to get some sleep." He moves his hand to my arm and starts rubbing slow circles there while he talks. Goosebumps pepper my arm immediately, and he laughs. "You're awfully reactive to my touch, aren't you?"

I bury my face into his chest, trying to hide the blush worming its way up my neck and face. "Don't be embarrassed, Callie. I like that I can affect you this way." He uses the arm that's wrapped around me and starts rubbing up and down my back.

We're interrupted by the door opening. I glance back and see Kenna. "We need to get you ready, miss. The messengers are back."

Looking back at the beast, I give him a questioning look. "I need you to be my eyes and ears in this meeting, Callie. Now is not the time to show weakness. We're trying to prevent a war. The king of the opposing side being indisposed would not show a strong front." It's the most kingly thing I think I've heard him say.

I scramble out of bed and follow Kenna back to my room. Today, she has a different type of attire for me. She dresses me in what I imagine must be men's clothing here. I've only seen the women wear dresses. "One of the servants brought this from his son's clothes for you to wear today."

The pants cut off mid-calf. She lets me wear the bra from my world beneath the rest of the clothing, a corset having no place with this ensemble. Again she braids my hair back, this time teasing it and making me look more fierce than I'm used to. She takes the time to braid it intricately. I look like a Viking princess.

I follow her down the hallway to the war room. When we have almost reached the door, I stumble. My hand connects with the wall as I steady myself, my heart pounding while flashbacks from the last time I was here scroll through my mind. The surrounding hall disappears, and I'm stuck replaying the moment he was shot over and over again. I grasp my chest, breath coming in quick gasps. A soft touch on my arm jolts me out of the memories and I look into the face of Kenna.

"Are you okay, miss?" She grips my arm more tightly, nodding her head in a show of support and understanding. Her hand glides down my arm to grasp my hand in her own. We walk the rest of the way to the door in this manner. Fingers tighten on mine one last time before she lets go and opens the door to the war room.

All eyes in the room turn toward me when I enter, back straight, steps sure, faking confidence as much as I can. The messengers are the only ones who seem surprised by my presence here. The rest of the men nod in acknowledgement and go back to what they were discussing. I approach the table they surround, and I can see how the other kingdom has moved since the last time I was here. They have covered significant distance and have arrived back at the edge of the water.

The messengers let us know that their sources have still not reported any boats or larger ships on the water. They tell us they continue to watch and have been instructed to ride as fast as possible to report in if they see any.

"And what of the scouts sent looking for other settlements?" I ask, hoping they have found signs of other life.

"What is she even doing here?" one of the men asks with a sneer.

Kenna surprises me when she steps forward and responds in a stronger voice than usual, "You will respect your king's request for Callie to sit in on these meetings."

The man averts his eyes, and I look back at her. I didn't realize she had entered the room with me. Their response to who I thought was just a maidservant confuses me but, who am I to look a gift horse in the mouth?

"No one has returned yet, miss." Beady Eyes looks away, I'm sure hoping I don't explode like I did the last time.

"They've been traveling, what, about a month now?"

"Yes, miss. It took only a couple of days to prepare them for the journey. They left as soon as we had sufficient provisions for a long journey," the tall one answers.

Every time I see these two, they seem to speak with one mind. I assume they have been working together for a long time to answer questions on the same topics so succinctly.

Raising my eyes, I look at the man who seemed to be in charge the last time. "What is your name?"

He blinks back at me for a second before realizing I've asked him a question. "Theodore, miss."

"Theodore, I'd like you to report directly to me or His Majesty if there is anything else you think we need to know." I turn and walk out of the room after his nod of acknowledgment.

Kenna follows me out, and I deflate as soon as the door closes behind me. She walks with me as we go straight to his room. When we enter the room, my hand flies to my mouth. He is out of bed and walking slowly across the floor, supported by one of the men who has been looking after him. His eyes find me and he stumbles. The man helps him sit in a nearby chair.

"You're standing." A wide smile spreads across my face as I make my way to him and fall to my knees in front of his chair.

His hand rests on my cheek, thumb brushing gently back and forth. "Leave us," he says, eyes focused on me, not looking at the other people.

Behind me, I hear the door click closed. I lay my head on his uninjured leg, allowing him to continue stroking my cheek.

"Tell me." Immediately, I know he wants an update on the other side.

"They have moved back to the water's edge. No boats have been spotted. And there has not been a return of the people sent looking for settlements." I feel a quick and complete description is best. "And Theodore will find either of us if any more information needs to be shared," I finish.

"Theodore, huh? Why him over the other men?"

"He seemed the one to know the most, the one who was actually processing the information."

"He's been with me the longest. He will make a good general if I'm not better in time."

"Don't say that."

"Don't say what, Callie? We don't know if or when this is going to happen. I can barely walk ten steps in a row. No one knows whether or not I'll be able to support my own weight for any length of time, let alone ride a horse."

"Then I suppose you better get back to practicing, huh?" I stand and extend my hand to him.

He smirks before engulfing my small hand in his own.

As we pace back and forth across the room, he grows increasingly tired. Finally, I force him back into bed with the promise of staying with him again.

The open window reveals it grows closer to dinnertime, and right on cue, my stomach growls. The beast chuckles.

"It's not funny," I mumble.

"I've never heard a stomach make so much noise before."

"Lucky me," I say under my breath.

A few minutes later, Kenna comes in holding a tray with enough food and tea for the both of us. She sets it on a side table and smiles at me before leaving the room.

Her coming here reminds me to ask him, "Who is Kenna?"

"What?" he responds.

"In the meeting, the men started to question me and Kenna stepped forward and defended me." His frown returns at my words. "They listened to her. Which makes me wonder, who is she? Because up to now, I was under the impression she was just a maid."

"Kenna has been here longer than I have. She is well respected by our people. She survived on her own here for a long time."

"Is it possible *she* knows about other settlements?"

"I don't think so. She told us she kept to herself, mostly. Until she moved in here, that is. How about that dinner?"

I climb down from the bed and hand the tray to the king to set on the far side of the bed, so I don't accidentally knock it over while I climb back onto the high mattress. Then he grasps my arm, helping me up. Thankfully, the pants I wear make this maneuver easier than a dress would.

"What exactly are you wearing?" He looks down at my ensemble.

"They thought I needed to dress the part." I grab a grape from the tray and pop it into my mouth.

He grabs another one and holds it in front of my mouth, waiting for me to eat it from his fingers. When I've finished the one in my mouth, I wrap my lips around the one he's holding, biting into the sweet, juicy globe. He brings his fingers to his mouth and licks the juices off before grabbing and popping one into his own mouth.

We continue much in the same way, alternating between feeding ourselves and each other. When we get to the tea, we opt to drink from our own cups, not wanting to make a mess across the bed.

Once the tray is empty, he leans back against the headboard, drawing me into his side. "I'm glad you're alive," I say, my face downturned so he can't see the unshed tears welling in my eyes.

"I'm rather fond of being alive myself." He chuckles and I gently punch his stomach.

"You know what I mean."

He sighs before saying, "Yes, I know what you mean."

CHAPTER 19

What Christmas Means to Me

A tear glides down my face when I feel my soft pillow under my cheek. I'm not ready to be back here. I want to go back.

Squeezing my eyes tightly closed, I pray to whatever god will listen to send me back.

Send me back to the beast.

Don't make me stay here alone.

Don't make me wait another month to see him again.

I open first one eye, then another. My heart clenches in dread when I'm still lying in my room at my parents' house.

Throwing the covers off and draping my legs over the side of my bed, I stand and start getting ready for my day.

I hear my parents' hushed voices outside my door, but I can also hear two voices I don't recognize. Quickly, I change into my clothes, then tiptoe down the hallway to see what's going on. There are two police officers standing in my parents' living room.

"What's going on?" I ask.

Every eye in the room turns toward me. My mom's hand goes to her mouth, and she asks, "Where have you been?"

My dad wraps his arm around her shoulders and turns to the

two police officers. "It looks like she's snuck back in, officers. We're sorry to have bothered you," he tells them.

My dad follows the officers to the front door, and my mom comes to me and wraps her arms around me. "Where have you been, Callie? When you didn't come out of your room yesterday, we called the police. They made us wait twenty-four hours before they would come out and report you as a missing person."

"I need to tell you guys something. Dad, if you could come sit on the couch with us?"

When we're all settled, one parent on either side of me, I start from the beginning. I tell them again all about finding the journals. About reading the story inside. But I continue past what they already know, recounting my first journey to the journal world and me thinking it was just a dream. I tell them about the people there and about the impending war happening. I can't help but smile as I tell them about the beast until I get to the part where he was injured right in front of me.

"Oh, my God," my mom responds.

My dad reaches across me to grasp her hand before asking, "Why did you leave on Christmas night?"

I look down at my hands, fiddling with my top, nervous energy needing to be released somehow. "I can't control when I go. Or at least, I haven't figured out how to control it yet. I was here for a month after he was shot. Not knowing if he survived the... the..." I bring my hand to my mouth, take a breath trying to steady myself from the memory of that day, "wounds. And when I finally got back there, the infection had almost killed him."

"You love him, don't you, Callie?" my mom asks. My eyes snap to hers. I look at her through tear-filled eyes. "We don't always know why the universe chooses us for things. My ancestors never knew why they were the ones gifted with the chest. Just as you will probably never know why you are the only one of us able to travel to the prison world. But I have faith that you will figure out what you need to do in time."

My phone rings in the other room, and I stand to get it and answer without looking at the screen. "Hello?"

"Callie." That's the only word out of his mouth, the only thing he says before waiting for me to respond.

"Where the *fuck* have you been?" I am pissed. He's been missing for over a month, not responding to any messages or phone calls. I assumed he had just ghosted me and I was resolved to never hear from him again.

"I'm sorry." I scoff at the lame words. He has a whole lot of explaining to do if he expects me to give him the time of day again. "I was... injured. Today is the first I've been able to use my phone since it happened."

"And?"

"And what?"

"Mason, you've ghosted me for over a month and the best response you have is 'I've been injured and couldn't use my phone'?" If I could spew fire like a dragon, it would be coming out of my nose and mouth right now.

"It's the truth, Callie. I haven't been able to use my phone in... a month? Has it been a month?"

"Yes, Mason, it's been a month. A month of unreturned phone calls. A month of unanswered texts. A month of me assuming you'd just ghosted me. You missed Christmas with my family, by the way."

I hear a sharp intake of breath on the other end of the phone. "Callie, I'm so sorry. Tell me what I need to do to make it up to you?" he pleads.

A soft touch on my back makes me turn around. My mom is standing behind me. "Give me a second, Mason," I say into the phone, hitting mute so he can't hear whatever my mom has to tell me.

"Give him a chance, sweetie. Maybe he really was hurt?" If my mom wasn't standing right there, I would tell Mason to fuck off and block his number. But with my mom's eyes pleading with me, I can't just be the bitch I want to be.

Hitting the button to unmute the phone, I bring the phone back to my ear. "Are you doing anything for lunch?"

He takes a moment to respond. I'm sure feeling a bit of whiplash from my sudden tone change. "I was going to just cook some ramen and settle on the couch. Why, what do you have in mind?"

"Why don't you come eat with me and my parents?" That way, I have some backup if he doesn't show.

"Text me the time and address, I'll be there," he says, and I end the call.

"If you think I'm in love with the beast, why would you push me toward Mason?" I ask.

"Because, sweetie, the beast is trapped in a prison world we don't know he'll ever make it out of. And if the two never meet, they never have to know about each other, right?" She winks at me before laughing her way out of the room.

As soon as she's gone, I pull out my phone and open up the Besties Group Chat.

ME

Guess who decided to call?

STACY

Oh, Callie!

JEN

Casper

HUXLEE

Did you tell him to get fucked and block his number?

ME

Mom made me play nice. He is coming to lunch. He tried to feed me some line about being hurt and not being able to use his phone.

HUXLEE

Bull! It's called voice to text.

JEN

Weird.

STACY

Maybe he was?

JEN

And that is why you are the favorite
daughter-in-law.

He's using a crutch and limping when he gets to my parents'
place. A large bandage is wrapped around his thigh. "Oh, my
God, what happened?" I motion to his leg.

"Uh... farm accident." I decide for my mom's sake to take his
answer at face value, although I would really rather probe a little
more.

After helping him get settled into a chair, I go into the kitchen
and help Mom get lunch ready. "I hope you like leftovers," she
says, carrying a tray of various things leftover from our Christmas
feast.

"If they taste as good as they smell, I'm sure I'll never want to
leave," he answers.

We all settle around the living room. Dad turns on a movie
channel that plays continuous holiday movies this time of year.

I sit far away from Mason on the couch, both because I'm still
a little angry at him for ghosting me, and because I don't want to
jostle his leg. But when my mom comes in, she glares at me. Hard.
I excuse myself to go to the bathroom, grabbing my phone before
getting up. From my hiding spot, I open up the Besties chat.

ME

Okay, he is hurt. He has a huge bandage on his thigh and is using a crutch.

STACY

See. What happened?

ME

He said it was a farm accident but gave zero details.

HUXLEE

Suspicious!

JEN

And you let him get away with that? Go interrogate him right now!

STACY

Jen, honey... are you okay?

JEN

No. Stupid hormones.

ME

Have to go. Will report back soon.

When I get back in the living room, I sit closer to him.

He nonchalantly rests his hand, palm up on his thigh, an invitation for me to hold it. Reluctantly, I entwine my fingers with his. He squeezes them in response.

Out of the corner of my eye, I see my mom's slight smile as she steals a glance at us.

Overall, we have a pleasant lunch. He gets along with my parents well and other than the fact I keep thinking about him ghosting me for over a month; I decide to give him another chance.

This *will* be the last one.

He hangs out with us until well after dinner. Finally, I help him out to his car. He opens the driver door and shoves his crutch inside before leaning against the backdoor and grasping my hand again.

I let him pull me to him and rest my hands on his hips. Gently, he holds my face, sweeping my cheeks with his thumbs. "You have no idea how much I've missed you." I stare into his brown eyes.

"I really am very sorry, Callie. If I had any control over the situation, I would have been here. I swear it to you." His tone is so honest and raw, my heart thaws a little more.

Too soon, he's saying goodbye, and he repeats again, "It's important to remember, looks can be deceiving." Then he climbs into his car. I wrap my arms around myself while I watch him pull out of the driveway, going off into the wintery night.

That damn phrase is going to drive me crazy. What does he mean by it? Why does he keep repeating it? What does it mean? His injury is a lie? He really wears makeup to cover up his hideous face? Maybe he wears a toupee? But no, his short brown hair appears to be his own. The fact he has yet to answer me when I ask also concerns me.

When I'm lying in bed with the journal, I get a text from him thanking me again for letting him come over today. I reply and decide to put the journal away for another time.

Opening up the Besties chat, I send them a text.

ME

> Okay. He was really sincere, and I'm giving him one last shot.

HUXLEE

> Yeah! I like having free labor and a coffee bitch. I mean, that's awesome.

JEN

> Did you warn him if he ghosts you again he will have a crazy pregnant lady to deal with?

ME

Lol, no. I think I am a bit too old to have my girls threaten his life.

STACY

Never! I'm with Jen. He acts up again and we ride. I'll just need mom to watch the kids.

Smiling, I set my phone on the nightstand before falling asleep.

Just for Now

"Do you know how unnerving it is to have you disappear from my arms in the middle of the night?"

I smile, looking up into the face of the beast. "I've never encountered it myself. I just know how things feel on my side, and it's odd waking up in a bed you didn't go to sleep in."

He runs his hand up and down my spine and I rest my head on his chest.

"Does it feel like you actually get sleep?"

"Sort of? I've definitely noticed yawning more since the world traveling started. But I haven't fallen asleep at any inappropriate times like while driving my car or anything like that."

He doesn't speak for a moment before asking, "Car? What's that?" I remember that he's from before the time of cars and never would have seen one.

"It's kind of like a carriage that can drive itself."

His face scrunches into an expression I haven't seen from him before. "Why on earth would they want to do that?"

"I have a feeling there are a lot of things you would be surprised by now." I grunt as I roll over and get out of the bed, extending both arms over my head and stretching my back.

He groans from the bed. I look up to see him staring at me,

more specifically at my chest. I look down and realize the night-gown I went to bed in leaves little to the imagination. Probably should have worn the flannel pajamas. *Too late now.*

"The messengers are supposed to be back this morning," he says.

"What exactly do you want me to do with them? They didn't have much to add the last time."

"Just for now, Callie, know that I trust you."

"What does that mean?" The repeated vague phrases are driving me crazy. First Mason, now the beast. What the hell do I know about war?

"It means that I trust you to be my eyes and ears, Callie. I trust your decisions during this time. I am on your side."

"You barely even know me. How could you trust me with your entire kingdom?"

He shrugs in response, which frustrates me more than anything he could have said.

I turn and leave the room, heading to my room to get dressed properly.

On my bed, Kenna has again laid out some kind of pants outfit for me to don to head downstairs. This time she does not help me into the clothes or with my hair and I struggle to replicate the braided style from before. Instead, I settle for just braiding it in a basic braid down my back and find a piece of cord on the vanity to tie around the end.

I'm grateful when I enter the war room to see someone has brought in breakfast for the men present. Snagging a pastry, I walk up to the table all the men surround. No one looks up at my approach. They continue discussing the movements of the men across the water.

Thankfully, still no ships or boats of any kind have been spot-ted. I look down at the map. It's different from the one that was here before. This one is a view from further out. It shows us on a larger mass of land, the people across the water on some sort of large peninsula. "Has anyone been to the other side to see if they're hiding boats from us?" I ask.

"We've sent scouts, they have not returned yet," Beady Eyes says.

"What's your name?" I ask, because really it's rude that I've just been calling him "Beady Eyes" in my head this whole time.

"Steve, miss. My name is Steve."

I extend my hand to him and he grasps it in a firm handshake. "Nice to meet you, Steve, I'm Callie."

Next, I reach out to the tall one, "James, miss, at your service." He bows his head to me. "Lovely to meet you formally."

I make my way around the room, repeating the process for each of the men there. They seem to heave a sigh of relief when we've all been introduced. "Now that we've all met, we can talk as friends, right?" I smile at each of them as I look around the room. In return, I get nods of respect from most of them. "What's next?"

"I would recommend we prepare as if something is going to happen. It would be better to be prepared and not need it than to be caught with our pants down," Theodore says.

"I agree. What do you need from me to get that done?"

"Just your approval, miss. The king has given express instructions you are to be his proxy for the time being."

"Consider it approved. Anything else?" I look around the room at each of the men. When none of them speak I say, "If that will be all for today, gentlemen, I'll excuse myself. Please let me know if there is anything else requiring my attention."

Turning on my heel, I make my way back out the door. These men seem capable of organizing things. I'm unsure why my presence is even necessary but, I'll be here if I need to be.

At the bottom of the stairs, I stop short when I see the beast being helped down the stairs by the doctor and another man who has been helping in his rehabilitation. "We're on our way to the library," the beast says excitedly.

"Tired of being cooped up in your room?" I ask with a smile.

"Something like that. How am I supposed to court you properly from my bed?"

"It seems that is a good place to end up, wouldn't you say?"

The doctor chuckles at my cheekiness. "You've got your hands full with this one, haven't you?" He laughs harder when the beast gives him a dirty look.

I follow the men into the library, settling onto the sofa I usually sit on and picking up my book from the side table, starting from where I left off.

"You're not going to offer to bring me something to read?" he asks after they've left.

"Wouldn't want you to think I wasn't helping in your recovery." I giggle at the dirty look he throws my way. He struggles to his feet, limping as he makes his way to one of the shelves. He runs his finger along the spines while he decides which one he is going to choose. Finally, he selects one and limps his way to sit next to me on the couch. He sits so close to me, his thigh presses against mine.

"I rather think you wear those pants well." I glance down at myself, remembering the outfit I put on before meeting with the messengers. "Anything new to report?"

"They are going to start preparing for battle." I glance over at him, unsure how he's going to react to this information.

"It has become inevitable?" His brown and blue eyes look directly at me.

"Movement across the water would seem to indicate it would be smarter to prepare than lose unnecessary lives."

"Any life lost would be unnecessary." He turns back to his book and opens it to the beginning. I can't help but agree with him, but it seems there is little choice we will have in the matter soon. His men at least act like they know what they are doing, and I know nothing about war.

"How many wars have you had to prepare for?" I ask.

"Does it truly matter how many? Any war is senseless." It's impossible not to agree with him.

"Will the villagers fight?" I can't imagine the kind people I met down in the village wielding weapons of destruction.

He grabs a piece of paper from his side table and places it in his book, marking his place. "Do you always ask so many questions?"

I clench my jaw closed and open my book up to the page I stopped on last. His first finger and thumb gently grasp my chin, tilting my head to look at him. "Yes, Callie, the villagers will fight. The ones too young to fight will stay here, but some will inevitably escape the protection of the mountain to help in the battle. War changes everyone, and I fear this is not the last one we will have to fight before this is all over."

"All over?" How could he possibly know *another* war is coming?

"If you are the one from the prophecy, and I truly believe you are, I fear there is another war coming, one that will make this one look like a silly squabble. After all, the person who's been sending us all here for hundreds of years isn't just going to be content with us all waltzing out of here, now will they?"

"How will we figure out who has been sending you all here?"

"That, my dearest Callie, is a problem for another day. First, we must focus on the most immediate threat, then we can look to the horizon for the next."

They bring our dinner to the library. We spend much of the rest of the day dividing our attention between occasionally reading and trying to figure out who could possibly be the one in charge of this world.

I can't help but wonder why *my* family was chosen to be the gateway to this world, the keepers of the journals for its occupants. And what will I have to do to save everyone?

CHAPTER 21

Seasons of Love

Today is my birthday. When I open my eyes to my world, I wonder, now that I've come of age to know about the prison world, will I be able to get back there?

As I get ready for my day, I think back on the last year and how I've grown. My mind also wanders to the last month or so and the people I've met in the prison world.

The anxiety I feel as I think about what my life will be like if I never get to see any of the people from the prison world again. I've grown to care for the beast, Kenna, and the various other people I've met there. How would they fare if I could not return?

My phone goes off and I look down to see a text.

MASON

Hey, I wanted to be the first to wish you a happy birthday.

ME

Thanks! Will I get to see you today?

MASON

I forgot to mention yesterday, but I've got to go away. I'm so sorry. It's important to remember looks can be deceiving.

I just can't with this man anymore, and what the fuck is up with that damn phrase? It feels like he's got a secret family or something the way he pops in and then disappears.

ME

K

I don't even have it in me to be mad at him. I also don't have it in me to keep trying with him. There are too many other things going on that I need to spend my time and energy on, and if he wants to take himself out of the equation, good riddance.

He never responds, and I don't blame him. I generally avoid responding to one letter messages too.

My phone rings and I smile when I see Huxlee's name on the screen. "Hey!" I answer as cheerfully as I can.

Huxlee immediately hears in my voice something is off. "What has you so out of sorts on your birthday?"

"Don't worry about it, I'll be fine." Really, I should have just come out and told her from the beginning because she full-names me on my birthday.

"Callie Gabrielle Dubois, you tell me right now or I'll drive there, ice and all."

I roll my eyes before heaving a sigh and answering her. "It's Mason—"

"What did that boy do this time?"

"Well, he came over yesterday, but then today he tells me he's got to go away."

"And he mentioned nothing about this yesterday?"

"No, I kind of assumed he would come back today for my birthday." A tear glides down my cheek and I angrily wipe it away. He doesn't deserve tears from me.

"I'm sorry, Callie. You know I'd be there if I could. Me and the store both miss you," she says in a silly voice. It makes me smile, which was her goal, of course.

"I love you, Huxlee."

"I love you, too, Callie. Tell those parents of yours to spoil you today, okay?"

"You got it," I reply before we say our goodbyes.

Before I get another call, I use the restroom and get ready for the day. In the kitchen, mom has already made coffee and I pour a cup before making my way into the living room.

"Happy birthday, beautiful girl," she says when I settle myself on the couch in front of the fireplace that already has a roaring fire this morning.

"Thanks, Mom. Where's Dad?"

"He ran into town for a surprise." She hides her face with her coffee cup and she takes a drink of the magical juice.

When my dad comes back, he has a box from my favorite bakery. As soon as the smell of the ooey, gooey chocolate explosion cake hits my nose, I can't help but smile.

"You're the best!" I run up to dad as soon as he's set the cake on the table and I throw my arms around him, hugging him tightly.

He wraps his arms around me, laughing at my exuberance. "I thought my girl deserved her favorite birthday cake." He kisses the top of my head before releasing me.

"We thought you'd had a weird couple of weeks. You deserved something a little normal for once," Mom says, entering the kitchen and getting a kiss on the cheek from dad.

"It has been a crazy couple of weeks, hasn't it?" A few short weeks ago, I thought my life was boring, predictable. There is no way I could have predicted traveling between worlds and a family secret that would turn my world upside down.

Mom grabs some plates and forks and cuts us each a slice. "Cake for breakfast?" I ask.

"It's your birthday, we can do what we want," Mom replies.

The first bite I take, I moan. This is the best chocolate cake I've ever had. It's even better warmed up with some vanilla ice cream, but we'll have a couple of days to enjoy it in other ways.

"What do you want to do for dinner, Callie?" Dad asks. "It's your special day. You get to choose what's for dinner."

"How about some of Mom's special mac and cheese?" I look at her and beam my best pleading smile. She makes *the* best baked mac and cheese.

"Of course. I think I've got everything I need here already." She moves to start pulling ingredients out of the cabinets to get them ready for dinner.

"You don't have to start cooking now." I laugh.

"I was thinking we could have a movie marathon today? I can pull out the old *Anne of Green Gables* movies we used to watch," Mom suggests.

Dad groans. "Not those girly movies! What about some *Fast and the Furious*?" Mom and I both laugh and shake our heads at him. She pulls the stuff for popcorn out and makes us a big bowl of buttered popcorn to enjoy while we binge all six movies.

Despite dad's protests, he stokes the fire in the fireplace and settles down in his favorite recliner. We're not ten minutes into the movie before he's snoring and Mom kicks him out of the room to disturb somewhere else.

Mom pauses the movie we're on to get dinner ready. I help to make things go faster. We'll be finishing these movies late into the night but, it's been several years since we've spent this much time just hanging out together.

"I love you, my Callie girl," she says.

"Love you, too." I wrap my arms around her, accidentally knocking over the popcorn bowl that was perched on the couch between us. "Oops." I shrug, collecting the fallen pieces and popping them into my mouth.

"You don't have to eat those, we can throw them away."

"Wouldn't want to waste perfectly good popcorn. Besides,

five second rule." I shove the last fallen piece in my mouth and turn back to watch the movie.

When dinner is ready, Dad comes out of his hiding place and we dish up the cheesy goodness. All of us settle back in the living room to watch more of the movies before bedtime.

"Don't forget, Callie girl, we need to make sure the chest goes with you when you head back home. It is officially your responsibility now," Mom says before pressing *play* on the movie.

At some point late at night, Dad went to bed while Mom and I stayed up finishing the movies. We hug goodnight, and as she releases me, she adds, "Callie, be careful. I have a bad feeling I won't be seeing you for a couple of days."

"How do you know?"

"It's just a feeling, sweetie. Be careful, okay?"

"Of course. I love you."

"Love you too."

It's so late, I don't read any of the journal before I burrow into my blankets and fall quickly to sleep.

CHAPTER 22

My Heart With You

Warm arms wrap around me and I smile, turning in the circle of his arms to face him. "Hi," I say with a smile.

"Hi." He squeezes me tighter and brings me closer to him. I relax in his embrace, nuzzling my face against his shirtless chest, his loose long brown hair tickles my face. "I've waited a long time for you."

"What do you mean? I was just here yesterday."

"But I awoke in the night and you were gone. It's a little unnerving to fall asleep with you and to wake up and you're not there."

We jump out of bed when we hear a loud *boom*, followed by the ground beneath us quaking. Furniture shakes, smaller objects rattle off their surfaces, and we hear objects shattering all around us.

"What was that?" My breath coming in sharp pants as my heart beats hard in my chest.

Looking over, he is quickly pulling his clothes on while I stand there, not sure what is happening. "That was the beginning of the battle, Callie."

"What do you mean?" I ask slowly, my brain not processing what just happened.

"I mean, they have just fired a cannon at the mountain."

The door opens before I've truly grasped the meaning of his words. One of the healers comes in holding a small vial. "It's time, your majesty."

"Time, time for what?" I look between the two men.

The beast nods his head and accepts the vial from the healer, removing the stopper and downing its contents.

"What is that? What did you just drink?" I ask as the healer takes the vial from him and leaves the room.

"A healing potion," he replies.

"Healing potion? Why the hell didn't you take a healing potion earlier?"

"Because magic has a price, and I will have to pay it later," he answers.

Kenna comes in, interrupting any further conversation and motions for me to follow her. "We need to get you ready, miss."

When I move toward her, a warm hand grasping mine stops me. I look up into the bearded face of the beast. He pulls me closer, wrapping his arm around me and holding me to him. "Be careful, Callie. My heart goes with you." He kisses my temple and releases me.

Kenna and I rush to my room. Laid out on the bed are the same kind of clothes I have been wearing the last couple of times I've been here. We take my pajamas off and I slide the breeches up my legs. Leaving my bra on, I pull the shirt over my head and tuck the loose ends in around my waist before lacing them up. Kenna helps me into the leather vest and then leads me through the castle, down, down, down, into tunnels that run beneath the parts of the castle I have never seen before.

It seems whoever spent time creating the castle also left some kind of tunnel system that runs underneath the mountain. I've lost all sense of direction, grasping firmly to Kenna's hand as she leads me left, right, left again, making our way deeper and deeper underground. The air is still here, and I wonder if we should be afraid of these tunnels collapsing if there are too many cannon blasts.

"The tunnels run under the entire mountain range, and the village. There are entrances all over leading down into them. I'm instructed to bring you to wait with the villagers, to keep you safe."

"Wait, what? I'm not just going to wait here and let everyone else take care of the problem!" I stumble in the torch-lit tunnels, releasing her hand and attempting to make my way back the way we came. Quickly, I give up. I don't know how to get back to where we started. Instead, I follow her the rest of the way and slide down a dirt wall as angry tears run down my face. "That bastard!" I spit and several eyes turn toward me before acting as if I don't exist.

From my spot on the floor, I watch the people move back and forth. More enter the underground cavern and I can't help but be jealous of them, of the fact they know these tunnels and can leave.

Kenna flits around like a bird, helping entertain the children, getting snacks for the adults, and she even sings for a little while.

Finally, I've had enough of sitting here and feeling sorry for myself. How dare he leave me out of this! How dare he leave me to sit here and do what? Pray he comes back to me?

Fuck that.

I stand from my position on the floor. Carefully, I skirt between the wall and the growing crowd. At the entrance, I snag one of the torches mounted on either side of the doorway.

As I get further in the tunnel, away from the noisy people, I slow to listen for footsteps, or any noises I can't explain. I close my eyes and try to picture the way we travelled here before.

Slowly I inch forward, hoping I don't die down here in some

branch of tunnel no one travels.

When I hear someone laughing, coming down this hallway, I turn around and quickly make my way down the nearest fork in the tunnel I passed just moments before. I do my best to cover the torch, because I know better than to leave myself without any light in these tunnels.

Where there are voices, there is a way out. I peek out of the branch I'm in and see two men I recognize. When they're right in front of me, I snag James's sleeve and pull him into the tunnel. Steve follows closely behind.

"Callie! We were just coming to get you!" James says.

"Why are you hiding in this little tunnel?" Steve asks.

Skeptically I ask, "Why were you coming to get me?"

"We don't think you should be left out. You've been the one with us planning this whole time. We don't agree with the king's decision."

I let out a sigh of relief at Steve's words. It seems being friendly has made me friends. James motions for me to hand over the torch, and I do.

"We must be quick. We don't want to run into anyone else on the way out of here," Steve says. He grips my arm just above the elbow to hold me steady as we hurry down the tunnel. A few times, we're forced to duck into side branches when we hear voices coming toward us.

Finally, we reach the door to the main part of the castle, and I gasp when I see what's waiting inside. They must have shot more cannonballs at the mountain. There is debris everywhere.

"First, we need to get you into some armor," Steve says. He takes me down a wing I have not been in before. Both of them do not falter in their path. They know exactly where we're going. Finally, James opens a door and Steve pulls me in after him.

I notice something as soon as I step in and the torch illuminates the room. Someone has set up a suit of armor in here. "What..." I trail off, my brain working quickly to process all the new information.

"We have an armorer in the village. They made this for you. His daughter is about the same size as you. He fitted it to her," James tells me. He sets the torch in a sconce and moves to stand next to the armor.

His hands make quick work dismantling it from the mannequin-like thing it rests on, while Steve helps to secure it around me. He is careful to tighten all the straps, making sure it's secure but doesn't hurt me. It fits like a glove.

When the last piece is strapped on, I run my hands over the smooth, cold surface. I admire the craftsmanship that went into making this.

"Now for weapons," Steve says. "What do you know how to use?" At my clueless expression, he moves to the side of the room where various weapons are laid out. With my attention focused on the armor, I hadn't noticed the weapons until now.

"Well, even unexperienced you should be able to figure out how to use these." James holds up a leather belt that has two sheaths hanging from it. He slides out each of the blades and hands one to me. Briefly, he shows me how to properly hold and use the weapon.

He puts each of them back into its sheath and demonstrates how to remove the blade. Only after I've successfully removed the blade several times do they both fasten all kinds of straps and things to me, and fit weapons into many places all over. They instruct me on how to pull each one free from its position on my body. Before we leave, they show me a few more moves for each weapon, and then tell me to be careful with all of them.

The last thing James hands me is a recurve bow after he fastens a very full quiver to my back. I hold the bow in position and pull back the string, being careful to hold it as to avoid getting slapped with the string.

"You know how to use one?" Steve watches me reach behind myself to pull out an arrow from the quiver and nock it, again drawing the string back to my chin. Slowly, I release the tension I've put on the string and continue to hold the bow to my side.

"It's been a few years, but at summer camp one year, I learned how to use one of these. I was the quickest to pick it up and won the summer games. I loved it so much, I joined the team at my school and continued all the way through college."

"I don't know what most of that means, but I'll take that as a yes."

Removing the arrow from the string, I place it back in the quiver, looping the bow across my back as well.

"Well, in that case," James begins removing the metal armor on my arms. "Why don't we put you in something like this to help you move better?" He pulls out a set of leather armguards that he secures around my forearms.

I pull the bow off my back again and test the movement. It's much easier to pull the string back without the armor hindering the motion.

I watch as they both strap on armor and outfit themselves with the leftover weapons.

We follow back hallways and exit out a door I've never seen before. Steve looks both ways before motioning for us to follow him. This side of the mountain looks out on trees and fields. When I turn around to look at the door, I think it must be the one the beast described in his journal.

"We came out on the other side from where they are getting ready," James says.

"We're hoping we can sneak in among them without anyone noticing who you are," Steve tells me.

"And if they do?" I fear if the beast gets wind of my being here, he'll be distracted, possibly even get himself injured.

"He may not know it yet, but he needs you." James tips his head at me, and a smile ghosts across his face.

We move at a quick pace until we can hear people talking. The closer we get, you can feel the energy, the excitement of what is coming. When we finally come around the bend, there are people as far as the eye can see.

I whisper to them both, "I still don't see any boats in the water. Where were they shooting the cannons from?"

Steve jerks his chin to the trees across the clearing, the business end of a cannon barely visible in the shadows of the trees. "Our guards were able to take out the men manning the cannons relatively easily. One of the first tasks is to get together groups big enough to bring the cannons over to our side of the line. But first we need to make sure there aren't other men hiding in the trees. That's what they're doing now."

I nod. "Where's the king?" Suddenly, a hush falls over the crowd, as if a wave of silence is making its way toward us. Above the crowd, we see a head pop up, and his eyes immediately lock on mine across the wide expanse of people. A scowl comes to his face, and his eyes move to either side of me, focusing first on James, then Steve.

"Oh, shit," Steve says.

He jumps down from his perch and we can't see anything for a minute or so, then the crowd in front of us parts and he marches his way through them. His gate shows no signs of the injury, and I'm amazed at how quickly he was able to recover with the "magic potion."

"What are you doing here? I told Kenna to take you down to the tunnels," he growls. Steve and James step behind me as he again glares first at one, then the other.

I step up into him, my armor brushing his. "How dare you!" My nostrils flare in anger. "How dare you think after all this time I would be content to sit on my ass while all of this happens above me? It seems you really don't know me at all." Shoving past him, I make my way to the rest of the crowd.

Behind me I hear him tell them, "If anything happens to her, I am holding you two personally responsible."

His shoulder brushes mine as he moves past me. My eyes follow him while he marches through the parting crowd to the front of the group. Steve and James settle in on either side of me. I reach out and squeeze each of their hands in a show of thanks.

CHAPTER 23

Little Drummer Boy

Slowly, we assemble in perfectly spaced rows. The men I recognize from the war room walk down the rows, moving us into place, instructing us on what to expect and what is to come.

Once satisfied everyone is in their place, the men make their way to the end of their respective rows, a hush falls over the group. A sharp *tap-rat-a-tat-tap-rat-a-tat-tat-tap-rat-a-tap-tap-rat-a-tat* comes from behind us. I turn my head and look over my shoulder, spotting a small boy of no more than ten with a drum strapped around his shoulders. He beats the drum with a smile on his face. The rhythm changes as he gets closer, becoming faster and faster.

When he reaches the back row of the assembled army, men on either side of me draw swords from their scabbards. I follow their lead and pull out one of my blades. We move out of the way to allow the boy to come through the crowd, the rows parting like a curtain. *Tap-rat-a-tat-tap-rat-a-tat-tat-tap-rat-a-tap-tap-rat-a-tat*, he continues as he moves further up the assembly.

He reaches the front where the beast is, and his drumming reaches a crescendo, his arms flying high above his head as he continues the rhythm. When the king raises his hand, palm out to the level of his head, the boy stops. I hold my breath, waiting for the signal to march. I look to my right, then to my left, down my row. I see everyone in a similar stance, weapons at the ready.

Tap-t-t-t tap-tap, goes the drum, and James nudges me. When I look at him, he jerks his chin at me. "He's calling the archers to the front of the line," he whispers.

I look forward and see men and women moving, bows standing over the heads of the crowd, all making their way to the front. The rest of the crowd moves to fill in the spaces vacated by the archers. I clench my jaw, raising my chin in indignation. I know the beast wants me to stay back here, but I can shoot a bow and I know I'm a damn good shot.

Steve grabs my wrist as I lift my foot. "Be careful." I nod to him and he lets me go.

It takes me a long time to make it to the front. The line parts to either side to give me space to stand. *Rat-a-tat-tat-tap-tap-tap-tap* goes the drum and the people on either side of me raise their bows, drawing the strings back to their jaws. I follow suit, preparing for... what? I do not know yet.

They come at us first from the tree line, swords raised above their heads. A battle cry echoes around the clearing as they charge at us. My heart pounds in my chest. The opposing warriors get closer and closer to us.

Rat-a-tat-tat, arrows fly all around me. I take aim at the man at the front of the approaching warriors and let my arrow join the rest. I gasp when it lands true, striking the man in the chest. My breaths come faster, panic setting in. I just killed someone, I just shot someone, I just ended a life. When I look around, I see that more than half of the group has fallen. Some clutch their wounds, others lie completely still.

The ones who remain standing stumble over fallen comrades but keep coming toward us. *Rat-a-tat-tat-tap-tap-tap-tap*, I pull another arrow from my quiver and nock it, drawing back to my jaw. I'm incredibly grateful for the protection on my arms. *Rat-a-tat-tat* comes in rapid succession. We all let our arrows fly, the remaining warriors fall, and I breathe a sigh of relief that they have stopped coming toward us. I try to think of anything but the fact there is now at least one person no longer alive because of something I did.

Rat-a-tat-tap-tap-t-t-t-t-t-tap echoes around the clearing. Our frontline moves through the archers, swords drawn to walk among the fallen. I turn the other way when I realize they will not take any prisoners. The king stands watch over his men, standing next to the boy with the drum. *Tap-tap-rat-a-t-t-t-tap-tap* echoes around us, and I sneak a peek behind me as the men among the fallen weave back and forth, swords stabbing into each man, assuring they cannot attack us unnoticed.

With each fallen man slain, the snow grows more red with their blood. The soldiers do their best to avoid stepping into the growing puddles.

When they're finished, they make their way back to their row and tears run down my face. I don't know what I thought this would be like, but for some reason, I never thought about the fact we would *kill* people. A hand on my arm startles me and I look down, following the arm up to the face of a woman. I was so focused on being where I needed to be I didn't even realize there was another woman standing there. Her eyes are kind and she nods to me in understanding.

Facing forward again, I avoid the eyes of the beast. I don't want to see the pity in *his* eyes. And I would rather avoid any criticism for being out here in the first place. Finally, I look up into his face, and his gaze is fixed on the back of our crowd. "Behind you, take arms!" The drum frantically beats *tap-tap-rat-a-t-t-t-tap-tap* over and over again.

From all the way up here, I hear the clash of swords. Swinging around, all I can see are swords raised over the heads of the crowd. I can't tell which side is which. Out of the corner of my eye, I see some of the archers dart into the lines of people. They pull arrows from their quivers and nock them as they run. A hand on my wrist stops me from following. "You will stay here," the beast demands.

I rip my wrist from his grip and glare at him. He holds a sword in one hand, it's only now I see that he, like me, has blades and other weapons strapped all over his body. He pulls a second blade out and I loop my bow across my back again. I pull two blades from random sheaths attached to my body.

He glances at me out of the corner of his eye, a smirk on his stupid face. The drummer comes to my other side. He also holds a sword, but one that is much shorter than the beast's. His drum is now lying on the ground.

"Stay safe," the beast says to the drummer boy, and he nods.

There is no time for him to run to safety. All we can do is make sure he stays safe within our ranks. The battle has begun. No more time for warning drumbeats. A few of the front rows face us, eyes trained on the forest behind us, to warn of an incoming attack.

From the corner of my eye, I see men running at us from the mountainside. I turn to face them as they come around the edge of the mountain and run toward us. The sound that comes out of their mouths does not sound human.

When one of the men gasps, I turn around to look at what he sees behind me. Another group comes at us from the trees. At the back of the group, they drag what looks to be another cannon. They stop at the tree line and load it.

"Can you hit the two loading the cannon?" the beast whispers in my ear. I glance at him to see him looking at the same point I am.

"I can sure as hell try." I quickly strap my weapons back into their sheaths and get my bow and arrow ready.

"Take the shot." The arrow flies from my fingers, true to my target. Before the first one has dropped, I have pulled another arrow from the quiver and nocked it, releasing it as the first man bounces off the ground. One of his comrades trips over the corpse when it bounces and his head slams into the ground. He does not get back up.

All of this happens in quick succession. The surrounding men come at us, unaware I have just taken out their cannon-loaders.

I'm jostled as people behind me make their way toward the attackers. The crash of armor and weapons as they collide makes me cringe. All I can do is pray for our success in the battle. Awkwardly, I hold my bow by my side, afraid of hitting one of our men with a stray arrow.

When I look around, I realize I'm standing on my own, as everyone else engages in battle. I loop the bow back around me and release the blades I had before. One blade will not come out of its sheath, and I struggle with it. While I continue to tug at the clasp, an arm wraps around my waist, the attacker's other hand coming over my mouth, keeping me from getting any sounds out.

I struggle with everything in me as I am dragged off toward the mountain's edge. When we're out of view of the battle, he finally knocks me over the head and the world goes black.

I wake up in a dark cave. I can hear men converse in hushed tones. I can't even see my fingers in front of my face. Without being able to track the sun in the sky, I have no idea how much time has passed. My stomach growls but, that's nothing surprising. My head pounds.

"Sounds like the king's whore is awake," I hear, followed by the sound of approaching footsteps.

"I am no one's whore," I spit.

"Could have fooled us the way you follow *His Highness* around like a puppy." I hold my tongue, knowing I don't need to prove myself to these thugs.

He comes through what must be the exit, holding a torch.

Another man follows close behind. They both keep an eye on me as they approach.

I reach for one of my knives and find they've removed my straps and the armor. I'm completely vulnerable to these two men, and I pray to whatever god rules over this prison world that he/she/they will keep me safe.

The second man keeps his mouth shut, while the first continues to taunt me with his vile accusations. They each grab one of my arms and drag me into a standing position. When they pull my hands above my head, I look up and see chains dangling from the ceiling. I start to fight back, not wanting to be tied up, not wanting to give up in the fight to get out of here. "He'll kill you, you know," I taunt, and the silent one falters briefly in his movements.

"He doesn't know where we are, you idiot. Secure her damn hands so we can get out of here. Do you want to be around when Hook gets here?"

Hook? Like Peter Pan's Hook? Of course, you idiot, they're part of a children's story, aren't they?

As soon as my hands are locked in the manacles, both men quickly leave the room, the only source of light going with them.

CHAPTER 24

Invincible

Jolting awake at more noises, I hear what sounds like boots stomping down the tunnel. I see the dim glow before any people make their way into the cave with me. The first person is backlit by a torch. His presence is intimidating. He wears an incredibly cliché pirate hat with a giant feather sticking out.

They enter the cavern, and he is illuminated. Though his arms are crossed when he enters, I see his hook hand gleam in the torchlight.

I suppress a laugh at how amusing his presence is. My bottom lip smarts as my teeth dig into it, doing my best to keep my laughter inside.

"Something amusing to you?" he asks. With every fiber of my being, I manage to keep my mouth shut. I do not want to give these men anything else to use against the king.

"It seems we have a bit of a problem. You see, your king has taken something that does not belong to him." While he talks, he walks around me, eyes wandering over my body. I shudder.

"Really? What's that?" I ask, wondering why the king would take something that isn't his. He never struck me as a thief.

"You." He now stands directly in front of me. Reaching out

with his filthy hand, he grasps my chin. I try to jerk it away, but the chains keep me from being able to move much.

"And why would you think I belong to *you*?"

"You see, we have a little, silent treaty of sorts..." He trails off in thought. "Every time a new prisoner comes here, we have always divided the captives evenly. But, you were to be *our* captive. It was *our* turn, and I heard through the... *grapevine* that there was a new person here. And to my surprise, I found out the rumors were true when you were spotted wandering among the villagers."

"There seems to be a teeny tiny problem with your 'silent treaty.'"

"Oh, really? And what's that?" He leans in to me, his warm, disgusting breath wafting over my face, and unfortunately up my nose. I suppress a gag.

Even though I know I'll regret this later, I use all of my strength and bring my knee up into his groin. The satisfying "oof" afterward makes it worth the backhand that jerks my head to the side, spit flying out of my mouth with the movement.

When he recovers himself, he spits in my face. He pulls the same arm back and lands the first shot to my body, and all the air whooshes out of my lungs. I gasp for breath as he lands a couple more shots to the rest of my body, thankfully not using his hook hand. Then he stomps back out of the cavern, his lackey following behind him, taking away the source of light again.

Tasting blood as it pools in my mouth, I spit to rid myself of the taste. Now I need to figure out how to get myself out of the chains. Unfortunately, with both hands tied so far above my head, I can barely stand flat-footed without the manacles digging into my wrists. I hiss at the pain as I try to tug them and see how tight they are.

I'm unaware of how much time passes while I drift in and out of consciousness. My head jerks back as someone grips my hair and yanks my head back, making my face accessible for more vile words.

Several more men come and go while I hang from the chains,

laughing at the tears that won't stop. They all take their turn, landing punches over and over in my ribs, more to my face. I'm almost certain my ribs are broken. I pray to any god who's listening that they're not.

No matter how much I wish I could wrap my arms around myself to make the pain go away, I am instead forced to stretch painfully. Each breath brings pain. Despite this, I go several more rounds with the many people who come in. They try to get information from me, employing various torture techniques I've only seen in movies, thankfully stopping short of slicing into my skin. It seems they don't want to mark my skin, damaging the "king's whore."

Every breath I take hurts. I'm *sure* now they've broken several of my ribs. I do my best to take shallow breaths. My shoulders are killing me from being tied above my head for so long. And my wrists have started to chafe and bleed from the cuffs. I lost feeling in my feet some time ago, hours, days, weeks? Time has lost all meaning to me.

I open my eyes at the sound of a new person entering the room, and I blink my swollen eyes open the best I can to see who approaches. "Oh, dear, look at what a mess you are. Here, let me help you," he taunts. He sounds young.

He brings a chair from one of the walls to touch the backs of my legs and moves to the chain holding my arms above my head. Slowly, he lowers my arms just enough for me to sit in the chair. I fall into it gratefully, tears flowing down my cheeks at the immediate relief in my legs. Gently, I flex and point my toes to help get some feeling back into the limbs.

He pulls up a second chair and sits across from me. "I'm truly sorry for the way my people have treated you. I assure you, I was unaware of the depth of their depravity, my dear." I'm now finally able to get a good look at him. While his body is the size of a man, his facial features are more childish, but the venom in his tone leaves no doubt in my mind he is a fully mature asshole of an adult.

I keep my mouth shut. If his men are the ones who have been repeatedly abusing me, I don't trust a word that comes out of his lying little mouth.

He gestures for me to give him my hands. Stubbornly, I tuck them up against myself as best I can. "You're a stubborn one, aren't you?" He snickers at the dirty look I throw his way. "Perhaps I should introduce myself. My name is Peter." He holds his hand out to me as if he wants to be fucking friends or some shit.

At my refusal to acquiesce to him, he leans forward and yanks my hands toward him. "Really, what could your king have expected? You belong to *me*."

"I belong to *no one*," I growl. His eyes shine with mirth, like he thinks this is all some kind of joke.

"I assure you, my dear, you will tell me what I want to know, or you will not like the consequences." He actually kisses the back of my hand and I spit on whatever part of him I'm able to hit.

He abruptly stands and throws his chair across the room. "You really shouldn't have done that!" he roars, moving swiftly back to the wall pulling the chain fast. I am forced back into a standing position, my chair flying backward. I cry out from the pain in my sides. He continues to pull on the chain until this time I am standing on my tiptoes. My shoulders feel the pressure of the new position and I hiss in a breath as pain shoots throughout my bruised torso.

He leaves me alone and I lose track of time again. My mind can't focus on anything other than the unbearable pain throughout my bruised body. I can't keep the sobs from escaping. I feel a warm liquid trickle down and know the new position has torn open the flesh of my wrists. The blood runs down both arms in a steady trickle, and briefly I wonder how long my body can take it.

My calves begin to cramp, forced to hold most of my weight on my toes.

First, I pray for rescue.

As the time continues to drag by, I promise anything I can think of to whatever god will listen if only someone will save me.

Next, I pray for relief.

If I could only have a little bit of relief from the pain, I could make it longer. I could handle it if it just hurt a little less.

More and more time passes and I don't hear a single sound other than my own labored breathing.

Finally, I pray for death. A swift, sweet, painless death.

I jolt awake sometime later when I hear footsteps coming down the hallway. I cringe, wondering who's here to abuse me this time. My sides ache from the rounds I took with the fucking pirate and the other men. My eyes are nearly swollen shut. I'm not sure how much more I can take.

When they round the corner, I recognize the voices of James and Steve. I let out a sob of relief and try to stand up as straight as I can to relieve the pressure on my wrists. Tears roll down my face when the next person around the corner is *him*. In my current position, I can't even cover my mouth to hide the sob that escapes my mouth.

He comes to me and lifts my body in his arms. With my hands still secured above my head, I do my best to hide my face in his shoulder. "Get her down," he demands and Steve moves to the wall where they've secured the chain, releasing it from its place. My arms slowly lower and James produces some weird twisted piece of metal, using it to pick the lock on my cuffs.

As soon as my hands are free, I try to wiggle down from the beast's arms. Instead of letting me go, his arms tighten around me. "You're not going anywhere, Callie," he whispers in my ear. "They will suffer for what they've done to you."

Steve and James exit first, the beast following closely behind with me in his arms. They methodically check each branch of the tunnels we pass on our way out, looking for any other people down here. "How did you find me?"

"Shhh, we'll answer all of your questions when we're out of danger," he breathes into my ear. The words are barely audible over the nearly silent footsteps of our small group.

We finally exit the tunnel, and are surrounded by trees. I don't recognize the area we're in. "Are you okay to walk on your own?" he asks.

"I don't know..." I respond slowly. "How long have I been gone?"

"Too damn long." The beast carefully lowers me to my feet, wrapping his arms around me in a hug. I yelp out in pain and he immediately stands back, inspecting my body. "Show me where it hurts," he demands.

"Everywhere," I sob.

He whisks me back up into his arms and motions with his chin for James and Steve to continue to lead the way. They both hold a blade in either hand, and for one ridiculous second, I wonder where my bow is so I can help them scout the area.

All three heads swivel back and forth as they continue to move through the forest. Finally, the quiet and the rocking motion of being in the beast's arms lulls my exhausted body to sleep.

When next I wake, we're in some kind of tent. They've wrapped my wrists in bandages and through the slits I can see that someone tried to clean the blood off my arms.

I can hear hushed voices nearby, the growls of the beast, and what sounds like a woman's voice. "She's awake," she says, and I hear them move closer to me. "How are you feeling, dear?"

Coming into focus, I see she's elderly, wrinkles at the corners of her eyes and around her mouth. Her eyes are kind and she reaches out to hold my hand in hers.

"Water," I croak out. Out of the corner of my eye, I see the beast move to grab a cup from a nearby table. He brings it to me and they help me lean up to drink some of the cool liquid. I wince at the pain in my ribs.

When I've had my fill, they lower me back down onto the mattress. "Now, dear, tell me how you're feeling."

"As long as I don't move, it's not too bad." Next to me, the beast makes some kind of indistinguishable grunting, laughing noise.

"You've had quite the ordeal, dear. I've treated your wounds and bandaged them as best I can. Unfortunately, the rest of the healing will take time." She moves to the table where there are some jars lined up. "I've instructed the king on how to apply the different salves and how to wrap your wounds, should you be unable to handle it yourself. I'll be nearby if you need anything else."

"My ribs, are they broken?"

"Oh no, dear, I assure you they're pretty bruised but, you'll recover." She nods to us and then leaves through the opening in the tent flaps.

"How are you *really* feeling?" he asks.

"Like I've been repeatedly beaten and hung from my wrists for days."

He grimaces at my honesty. "If only I could have found you faster, sooner, protected you better..." His voice fades out as he talks. I gently wrap my hand around his wrist and he looks down at my hand before looking into my eyes.

"Did you do everything you could? Did you know where they had taken me?"

"Well, no."

"Then stop beating yourself up over it. You saved me when you could."

"But maybe if I had seen you go missing, I could have gotten to you sooner. I could have followed th—"

"And probably gotten yourself captured in the process," I cut him off.

He moves to me and brushes hair out of my face, his warm fingers lingering as he follows the various bruises down my body.

"How long until the ribs heal?" I ask, grimacing when I try to turn over to face him. His long brown hair looks like he's been running his hands through it over and over.

"Several weeks."

"When do we need to move?" I'm not even sure which side of the line we're on now.

"We have to move tomorrow." He stands and moves to the table, grabbing a spoon and two of the bottles. When he reaches my side, he says, "I think it would be a good idea for you to take these."

"What are they?"

"This one is a kind of tonic to help you sleep. The more you sleep, the better for your wounds to heal." I nod and he carefully pours some tonic into the spoon, bringing it to my mouth slowly to avoid spilling it. It tastes like some kind of berry and I lick a stray drop off my lips. When I look up, the beast's multi-colored eyes are glued to the spot my tongue touched. "And this one is the same healing tonic they gave me. Normally, I wouldn't recommend this one. All magic comes at a price that will have to be paid back, eventually. But since we don't know what awaits us in the morning, I think it wise to take it now and we can both deal with the consequences later." He uncorks and hands me the second bottle, which I drink and hand back to him.

"Thank you."

"It won't take away all of your pain, but it will drastically reduce it, for a time."

It doesn't take long for the tonic to kick in and I start to drift off. A big yawn escapes and I reach up to cover my mouth. I take a second to inspect the bandages on my wrists again. When I've settled them carefully back across my stomach, my eyes close involuntarily and I fall asleep.

Briefly, I stir when I feel the bed dip behind me. Warm arms draw me in, and I let out a sigh of contentment, relaxing into his arms and falling into a deep sleep.

CHAPTER 25

I Saw Three Ships

The next morning I'm awoken by sounds around camp. Best I can tell, they're deconstructing the surrounding campsite. "Mmmm, good morning," he says behind me, kissing my hair before releasing me. When I rotate onto my back, groaning as my bruises and ribs ache, but thankfully less with the potion, I see him sitting up and stretching his arms over his head.

"Good morning. I am so sorry to ask, but can you find the lady from yesterday? I really need to use the bathroom." I'm beyond embarrassed to have to ask him for this, but I would be even more embarrassed to have him help me.

"Let me see if she's still here." He pulls a shirt over his gorgeously muscled back. He stands and moves to the door, peeking out and saying, "Has Althea returned to the castle yet?" I hear some muffled words in return before he ducks his head back inside the tent. "It seems all the women left together at first light."

I let out a sigh, grunting as I try to get out of bed myself. When I look up, I see him extending a hand to me. I accept and he helps me to stand. "Chamberpot?" I ask.

He looks around the room and spots the pot under the table of salves. Bringing it to me, he looks away as best he can while helping me to lower over it. My bladder has never felt so full, or so much relief after a trip to the bathroom before.

When I'm finished, he helps me to stand again and brings me some clothes. I sit on the edge of the makeshift bed while he helps to get the pants up my legs. Then he helps me to stand and pulls them up around my waist. I tie the strings myself, leaving them slightly looser than previously, so they don't press against my bruises too much.

When I lift my arms over my head to get my shirt on, I cry out as I feel my bruised sides stretch. "I'm so sorry, Callie. I wish it had been me. This never should have happened." He reaches out to help me get my shirt on and tucked into my pants. Next comes my vest, which he also helps me get into.

"Hush now, if it had been you, there's no way I could have carried you out of that place. I can't even imagine how bad it would have been without the potion." I reach my hand up to his face, rubbing my thumb back and forth across his bearded cheek. "You did everything you could. Now let's get home." I grin and he puts shoes on my feet.

"Would you like to walk, or would you like me to carry you?" he asks.

I test my weight on my feet, and take slow steps around the tent. "I think I can walk a short distance, but if I'm walking back to the castle, I'm not sure I can make it the entire way."

He lets me lean on his arm and we make our way out of the tent. He helps me up into one of the wagons. I sit, watching while they finish taking the camp down, loading the equipment into the wagons. Finally, he comes to sit next to me on the seat and grabs the reins for the horses. Clicking and tapping their behinds with the reins, he is able to get the wagon moving.

At the first bump of the wagon, I wrap the hand not grasping the edge of the wagon around my torso. I try to hold back my grunts and groans of pain as we make our way to the castle. When we hit the particularly large bumps, I can't help it. Several times I catch the beast looking at me and grimacing after any of the particularly big bumps. He starts to warn me when he can see them coming. It doesn't help them hurt less, but I figure he feels like he's helping, so I try harder not to make any noises of pain.

We finally get out of the trees and pop out onto the shore. The sun reflects off the water and I squint my eyes against the bright light. Suddenly, there is a little boy running up to our wagon, and the beast pulls back on the reins to stop the horses. "What is it?" he asks.

"Your... Majesty," he pants. "I saw... three ships."

"Are you absolutely certain?" he demands, and the boy nods.

"Yes, your Majesty... they're just... around the bend."

The beast reaches behind me and lifts the canvas-like material covering everything in the back of the wagon. He pulls out several blades, followed by my recurve bow and quiver.

"Callie, I know you're still hur—"

"I can do it," I blurt.

He jumps down from the wagon and places all of his blades on the seat, motioning for me to come to him. Carefully, I stand and move past the seat without knocking any of the weapons off. He places his hands on my waist and helps me down without further injury. I try to keep any pain off my face, and take a relieved breath when I'm back on the ground.

He then reaches up and starts bringing the blades down one at a time, strapping them to us until he's gone through the whole pile. "We don't have your armor. We weren't able to find it in the tunnels."

"I'll do my best to stay back then." He nods in confirmation before helping the boy up into the wagon. I'll also have to be very careful not to get slapped by the bow's string without the protection of my armguards.

"I want you to ride straight back to the castle. Take the safest route. There should be someone to help you put the horses away when you get there."

The boy nods in return.

We move back into the trees and stay just inside the tree line as we make our way to where the boy indicated the ships had been spotted. When we get to the very edge of the trees, he motions me forward, pulling me into a crouch. "Be careful," he whispers, brushing my cheek with the back of his fingers.

"You too." The smile I plaster on my face is a complete and total lie. I'm terrified of being captured again. I'm terrified of being beaten more. I'm terrified of never seeing the beast again.

He stands and draws two blades. I clench my teeth against the pain as I reach back and pull an arrow from the quiver on my back and nock it. We step out of the trees at the same time, the large ships clearly visible at the edge of the water. Men, filthy pirates, and women make their way from the ships, armed and ready for battle.

Our people are there and waiting, already engaged in battle with whoever makes it within view. I immediately make my way to the other archers and join them in their barrage of arrows. After the first few shots, adrenaline flows through me, dimming the pain in my sides. My aching arms and shoulders protest at the motion of firing my bow over and over and over again, but I know I would regret standing on the sidelines. I would regret not helping. I would regret not being here if, God forbid, something were to happen.

According to the men who captured me, all of this is because of *me*. How could I just stand by and let a battle be fought because of me?

CHAPTER 26

White Winter Hymnal

Arrow after arrow I shoot. I ignore the soreness in my ribs, arms, and shoulders. I pull out my blades when I run out of arrows. I ignore all of my aches and pains, taking deep breaths to keep oxygen in the muscles that are fighting to defend the beast's kingdom.

When we have finally defeated anyone who has emerged from the ships, some people from our side board the ships and kill any remaining enemies.

The beast comes back to my side. He glances over at me as if to make sure I haven't been captured again.

"I'm still here." I look up at him.

He wraps his arm around my shoulders and gently pulls me to his side.

I feel him kiss my hair and I wrap my arm around his waist, being careful not to nick him with one of my blades. We turn when we hear the sound of horses coming from beside us, the opposite direction from where everything started just a few short days ago.

I recognize some of the men leading additional horses behind them from the village. "We have to travel around the water, make sure that there aren't any more getting ready to attack," the beast tells me. I nod in confirmation. "Will you be okay to come, or do you need to go back to the castle?"

"I'm coming." Quickly, I slide my blades back into their sheathes and move to one of the horses in front of me, attempting to get my foot into the stirrup. My muscles protest the movement.

"Here, let me help you," he says behind me. When I turn around, I see the beast kneeling down and offering me his hands to use as a step. I place one hand on his shoulder, and the other on the saddle horn, step into his hands, and he helps me onto the horse.

I shift my weight in the saddle, trying to get in a comfortable position. The beast quickly mounts his horse and rides up next to me, reaching out between our horses. I take his outstretched hand and he squeezes my fingers. "Keep a long blade in your hand, the shorter blade tucked away in case we're thrown from our horses."

Briefly, I pray that doesn't happen. I'm not sure if my body can take being thrown from a horse after all my other injuries. I nod to him and pull a blade from its sheath, holding it against my thigh and grabbing the reins in my other hand.

Our group splits in two, going around the water in either direction to make sure we find any stragglers from the other side. We all travel just inside the tree line, barely within sight of the water, to avoid being seen by anyone walking along the shore. The beast comes to my side and stays near me the entire trek.

We follow the rest of the pack, and when we're about a quarter of the way up our side of the water, we see them. In front of us, in the trees, is a group of men. They're circled up around a fire. Unlike the pirates from the ships, these men are all dressed warmly for the snowy weather. They're bundled up and even have some kind of scarves wrapped around their necks.

"Do we have to kill all of them? What if we can make some kind of deal?" I whisper to the beast. He shakes his head at me in return, motioning with his finger for me to be quiet.

I face forward again and continue to follow the men in front of me.

We stop moving, and my group moves back just out of sight of the men. Some of the people dismount and draw their weapons, attempting to sneak up on the enemy men. I remain on my horse, unsure if I could handle having to dismount and remount again.

The beast dismounts and joins the rest of his men. From my position, I hear shouts and the clashing of blades, but can't see anything happening. I look around me to see what I can and the other people remaining on horseback do the same. It's then I spot them, a second group of men coming straight for us, blades raised.

"Get ready!" I yell, bringing my blade up, getting ready to strike.

The first one who reaches us is taken down by a woman holding her sword in both hands as she brings the blade down. Her single strike decapitates the man entirely, and I gasp as his head bounces off the back of his horse and lands at its feet. His body tumbles off shortly after, his foot caught in the stirrup as his horse takes off at a run, dragging his body behind it, a trail of blood left behind in its wake.

When finally one of them reaches me, the woman's teeth are clenched as she tries to bring her blade down on me. I strike first, hard and fast, adrenaline masking any pain in the rest of my body. Somehow my blade hits where I've aimed, at her neck, and she tumbles off her horse.

Before I have much time to look, another one comes at me, and I'm knocked from my horse, hitting the ground with a grunt. At the sound, one of our men turns and helps me up before continuing to fight. I run between the horses, ducking and slashing out my blade at any enemies I see. My maneuvers do not take down anyone but, I do see several get taken down by the next person they come into contact with. Their injuries from my blade distract them enough they don't notice the next guy they run into.

When there is a small break in the attack, I pull a second blade from its sheath. I look up just in time to avoid my head joining the others in the snow. Instead, I slash out my blade and slice the leg of one of the riders, causing him to yank on the reins and the horse bucks him off, kicking the rider in the head as he runs off.

What seems like hours really only takes us a few minutes and we see our other men coming back to us. From what I can tell, they all survived their part of the attack. The beast leads them back to us, and he approaches me slowly. "Are you okay?" He pulls me to him and scans up and down my body.

Finally, I look around at the damage we inflicted on the riders that came at us. I approach the woman I slashed at the beginning of the battle. Her gasps growing more shallow.

Vomit rushes up my throat so quickly, I barely have time to bend over before what little remains in my stomach is heaved onto the snowy ground. The beast runs his hand up and down my back. He also attempts to pull my hair out of the way while I continue to heave. Standing back up, I glance around at the remaining bodies.

For the first time since I woke up this morning, tears flow from my eyes. "I'm so sorry. It was my fault," I cry.

"It was not your fault, Callie. This is war. These things happen," the beast says, resting his hand on my shoulder.

I jerk my shoulder away from him, angry at his nonchalant behavior. "These things do *not* happen in *my* world!"

The beast gestures for me to hand him my blades. He reaches down and wipes them off on one of the fallen men's clothes before helping me to secure them back in their sheaths.

I move to my horse and attempt to get back in the saddle. It's on my third attempt I notice red out of the corner of my eye. I look over and see the blood pooling in the snow from the woman I killed.

What makes me do it, I'll never know, but I look around the rest of the clearing and search for the other blood pools staining the snow. I move to the woman and kneel beside her. "I'm sorry," I whisper to her corpse.

Around her neck, I see a necklace, and I quickly remove it, shoving it into one of the pockets in my coat.

The beast helps me to mount my horse again and we have to continue traveling the rest of the way around the water through the trees.

"Someone will come back to bury the bodies," the beast tells me.

I glance over at him and nod. Facing forward again, I do my best to ignore the excited chatter all around me. Inside, I feel anger, sadness, and a mix of other emotions I can't name. I can't believe I've killed so many people in such a short amount of time. I'm not sure I'll ever be the same again.

We stand just inside the trees, a small distance away from the land bridge to the other side's castle. Finally, the other group who went around the other side on the opposite bank from where we started arrive.

We all dismount to discuss what to do next. They tell us they also encountered men, but theirs were all on foot.

"What about Hook and Peter?" I ask.

"Who?" the beast replies.

"They're the ones who captured and tortured me. At least, they said they were the ones in charge. I don't believe I saw either of them at the boats, or in the woods."

"What do they look like?" Steve asks, part of the other group.

"Peter has boyish features, and Hook wears a ridiculous hat, and has... well, he has a hook instead of one of his hands," I gesture above my head in some pathetic imitation of his hat.

They ask around to see if someone encountered anyone matching their descriptions. No one remembers seeing anyone like them.

"Maybe they never left their castle," the beast says.

"So they're cowards," I reply between clenched teeth. "Only willing to join the fight if their opponent is chained up."

The beast rests his hand on my shoulder. This time, I don't shrug him away. "They may have never left the tunnels they took you to. We're not exactly close to where we found you."

Two of our men come running up, out of breath. "It's abandoned," one of them says.

"There's no movement at their castle, no smoke can be seen in the air. It's as if they all just... disappeared," the other one finishes.

"Did anyone notice these guys seemed a little disorganized? Almost like they weren't entirely prepared for any of this," James states.

"What do you mean?" I ask.

"Remember how our group was lined up at the beginning? We were all together, and while they approached us from behind, we were quickly able to disarm and kill them," Steve says.

"Okay, if you say so. What does that mean?"

The beast looks down at me and responds, "It means, that all the things they were preparing, the last several weeks they've been crafting weapons, there's no way that the men that we've taken out today were carrying all of those. There is either a stockpile of weapons somewhere, or a larger army waiting. Probably both. This felt like they were testing the waters, seeing how prepared *we* are."

"Which means?"

"It means, miss, that there's a bigger war coming, and we don't know where they hide in wait, or when they plan to strike," Steve answers.

CHAPTER 27

Light in the Hallway

We all ride into the forest at a punishing pace. My ribs and body ache as we push further and faster into the woods. I grit my teeth as we move. I try to ignore the pain as I duck my head down under branches, doing my best to not get knocked off my horse.

The beast stays beside me as we continue running through the forest. My terrible sense of direction means I don't know where we are in relation to our castle, or where the bodies we left in the dirt are.

Finally, we come to some kind of large house. Bells hang along the porch, tinkling in the slight breeze.

"Where are we?" I ask when we stop, dismount, and tie our horses to the rail of the porch.

"This is one of our outposts. We need to look at the maps of the area to see where the other army could have gone to," the beast replies.

I follow everyone inside the small building. Steve nudges my shoulder as we approach the center table covered in a large map. "This is also where James and I usually stay when we're not on scouting missions, or home with our families."

"You don't live in the castle?" I ask.

"We prefer the solitude out here," James replies. "Plus, it gives us an extra strategic location when we need one."

While they all talk over possible locations the rest of them could hide in, I curl up in a chair and try to shove the images from the last couple of days from my mind.

Warm arms lift me from the chair sometime later and I curl into the beast as he carries me into another room. While they were talking, I must have fallen asleep. I jostle slightly when he opens a door and then he sits me in another chair.

My eyes fly open when I feel him start to unlace my shoes. I look down and watch him as he carefully removes them from my feet. He continues removing articles of our clothing. I help him when I need to, but sitting still in the chair has caused all of my muscles to tighten and it hurts to move. Especially my shoulders and my ribs. All of my clothes are soaked in sweat and blood. He leaves my bra and panties on since we don't have any kind of replacements here.

The muscular lines of his body are revealed the more he removes, and I feel the heat of a blush crawling up my face. He moves over to the washstand and brings it and a cloth of some sort over. First, he carefully washes his hands, then somehow manages to wash my hair, brushing it through with his fingers to remove the tangles from riding horses through the forest all day. "There, all back to blonde," he murmurs while he braids my hair and somehow ties it up on top of my head to keep it from touching my filthy body.

It's only when I look back into the bowl that I realize how covered in blood and dirt we both are. When he washes down my arms, I cringe as he leaves circular clean splotches among the brown and red-caked skin.

When he's finished cleaning me from head to toe, he dumps the bowl out a nearby window and fills it again from the pitcher with fresh water. I watch as he follows on his body the same cleaning path he used on me, ending with cleaning the dirt from his feet. He dumps his dirty, bloody water out the window before filling the bowl for a third time, just in case we need it later.

Only when we're both as clean as we're going to get does he gently pick me up and place me down on the bed. He climbs in behind me and carefully pulls me into him. I rest my head on his arm and fall quickly back to sleep.

During the night, I wake up and see a glow under the door. Someone has left a torch lit in the hallway. Maybe they never went to sleep. I slide out of bed, careful not to disturb the beast. They've left us a tray with some food and drink on it and I gratefully quench my thirst, following it with some of the delicious food.

I'm attempting to use the chamberpot, when I hear from the bed, "Did I just hear you eating something?"

"Yes. Why, are you hungry?" I tease as I stand up and wash my hands the best I can. On my way back to the bed, I grab the tray and bring it to him.

"Thank you, I'm starved." He digs into the food and finishes everything left on the tray.

Setting it back on the table, I turn around and see the beast smiling at me. "What?" I look down at myself subconsciously.

"You're beautiful." He takes my hand and pulls me between his legs where he sits on the edge of the bed.

"You're a liar." I smile, and he helps me to climb back into bed. "How long do you think it will take me to heal from all of this?" I gesture down at my body.

"The soreness from the battle? I would guess you haven't even felt all the soreness yet. You'll need to see a healer when we get back to the castle. As for what the magic helped fix... that pain will come back at some point, as will mine."

"Why did we come here instead of going back to the castle?"

"This was closer," he says simply, wrapping me back in his arms. He runs his fingertips up and down my side. Goosebumps break out all over as he continues the movement over and over.

Eventually, I fall back to sleep, wrapped in his arms.

New Year's Day

CHAPTER 28

New Year's Day

The sun is shining through the window when we next awake. I hear people moving about in the rest of the house. "It sounds like everyone is awake"

"Mmmm, I would say that sounds right." He pulls me backward into him and I hiss as his arm crosses some very sore areas of my body. "Callie, I'm so sorry, I didn't think—"

I place my hand on his arm to still him from his panic attack. "It's okay, it's going to take me a while to remember I'm covered in bruises, too."

A knock sounds on the door, and we quickly sit up in bed, both cringing at how sore we are from yesterday's battles.

"Your Majesty, we're just about ready to head back to the castle," Steve says from the other side of the door.

"We'll be out in a moment," he returns. After getting out of bed himself, he helps me to climb out and moves to a wardrobe I didn't notice last night. He pulls out two sets of men's clothing and places them on the bed. "You'll need to tie the laces on the breeches extra tight to keep them from falling down your body."

"Whose clothes are these?" I ask.

"I believe we're in James's room."

"You kicked him out of his own room?"

"We all agreed you needed one of the beds after all you've been through the last couple of days," he replies. "If it makes you feel better, Steve also let one of the women take over *his* room."

It takes me some time and help from the beast to get the clothes on. Everything hurts. Muscles that haven't been used probably ever. Getting beaten and tortured. Riding the horse through the woods all damn day yesterday, I need a break.

When we walk out of the room, everyone else is already outside. "Here we go again," I say sarcastically, hoping we are close to the castle and we don't have to ride for long.

Thankfully, the house we stayed in last night is somewhere in the trees between the two castles and we get back home within a few short hours. When I dismount, I awkwardly limp to the man waiting to take my horse back to the stables, wherever they are.

Kenna runs up to me as soon as I hand off my horse and wraps her arms around me so tight, I can't keep a groan of pain from escaping my mouth.

"You had me so worried! I can't believe you snuck away like that!" she says too loudly. Then her eyes roam down my body and the awkward way I'm holding myself. "What happened to you?"

"Kenna, can you please take Callie to the healer? She will need her wounds tended to as soon as possible," the beast tells her.

Kenna nods to him and loops her arm through mine, leading me into and through the castle.

She takes me to the petite healer, Althea, who does her best to help me. She gives me some herbs and salves to apply as needed for my various injuries and something for Kenna to add into my bath.

Next, Kenna takes me up to my room and my jaw drops when I see the beautiful gown hanging from the open wardrobe door. "Kenna, what's that?" I ask.

"It's New Year's Eve, miss. There's going to be a ball to celebrate the end of the battle and the new year."

"I'm afraid I won't be able to wear that." I gesture down at my body, now covered up, but she just saw all my bruises when we were with the healer.

"Oh, we can get you into it without a corset, miss. I'll make sure not to lace it too tightly as well."

She moves into the other room to prepare the bath, adding the herbs from the healer into the tub before several people come into the room carrying buckets of water with steam rising off the surface. Then she helps me to get out of the men's clothes.

Slowly, I ease into the water, holding onto the sides to keep myself from slipping on the smooth bottom of the tub. Kenna comes in and helps me wash my hair. She scrubs extra hard and laughs as she pulls out various twigs and leaves tangled in it that somehow accumulated in our short ride today.

I scrub as hard as I can with the soap she hands me, doing my best to remove any residue left over from the previous day. Once I feel like I can't get any cleaner, Kenna has me stand in the tub and dumps several buckets of clean water over my head to wash off any remaining bloody bathwater.

I climb out and dry off, and we add as many layers as she thinks I can handle. Then she leaves everything as loose as possible without the dress falling off or looking like a giant, beautiful burlap sack. Thankfully, the potion healed me enough where I don't have to wear bandages, but the skin around my wrists is still tender. The bruises along my torso are still visible, and my ribs are still bruised. The bath seems to have helped all of these things, including the muscle soreness from shooting so many arrows and riding a horse for so long. But, unfortunately, as everyone keeps telling me, it's just going to take time to heal properly.

While my hair dries she does my makeup beautifully. Then she pins and tucks my hair in an elegant updo. "What about you? Don't you need to get ready?"

"Of course, miss. I'll be going to my room as soon as someone comes to take you down to the ballroom." When she reaches the end of her sentence, we turn at a knock on the door.

Steve pokes his head in. "Your carriage awaits, madam." He bows low and ridiculously moves his arm in an arc toward himself before standing with a big smile across his face and holding his elbow out in my direction.

Quickly, I squat down, snag the necklace from my coat pocket, and shove it into a hidden pocket in my dress. I don't know what makes me do it, or why I felt the need to take the necklace off of the woman I killed. But something inside me tells me to keep the necklace with me, so I do.

Carefully, I stand from my crouched position and move toward him. Thankfully, there were some flat shoes in my wardrobe so I can minimize tripping over my own feet and further injury.

When we reach a large set of double doors I've never seen before, James stands beside the door. He opens it and announces, "The honorable Miss Callie has arrived."

I feel the heat move up my neck and cheeks. Inside, it appears there are stairs going down into a large ballroom. All eyes are on me while Steve helps me down the stairs. Thankfully, he keeps me from tripping the entire way down.

"Seriously, who built this place?" I wonder aloud to myself.

"I couldn't even begin to tell you," he replies.

It's hard to believe they created a ballroom under this mountain, but I guess when you're digging down, it's easier to fit things.

At the bottom of the stairs, the beast waits for me. His jaw drops while he watches me descend the staircase. "Here she is, Your Majesty," Steve says, passing me off to the beast.

"Thank you, Steve. You may go be with your family now," the beast tells him.

"Your family is here? I would love to meet them!" I say and both of them look at me and chuckle.

"Later, Callie First we must kick off the dancing."

"I'm not sure I know your kind of dancing." It's been a long time since I've done any dancing. I'm afraid I probably won't know any of the ones that were around back when these guys started getting banished here.

"Don't worry, you can follow my lead." He winks at me.

Taking my hand, he leads me out into the middle of the dance floor. He takes one of my hands and places it on his shoulder, then he rests his hand on my upper back before grasping my other hand in his. Off to the side sits a small orchestra, they start playing, and the beast waits a few beats before starting the dance.

We move across the floor, and he leads me beautifully. I feel like a princess. The others join in a few bars into the song, and we twirl and swoosh around each other.

The men are dressed in their best suits, the women wear beautiful gowns. Running around the room, even the children are dressed up for the occasion.

Several dances later, we move out of the dancing area to get some punch and refreshments from tables off to the side.

"I don't believe I've thanked you for your help these last few days, Callie." He looks at me over the top of the punch cup he holds.

I take a sip of mine before responding, "I don't believe I've thanked you enough for rescuing me from Peter and Hook."

"Truly, Callie, I've never been so terrified in my entire life."

"Not even when you first came here?"

"That wasn't terrifying, it was just an adjustment. When I turned around and I couldn't find you, my heart stopped in my chest. I thought for sure they were going to kill you."

"They almost did," I mumble. He draws me into his side and kisses the top of my head.

One of the young archers comes up and asks for me to join him in a dance. The beast nods for me to join him. I hand my cup off to him before extending my hand to the young man. While he is not as skilled at leading as the beast, I manage not to further injure myself.

When we finish the dance, another man comes up and asks me to join him. I look at the beast on the sidelines and he nods to me again. Then, a woman comes up and asks him to dance and we spend the next several songs trading off partners.

Finally, Steve and James approach me at the same time and Steve says, "Callie, we'd like to introduce you to our families." I nod to my most recent dance partner and follow the two men to where their families stand.

The wives call to their children, who are running around the perimeter of the room with the other children.

"Callie, this is my wife Abigail," Steve says.

She curtsies to me and I nod in return.

"And this is my wife Imogene," James adds.

Looking between the two, I recognize the similarities and ask, "Are you two sisters?"

"Yes, miss," Imogene replies.

"We've always been told how much we look alike," Abigail tells me.

"The boys are running around here somewhere. I'm afraid they're having too much fun running around the ballroom with their friends."

"Probably off somewhere picking on our daughters," Steve chimes in.

"It was lovely to meet you, Callie, but I must get James out onto the dance floor," Imogene says, and James holds out his arm for her to take.

"You'll come over for dinner some night, won't you?" Abigail asks.

"Of course," I respond, and Steve whisks her out onto the floor as well.

Theodore approaches me and extends his hand to me. "May I have this dance?" I nod, grateful to dance with someone I know better than those I met just days ago because I stood beside them on the battlefield.

"Are you married, Theodore?" I ask while we twirl across the floor.

"No, ma'am. I've never found a woman worth settling down with." I nod in understanding. He spins me one last time, straight into the waiting arms of the beast, who immediately whisks me off the dance floor, back over to some refreshments.

"I have something to ask you, Callie," he starts, but our attention is diverted when someone yells that we have ten minutes until the new year. "But first, I want to show you something."

He takes my cup and plate and places them on the table, grabbing my hand and leading me back up the stairs. We move through many tunnels and up many staircases in the mountain, moving up all the time.

I hear a shuffling behind me and realize everyone is following us up to wherever we are going.

At the top of the last staircase, he pushes open a set of double doors and we enter a large room, one entire wall made of glass. And I think we must be on a side of the mountain I haven't seen before. I would have noticed this much glass on the side of the mountain.

"Whoever built this place had some amazing technology. It took me forever to figure out how to open the false rock covering the windows," he whispers in my ear as he moves us right up to the window.

I touch the cold glass and look out at the surrounding land. There are trees as far as the eye can see, and the river I encountered can be seen flowing in the distance, the moon glistening off the water.

"Why are we up here?" I ask.

"You'll see." He moves to stand behind me, arms gently wrapped around my waist. His warm breath across my cheek gives me goosebumps as we wait.

"Five." His breath skates across my skin, my hair tickling me as it gently moves against my neck.

"Four." His arms pull me closer to him and I hold my breath in anticipation of what is to come.

"Three." His arms leave my waist and he trails his fingertips down my arms, hands entwining with my own.

"Two." He releases one of his hands and runs his fingers down my neck. I tilt my head to the opposite side to give him access.

"One." He leans in and kisses my neck. Tingles reach all the way to my core and I gasp at the contact.

"Happy New Year!" everyone shouts together, and as soon as they finish, fireworks, or something that looks like fireworks, fly over the water, and the enemy castle. Their reflection on the still surface makes them look even more magnificent.

I gaze at the beauty of the different colors lighting up the world outside the large window. I release his hand and move closer to the glass, touching its cold surface.

The beast comes around my side, and I turn to face him. "Happy new year, Callie," he says as he gently places one palm on my cheek. His other arm wraps around my waist and he pulls me into him. I can feel the warmth of his body against my own.

"Happy new year," I reply, moving my hands to wrap around his neck, fingers clasping together, his braided brown hair not allowing for me to run my fingers through it as I want to.

He moves closer to me, giving me the opportunity to move away, to stop this from happening. Everything around us fades away and we stand in our own bubble of whatever this is. Too slowly, he presses closer to me. If he could pull me any closer to him, he would, though my dress prevents it. My own blue eyes flash back and forth between his brown and ice blue ones.

It feels like it takes forever and finally I pull his face to me, closing the remaining distance between us, tired of waiting for his slow descent. As soon as I feel the warmth of his lips against mine, they're gone. His warm arms falling away in the blink of an eye.

The smell of him is suddenly an echo on the breeze. An icy chill whispers across my skin and I wrap my arms around myself, tears falling down my cheeks. I open my eyes to my bedroom at my parents' house.

PART SIX

The Next Year

Where Are You Christmas?

JANUARY

I take the necklace from my pocket and clutch it in my hand as I curl up on the bed, still dressed in the ballgown.

How did that happen? I've never travelled while awake before. When the first tear falls, I don't even have the energy to wipe it away. Everything pours in all at once, the war, being captured, tortured, so many men dead, and finally the kiss that ended too soon.

The next morning, a gentle knock on the door wakes me up. The door cracks and I open my eyes to see my mom peeking her head in. "You're back," she says quietly and moves to my side. "Oh, sweetie, was is really so bad?"

I reach up and swipe the tears off my cheeks, but the damn things won't stop falling. My mom wraps her arms around me, cradling me to her as she rocks us back and forth.

"What's that you have there?" She reaches to touch the golden necklace in my hand.

"I..." I trail off, not yet wanting to tell anyone about what all has happened to me over the last couple of days. "I found it," I finish lamely.

"It's beautiful," she says. "So is this dress!"

I look down and admire the ballgown I still wear, running my hand over the silky fabric. "Can you help me get out of it?" I know there is no way I can unlace the back by myself.

The material slides down my body and I hear my mom inhale sharply. "What happened?" she breathes.

"There was a battle... I was captured and held until they found me and saved me." I don't need to tell her I was beaten. The bruises covering my body are proof enough of that.

She wraps her arms around me from behind gently, and I turn around in her embrace. We stand there for several minutes just hugging each other before I step back and say, "Why don't we wait until I have some clothes on before talking more? I'll be out soon."

When she closes the door behind her, I pull out the most comfortable undergarments I have and carefully pull them on. Thankfully, I packed some sweats. I pull them over my battered body and make my way to get something for breakfast.

Across the table, Mom and Dad watch me while I slowly consume the food in front of me. Mom brings me coffee fixed just the way I like it and watches me over her cup as I slowly drink the warm liquid.

The coffee helps to wake me up, but does nothing to cure my broken heart. Mom reaches across the table and pats my hand. "You just tell us when you're ready."

The tears continue to fall as I take deep breaths. "I woke up in the prison world..." I start. Pausing to gather my thoughts before telling everything that happened while I was there. "You were right, Mom, bad things happened.

"As soon as we woke up, the mountain shook when a cannonball was shot at it from the outside. At first... he tried to send me down into the tunnels with the children and elderly. But, after all the planning I helped to do for the battle, I couldn't just stand by and watch. So I tried to make my way out of the tunnels only to get lost and have to wait until Steve and James came down the tunnels looking for me. They brought me to a room and helped get me outfitted with armor and weapons.

"You'll be glad to know all those years of archery clubs and horseback riding lessons came in handy." A maniacal laugh escapes me when visions of shooting people play through my head. "I killed so many people, Mom."

"Shhhh, honey, it's okay." She stands and comes to wrap her arms around me. "Why don't we move to the couch?"

We stand and get comfortable on the couch, Mom holding my hand while we walk. A fire warms the room and I stare into the dancing flames as I continue my story.

"It was all so fast. They came up behind us and everyone turned to kill the attackers. They captured me. Not a soul saw me being dragged away." I clutch my chest, taking deep breaths to calm my breathing. My mom rubs my back, the circles soothing my anxious heart. "They... hit me... beat me... left all these bruises. And when I didn't keep my mouth shut, he pulled my chains until I could barely touch the ground on my tiptoes." Unconsciously, I rub my wrists, the memory of the experience coming back to the surface.

My dad moves from the recliner to sit next to me, pulling me to him in a side hug.

"I didn't think he was going to come for me." I choke back a sob. "I'm still not sure how long I stayed there."

Looking up at my mom, she has tears on her cheeks. "But he came for me. He saved me from them. But the next day we had to make sure they were gone."

"Why didn't that son of a bitch send you back to safety?" my dad asks.

"I wouldn't let him. I couldn't stand to be trapped in the

castle, not knowing if he... if he... survived. It was like him being shot all over again. I couldn't bear the thought of him lying in the dirt, dying alone."

Mom nods in understanding, and I feel a sort of kinship with her. My mom is one of the strongest people I know and I feel like if she were in the same situation, she would have done the same.

I finish my story, and dad turns on the TV to drown out the silence.

A couple of days later, my body is still covered in bruises and Dad helps Mom put all the Christmas stuff away.

I can't bear to be stuck in the house with their pitying glances, so I drive back home. I'm forced to leave the chest at their house until I'm able to lift anything without excruciating pain.

When I get home, I text Huxlee to let her know I'll be back at work in the morning.

HUXLEE

Thank fuck! My sister is about ready to drive me crazy!

ME

See you in the morning. I'll bring the coffee.

HUXLEE

Employee of the year!

When I get to work the next morning with a coffee cup in each hand, I struggle to open the door and jump when a hand reaches from behind me to open it for me. I quickly turn around to see the intruder and stare into the face of a man I've never seen before. "It looked like you were struggling. I was sitting just over there." He points to a table at the café where a woman sits and waves at me. I smile and raise my coffee cup in greeting.

"Thank you." I go through the door, which closes behind me as he releases it to go back to his table.

Huxlee looks up from the book she's reading at the counter when I approach. "Oh, my God! What happened to you?" She watches me walk in awkwardly with my all-over soreness.

I can't help the tears that start falling down my face. She comes around the counter and takes the cups from my hands. "Come on, let's go to the back."

I nod in agreement and let her lead me. Then she sets our cups on the table and tugs me to sit beside her on the couch.

"Spill."

For the second time in less than a week, I share what happened to me in the prison world. Huxlee holds my hands the entire time, nodding occasionally as I continue talking.

When I get to the part about the healing potion, she asks, "So, what does a magic healing potion taste like?"

"I don't know, like someone ran too many herbs through a blender? I was a little focused on the pain at the time." I laugh.

She motions for me to keep going with the story. The next time she stops me is right as I finish, ending with me in my parents' house.

"Wow, Callie. So how was the kiss?"

I bark out a laugh. Of course, that would be the thing she asked about.

"Huxlee, I swear to you, the *second* our lips touched, I was back at my parents' house. And since I still have no fucking clue how to get back there, I'm forced to stay here."

"Ouch," she says, hand to her chest in mock hurt.

"You know what I mean."

She pulls me into a hug and I can't stop the floodgates anymore. She lets me cry on her shoulder until my eyes dry up. "Are you sure you want to be here today?"

"Huxlee, I couldn't bear to see my parents' pitying looks anymore. And I definitely don't think I can be left to my own thoughts right now." She nods and squeezes my hand one last time before standing up and grabbing her coffee.

"Well, then I guess it's time to get to work to take your mind off it, huh?"

I spend the rest of the day pushing boxes around on our book cart as I fill them up with the various Christmas decorations we strung around the store such a short time ago.

Several customers come in and I can barely muster a, "Welcome to Enchantments and Fancies." Huxlee helps everyone who comes in and helps me between customers.

About a week later is when I can tell the magic potion's price demands a full refund. My bruises change to darker colors instead of getting lighter like they should. It hurts me to lift or do *anything* that requires moving my torso. And my calves cramp like I've been doing calf raises forever.

When I walk into work that morning, Huxlee immediately asks, "What the hell happened to you?"

"My guess? That damn magic healing potion has left my system finally."

"Yikes, well if you need to go home for the day, you know you're welcome to."

"Thanks, I think I'm going to try to stay as long as I can stand it."

We both go about our work for the rest of the day. Huxlee hugs me goodbye when we leave.

FEBRUARY

A month has passed and I have not woken up in the prison world again. Every night, I miss the beast unbearably. At every chance I get, I continue to read the journal.

Over the next several weeks, Zev honored his vow, dropping food at my door at every opportunity. This, in addition to my snares, has kept me fed.

I talked to myself while I wandered the halls. Today I found a room with various creatures inside. They all appeared well fed, so I assumed someone must have been feeding them. I also found a study with many books, and most afternoons find myself grabbing a volume and sitting with the animals.

Their presence makes me feel less alone.

Days have passed, and I started to hunt for other forms of nourishment. It's on one of these excursions Zev approached me in his human form, a woman at his heels.

"Sir, I found her wandering in the trees," he said. She curtsied to me, eyes staring at a spot on the ground.

"What is your name?" I asked her.

It's only then she looked at me and answered, "Kenna, sire."

"When did you arrive here, Kenna?"

"I've been here for over one hundred years, sire," she responded.

I nodded in acknowledgment and extended my arm to her. "Where have you been sleeping?" I asked.

"Under the stars, when I can. Sometimes I find a cave to sleep in, sire," she said, placing her hand in the crook of my elbow.

Wow, so that's how Kenna met up with the beast? I imagine the terror she must have felt being approached by a large wolf. I remember my own terror at encountering the very same wolf.

I place my bookmark in the journal and hold it close to my chest before dozing off to sleep.

Huxlee avoids talking to me at work. I've been a bitch recently and I don't blame her for avoiding me. Turns out bruised ribs take weeks to heal and apparently, when magic healing potions wear off, you get to feel the full brunt of all those weeks.

"Callie, just because you're alone and in pain doesn't give you the right to be a royal bitch," she tells me after one such tantrum.

I start at what she says, thinking back on my words and actions over the last month, realizing the way I've been behaving toward her is unacceptable. No one should have to put up with what I've been dishing out to Huxlee. "I'm... so sorry." I set down the books in my hands and make my way to the back.

"Wait, Callie, where are you going?"

Bewildered, I turn to face her. She has come out from behind the counter and looks genuinely confused. "I was going to go home. I've been a terrible friend, and I figured I would give you a break." My arms are wrapped around myself as I wait for her response.

"Callie, that's ridiculous. Sometimes all of us need a little kick in the ass to get us out of a funk. I love you. I'm here for you if you need me." She makes her way to me and holds out her arms.

Gratefully, I hug her tightly to me. "I don't deserve you."

"No, you don't. But I love you anyway." We both start giggling, and when a customer walks in amidst our chuckles, we laugh even harder.

After that, we go about the rest of our day like old times. I treat Huxlee to dinner somewhere nice, as an apology for having to put up with me. Over dinner, we reminisce about old times, sibling fights, and the ridiculous things our parents put us through as we grew up.

When I get home that night, I can't help but wonder if the big war has happened. Is everyone alive? Would I know if they were gone?

My phone ringing interrupts my thoughts. Looking down at the screen, it's my dad. "Hello?" I briefly wonder when or if I'll ever hear from Mason again.

"Hey, Callie girl, I just wanted to check on you. How are you?" he asks.

"All things considered?"

"All things considered."

"I still miss him, Dad."

"I know, Callie girl, I know. I love you, have a good night's sleep, okay?"

"Night, Dad, love you, too."

Every night, I fall asleep holding the journal against my chest. The necklace hangs in my bathroom and I wonder to myself sometimes whether this makes me a serial killer, collecting mementos from my victims. But there's just something about it I can't shake. The necklace itself isn't exactly remarkable. But the little golden journal hanging from the chain just seemed like too much of a coincidence with everything that has happened.

The woman haunts me in my dreams. Sometimes I wake up gasping for breath and am forced to start my day early because there's no way I can turn my brain off after another repeat of the gory scene.

She reminds me of someone, I just can't place who. Or maybe I just can't bear to consider my actions too closely. I know no one will blame me for the lives I took that day, but not having grown up fighting in battles, my heart aches when I think about the things I had to do.

Valentine's Day rolls around, and I take the day off work. I bought myself chocolates and ice cream before ordering a mushroom burger with sweet potato fries and curling up on the couch with a fluffy blanket to watch the most violent movie I can find.

Rom-coms can suck a big, hairy, lint-coated toe.

Before starting the movie, I shoot off a text to Mason.

ME

Hey, I haven't heard from you in a while but, I just can't handle a relationship right now. I'm sorry.

Over the last several days, I've managed to keep my sour attitude to myself. Opting for mostly reading and watching movies by myself. It's too cold to run outside, so instead, I find a store that has all kinds of bows and arrows and they help me pick which ones to get before showing me to their archery range.

I figure if there is going to be another war; I need to be prepared. My bruises have mostly faded by now, only a slight yellow hue in the areas that took the most abuse. Absentmindedly, I run my hand over my abdomen, pressing and feeling to see how much discomfort is still there.

MARCH

I walk into work, and Huxlee is waiting for me just inside the door. She stands with fists on her hips. "Enough is enough, Callie. I know it sucks. I know you love him. But you can't keep walking around here moping all the time. You're scaring the customers away with your bitchy attitude."

Her pep talk last month only lasted for a few days before I slipped back into bitch mode. I wonder how many times I can snap at her before she fires me?

Pushing past her, I start putting away a shipment of books that came in over the weekend. "Nuh uh, you will either talk to me, or you will need to go home." She takes the book out of my hand and sets it down on the shelf beside her.

I stare at my hands in my lap.

"Oh, Callie." She pulls me into her arms.

"I just miss him so much," I admit as she continues to hold me.

"He'll come back to you, I know it." While I appreciate her optimism, I'm not so hopeful.

I make an extra effort to at least appear happy on the outside, even though I still feel like I've lost a huge part of myself on the inside. I don't know what I'd do if I lost my job. Probably have to move back in with my parents, or worse, one of my brothers.

For the rest of the day, I do my best to make some lighthearted conversation, not wanting to irritate Huxlee any further. Maybe I should start seeing a therapist to help me deal with my feelings.

I decide I'll call around to some tomorrow. It may not help, but it's not like it could get much worse, right?

When I get home that night, my dad's truck is out front. "What are you doing here?" I ask.

"I had some business in town today, thought I'd stop by and take my only daughter out to an early dinner."

We load up in his truck, and he takes me to my favorite Italian place. I order my favorite, fettuccini alfredo, and he orders ravioli. One of the things I love about my dad, he's not a man of many words, but you always feel like he's there for you.

When he drops me back off at my place, he gives me a hug before getting back into his car. "I love you, Callie."

"I love you too, Dad. Text me when you get home, all right?"

"I will." I wave as he drives off, only making my way back inside once his taillights disappear down the street.

Several hours later, my phone chimes.

DAD

Home. We did not eat Italian without your mother.

ME

What Italian?

DAD

What did the spider tell the pig?

ME

Chin up!

Everywhere I go, I look for him in the crowd. Maybe some sign that will lead me back to the prison world. I continue to read the journal looking for any instructions for how to get back there but, there is nothing. He told me I was the only one who has ever been able to leave the world, figures he would have no idea how to travel back and forth.

And according to my mom, none of my ancestors have been able to travel back and forth either. I don't even know how I travelled, other than knowing it usually happens when I sleep.

Every day, I pray that my time in the prison world hasn't come to an end. My heart hurts. I miss the beast. I miss Mason. I hope I don't push Huxlee away.

Tonight, I decide to read something else, picking up my most recent dark romance from the end table. Before I dive into the pages, I place a delivery order from my phone and read until food arrives. Before I set it down on the end table, I shoot off a text to the girls.

ME

Okay, I have been out of the loop. What are we all reading?

JEN

Do budgeting books count as a genre?

STACY

You know me, Historical Romance.

HUXLEE

… everything…

ME

I feel like my TBR needs an overhaul

My food arrives, and I set my phone down before answering

the door. Tonight, I decided to order fully loaded nachos and I pour the cheese sauce over the top before taking the first bite.

I loathe getting food or drink on my book, so while I eat, I watch some of *You* on Netflix. This show gives me the creeps every time I watch it, but I love it.

The sky outside is beautiful tonight. I grab my blanket and my book before making my way out to my porch and read under the dim porch light for the rest of the night. The cold air nips my cheeks, but I don't care.

APRIL

Today is Easter. All the adults sit on the back porch at Mom and Dad's house watching the kids hunt for Easter eggs. Tucker is pointing out the easy eggs to Macie so she can get more in her basket while the bigger kids get the ones Jake and Andy hid higher up. Now that some of the kids are tall enough to reach, they hide some of them balanced on top of tree branches and on the fence line.

Huxlee's ringtone goes off in my pocket and I pull my phone out to see what she's got to say today.

HUXLEE

Happy Easter!

ME

LOL so cheesy. Happy Easter. Your family doing eggs?

HUXLEE

Yes. But mostly the kids are making themselves sick on chocolate bunny parts. You?

I tuck my phone back into my pocket and watch the kids run back and forth across the yard. With each egg uncovered, they get louder and louder.

Once all the eggs have been found, the adults circle around me. They've been eagerly waiting for me to tell my story since I got home.

Jen sits next to me, holding my hand while I relay the story for the third time.

I start from the very beginning from when I found the chest. Mom jumps in to tell everyone about the firstborn female in our family being the protector of the chest.

"Oh, that old dusty thing up in the attic?" Andy asks.

"Yes…" I reply.

"Yeah, we found that one year when dad made us clean the attic."

"I know. Jake told me months ago. I can't believe you guys found a mysterious chest with words on top and you didn't tell me?"

"Oh, little sister, you think we tell you everything?" Jake nudges me, laughing at my shocked face.

Throughout the story, they all gasp and *oooo* in unison when I get to a particularly exciting part of the story.

When I get to the battles and finally to the kiss, Jen squeezes my hand.

"Oh, Callie, I can't believe you actually lived that. It sounds more like a fairytale." Stacy presses her hand to her heart. "It's so romantic. I wish something that romantic had happened to me. Okay, maybe not the kidnapped and tortured part."

"Hey! I'm romantic!" Jake retorts.

"Oh, sure you are, sweetie." She pats him on the knee. He

crosses his arms in response. I can't help but smile, looking around at my family.

After we eat the burgers Dad cooked on the grill, and the potato salad and deviled eggs Mom made, there are hugs all around before everyone loads into their cars and head back to our homes.

I took today off work. My therapist has been telling me I need to do something for myself. So finally I decide to do something today. I picked up some picnic stuff and am sitting in a field of flowers near where I live. The springtime air smells wonderful, with all the flowers popping up with the recent rains.

I lay out the blanket I brought to sit on, sit and start pulling out the food items I brought with me. While I eat, I admire all the different colors of flowers. It reminds me of the painting I saw in the beast's castle.

My heart aches to see him again. I've been Googling random *How to travel to other worlds, Has anyone ever been to other worlds,* and any variation thereof so much I wonder if I'm on some kind of crazy person watch list.

When I finish eating, I lay back on the blanket and fall asleep in the warm sunshine. Something tickles my nose and I open my eyes to a butterfly staring back at me. I stay as still as I can watching it watch me.

When it finally flies away, I sit up and see all kinds of bugs flying around me. Bumblebees fly back and forth between the flowers, doing their job pollinating the various plants. Butterflies also land on the colorful surfaces. I marvel at the ecosystem in front of me, and take another deep breath to inhale the fragrance of all the flowers combined.

Finally, I pack up my things to head back home. My phone

goes off with Huxlee's ringtone right before I drive off. Pulling the phone from my pocket, I smile at her words.

HUXLEE

Hey, hope your day was good. The books and I missed you.

ME

What do you need?

HUXLEE

Lol, nothing…

ME

Huxlee Nicole Rochefort

HUXLEE

Nothing much. Can you stay after closing to receive a delivery? It has to be signed for. It's the bookcase nooks we ordered, and I promised I would do a thing with my mom.

ME

LOL yes. Of course. You know you just need to ask…

While I drive, I think about how therapy has helped me not be such an unpleasant person at work. Huxlee has even commented on how much more pleasant I am to work with now. It stung a little when she said it, but I appreciate her honestly.

MAY

I sit on my couch, *his* journal in my lap. In the last couple of months, I've read over it more times than I can count, trying to feel close to him.

The one thing I have not done is show the journal to Huxlee.

It feels like by sharing the contents of the journal with her, I would be somehow letting a piece of him go.

I stroke the soft leather, worn by the years. The pages have that wonderful old book smell I love.

When I first got back here, I hoped that by reading the journal I would somehow trigger going back to the prison world. But the more time goes by, I am starting to believe I will never get back there.

Maybe my purpose there is done?

"A woman will come, differently from the rest. And she will save us from this world, this prison."

I hear the prophecy echo through my head. It makes me wonder if he was wrong? Maybe I was just supposed to come and stir up trouble?

Setting the journal aside, I pick up my copy of *Peter Pan* and wonder how in the prison world Peter and Hook have come to work together. Maybe the author of the story had it wrong? It seems to me that each story probably has deviated from the truth. Several of these old stories were orally passed down before finally being recorded. Who knows how much the story changed from the originals?

Maybe the written version is always the original version and any resemblance to past oral traditions is only a coincidence? But that wouldn't explain Peter and Hook unless something happened to bring them together. I spend my days alternating between reading the journal and various fairytales. The Grimm tales are usually the most disturbing, and I wonder if every person within these books resides in the prison world.

JUNE

"Hey, girl, I brought you some iced coffee," Huxlee says when she walks in the door.

"Oh, thank God. I didn't sleep very well last night." I accept the cup from her outstretched hand and take a long pull from the straw.

"What do you say we close the store for the day?"

I look up sharply. I don't recall a time Huxlee has ever closed the store for no reason. "Why...?"

"I think we need a girls' day. I want to treat us to some massages, manis and pedis, and some junk food and movies afterward." She heads to the back, coming out with our purses and turns all the lights off as she moves toward me.

"What the hell?" I shrug and follow her out the door.

First, we head to the massage place. It's one of those "choose your level of comfort" places when it comes to how much clothing you remove. Huxlee, of course, goes full-on nudist, and I figure what the hell, let's do it.

She booked us for a couple's massage so we can be in the same room together and when they offer us champagne, I quickly down the first glass. I've never had a massage before, so I don't know what to expect and having some stranger's hands all over my body is starting to freak me out.

When two women walk in, I breathe a sigh of relief. These women don't look like much, but when the one working on me starts digging her elbows into my muscles to release the tension, I groan in both discomfort and relief.

We're there for an hour before we're ushered into another area of the building where the manis and pedis are done.

I'm grateful I shaved this morning when the woman pulls my pants up so I can dip my feet in the little foot whirlpool.

Huxlee has them paint her fingers and toes to match her current turquoise hair. I opt for a dark green. Green has always been my favorite color. Both of our phones chime and in unison we pull them out to see what's going on with the Besties.

JEN

Hey Andy is going to be in town for work at the end of the week. Are you super busy? I keep calling the store to place my Bed Rest Book Haul order, but no answer.

HUXLEE

Closed.

JEN

What?!

ME

Everything is fine. We took a day off.

JEN

Together?

HUXLEE

We needed some pampering.

JEN

NOT FAIR! What about "we all need a girls' day?"

STACY

Right?!

ME

After the baby, I promise we will all take a girls' weekend.

STACY

If Jen brings good coffee, mom and dad would keep all the terrors.

JEN

Deal.

When we're finished, we head to the store, hobbling awkwardly in our salon shoes through the store. We get every kind of junk food that sounds good. It looks like we're feeding an army. Then we head back to my house and pick a movie we both enjoy, settling on the couch with our food surrounding us.

At the end of the day, I think back on how long it's been since I've laughed so hard. Huxlee did her best to keep me entertained and my mind off of the beast all day. When she left, I gave her a big hug, thanking her for the day out. We vow to not wait so long before doing it again before saying goodbye.

Now that I'm lying in my bed, I clutch the journal to my chest and fall asleep.

CHAPTER 30

It's Beginning to Look a Lot Like Christmas

JULY

I mop the sweat off my brow as I finish my run around my neighborhood and walk back into my house.

I peel off my sweaty clothes, struggling to pull my sports bra over my head. Really, is there anything harder than getting a soaked sports bra off after working out? Gah!

I stand under the spray of the shower, letting it flow over me. My scalp gets some extra attention to make sure everything has been scrubbed away before I condition and wash the rest of myself. My big towel is waiting for me on the hook outside the shower as soon as I'm ready to step out. I wrap it around myself and get out of the shower.

A couple of days ago, Huxlee had me paint the front window for the Fourth of July and the firework scene across the front makes me smile as I walk past.

When the bell jingles above me as soon as I open the door, I hear Huxlee greet, "Welcome to—," before cutting off and saying, "Hey, Callie!"

"Hey, is that my coffee?" I motion to the two cups that sit on the counter in front of her.

"Yeah, I picked them up on the way in this morning."

My phone goes off as soon as I get to the back room. Pulling it out, I see a text from one of my brothers.

ANDY

Sad you won't be here for the bottle rocket war.

ME

Don't tell Jake I moved it. But the 60s soda bottle of dad's is in the back of my closet behind the Taylor Swift concert signs.

ANDY

You little thief. Love you!

ME

Jake cannot win or he won't shut up until next year.

After sliding my phone into my pocket and setting my purse down, I make my way to the front. Grabbing my coffee from Huxlee, I hold the cup in my hand, thankful she got iced coffee this morning. I much prefer my coffee iced during the summer months.

"Are you coming out to see the fireworks and the carnival tonight?" she asks.

"I don't know—"

"Come on, Callie! You'll be with me the whole time. I'll even let you drive yourself so you can leave when you want to."

"Deal!"

While we go about our day, I think about what I could possibly wear to keep me from overheating too badly. When I get home, I quickly change into some jean shorts and a breezy red and white top. Fourth of July colors represent. I roll my eyes at my ridiculous inner monologue and stuff my credit card and my phone into a small purse, walking out the door and heading to where the town has set up for the carnival.

Until I got here, I didn't even think about the fact that the last fireworks I saw were with the beast. When they start exploding over my head, the colors remind me of that night.

Huxlee wraps her arm around me at some point and I smile at her, thankful to have such a good friend.

When I'm finally home, I send a quick text to the Family Group chat. It's way less active than the Besties chat but, occasionally Mom or Dad send some ridiculous comment to the rest of us.

ME

Who won?

ANDY

Mom

ME

Mom??

JAKE

Mom.

DAD

Well...

MOM

No more bottle rocket wars! I thought I put an end to this last year when you kids nearly burned the shed down.

ME

What happened?!

JAKE

Well...

ANDY

Umm...

JEN

A bottle rocket went off the "expertly" projected path, chased mom, and ended up exploding under the porch.

STACY

It terrified Mr. Green's cat who was asleep under there.

DAD

The cat is fine. My friendship with Kevin Green is not.

MOM

Grounded… all of you.

I change into pajamas and settle into bed with the journal tucked close to my chest again. I breathe in the pages, imagining they smell like the beast as he wrote them, even though that was hundreds of years ago.

AUGUST

I drive to my parents' house for a joint birthday party for my parents. My brothers are coming into town for the event. My parents' birthdays are about a week apart, so we usually celebrate them at the same time.

Jen demanded Andy bring the older kids and leave her at home with the new baby. Something about him ruining her lady parts again and her not wanting to be stuck in an uncomfortable car for so long.

I can't wait to hold the sweet new baby in my arms again, a few hour visit right after she came home from the hospital is *not* enough time with my new niece.

When I arrive, Tucker runs out to give me a hug. "Auntie Cals! I haven't seen you in forever!"

"Hey, Tucker! Ready to go back to school?" He's at that great age where he still likes school.

"We start next week, Auntie Cals, I can't wait to be at the junior high."

I fake a pain in my chest before responding, "Oh no, they must have gotten it wrong. There's no way my little Tucker is old enough to be in junior high."

"Believe me, I wish it weren't so," Stacy says from behind me. "I swear these kids are giving me a new gray hair every day." She laughs before wrapping me in a hug. "How are you holding up?"

Tucker runs inside to play with the other kids before I answer, "I feel like I've lost a part of myself."

When we sit around the table together, I glance around at my family and I think about how much I love and appreciate every one of them.

My phone chimes with a text.

HUXLEE

Tell bonus parents happy birthday. I want pics of them holding their gifts.

ME

Done

After dinner, we all sit around the living room playing some game, laughing and enjoying the time together before we all make our way to our rooms for some sleep.

Following my normal bedtime routine, I hug the journal to my chest, taking a big whiff of its pages.

The next morning, someone picked up donuts before the rest of us woke up, and Mom was kind enough to get up early to make the coffee. We all sit on the back porch, watching the kids run back and forth in the backyard.

When I'm driving home later that day, I can't help but feel a small weight has been lifted off of me spending time with the family.

SEPTEMBER

While I love running outside, I end up joining a gym to help burn some of the energy brewing inside me. I also make many trips to the archery range, making sure that no matter what is to come, I'm ready for it.

In all the relationships that have ever ended for me, however willingly or not, I've never had a single one of them stick in my mind like the beast. It's unbearable how much I miss him.

I'm grateful the bruises are now gone from being kidnapped, but I'm one of the lucky ones to have survived the battle.

I close my eyes and envision I'm with the beast again. Wrapping my arms around myself, I imagine it's him with his arms wrapped around me. His smell and voice have begun to fade away, and that feels like a stab in the heart all over again.

I'd endure being captured and the beating all over again just to actually have him here with me.

Never have I dated anyone who made me feel so much an equal as he did... does, as he does. A tear slips down my cheek when I consider the possibility that I have served my purpose there for the thousandth time in the last nine months.

OCTOBER

When the temperatures start to drop, I start running outside again. Huxlee has set me up on a blind date for tonight. She cornered me and basically forced me to agree.

I have thought back on that moment many times in the last week. "Callie, I've got a hot date this weekend, but he won't go unless his friend has someone to take out too. Apparently, his friend is only in town for a couple of days, so no commitment is necessary. Please, please, please," Huxlee begged. I rolled my eyes before agreeing.

Now, as I stare at my reflection in the mirror, I can't believe the woman staring back at me. The purple circles under my eyes have grown more prominent in the last ten months.

I add extra concealer to hide them before applying the rest of my makeup. Since this is a one-off blind date, I don't worry too much about whether or not I've done everything too simple or over-the-top tonight.

My makeup is basic at best when I'm finished doing it, and I pick out the first thing I can find on the dressy side of my closet, a flirty red dress. Out of the corner of my eye I catch sight of the ballgown and I unconsciously move toward it, running my hands over the fabric.

Closing my eyes, I imagine I'm back there at the ball, dancing with the beast, our friends all around us. Letting go of the dress, I walk back out of the closet and get dressed for my night.

At the last minute, I decide to just put on some dressy flats. There's no way I can be trusted not to hurt myself in heels tonight.

My phone dings as I wait for Huxlee to get here.

DAD

Hey kiddo, was thinking about you, wanted to say I love you.

ME

I love you too, dad!

I back out of our text chain and am scrolling through my other texts when I realize I never heard from Mason all those months ago. I decide to text him again just to make sure he's okay.

ME

Hey, haven't heard from you, just wanted to make sure you're okay.

When I hit *send*, I hear Huxlee honk her horn outside. I grab my purse and lock my door behind me.

Why the hell did I let her talk me into her being the one to drive? I'll never know. It will probably end in me frustrated and wanting to leave but being stuck there instead.

But when I get to the car, it's just her. Which means we must be meeting the guys at the place we're going for dinner.

"Hey, girl! You look good!" she greets as soon as I duck into the car.

"Thanks," I reply. Her makeup is definitely more dramatic than mine. She's spent time making sure everything looks perfect. And she's definitely got a pushup bra on to make her already ample cleavage look even better. I remember how my boobs looked in the corsets from the prison world and I quickly shove down the wave of sadness that threatens to overwhelm me.

As soon as we get to the restaurant Huxlee runs to one of two guys standing outside. "Callie, this is Jason, my date, and this is…" she trails off, probably because she never thought to ask the friend's name.

"Michael, my name is Michael." He extends a hand to me. I place mine in his and he kisses my knuckles. Carefully, I take my hand back and give him a small smile.

We spend the rest of the night making small talk, and at some point, Huxlee and Jason disappear and Michael and I awkwardly chat until my phone goes off. I pull it out and bite my lip when I see the text.

HUXLEE

Can you please smile at the poor guy? You look like you did when I read you Twilight.

ME

UGH I am trying.

Huxlee's hair is disheveled when she returns. I have no doubt she and Jason were just off making out, at the very least. A pang of jealousy shoots through me and I'm thankful that she's ready to leave quickly after.

In the car, she chatters on about what a good time she had with Jason. I let her talk, not sure what I could say to her.

When I close the door at my house, I slide down it and my hands cover my face as I start to sob.

NOVEMBER

Several. She's now forced me to go on several dates and not a one of them holds a candle to the beast. Today we're preparing the store for the Christmas season again, and I can't help but hope that maybe since I started traveling to the prison world during this time of the year that maybe, just maybe, I'll be able to go back there soon.

"Hey, Callie, what ever happened to Mason?" Huxlee asks as we pull everything out of boxes to decorate the store.

"I have no idea. I haven't heard from him since before my last trip to the prison world," I say, keeping my head down. I don't know that I would respond to me either after essentially a break-up text.

"Huh, you guys seemed so close."

"I mean, I texted him months ago, letting him know I just wasn't ready but, it is weird that he never texted me back."

"Who needs men? You can just come stay with me. We can be the cool aunts to all our nieces and nephews forever."

"What, and deny you the pleasure of all those dates you go on? Never!"

We laugh and get back to work.

I said goodbye to her at the store today. Now, as I stand packing my bags to head back to my parents' house for Thanksgiving, I glance around for the tenth time to make sure I haven't forgotten anything. It takes sitting on my suitcase for me to be able to get the damn thing closed and I struggle to load it into my car.

Thankfully, the weather hasn't gotten too bad yet this year and I'm able to make it to their house in just a couple of hours. Before I get out of my car, I send a text to Huxlee.

ME

Here. Don't miss me too much.

HUXLEE

Please, how can I miss you when my sister is here… with tea… save me!

Thanksgiving morning, the insanity begins as Mom and I begin cooking everything for the family. Dad and my brothers are in charge of frying the turkey this year, and they were smart enough to tape off an area where the kids are not allowed to run.

We all sit around the table and follow the classic tradition of going around the table saying what we're thankful for. Several of us say family, but Tucker surprises us all when he tells the family he's thankful for his girlfriend. Stacy and Jake give him shocked glances and he hangs his head, knowing that they're going to have a conversation about this later.

I hide my smile behind my napkin, remembering my brothers getting the same talking-to when they first started to get interested in girls.

The men are kind enough to do the dishes while those of us who cooked head out to the back porch with wine.

Overall, I have a good time. And the next day when it's just Mom and me in the house getting everything ready for Christmas again, I enjoy the time with her. My phones chimes interrupting my thoughts.

HUXLEE

Come home now!

ME

What's wrong?

HUXLEE

She is trying to make me drink kombucha on BLACK FUCKIN FRIDAY!

ME

That is attempted murder. Call the police.

HUXLEE

Next year I'm closing the store.

ME

But the revenue?

HUXLEE

Kom Bu Cha…

Laughing, I tuck my phone back into my pocket, wondering if there will ever be a time when I'm trapped in the prison world as long as I have been trapped here.

The chest still sits in their attic since I realized I wouldn't be able to unload it at my place by myself. Before we finish up the decorating for the year, I run my hand over the words on the top of the chest, tracing each letter of *The Forgotten Ones* before making my way down the ladder.

For the first time in a long time, I'm able to take deep breaths. I can forget about the beast, if only for a short time.

DECEMBER

A year. It's been more than a year since I first met the beast. And all I can think about is the fact that I can't get back to him.

Why would this cruel world let me meet such a wonderful man, just to tear us apart from each other?

Why would he have been sent to the prison world in the first place?

Are we destined to forever be apart?

I broke the rules of the curse when I opened the chest and read the journals before I was of age. But does that really mean that I have to spend the rest of my life yearning for the one left behind, stuck there?

Sometimes, I find my thoughts wandering to Mason and I wonder whatever became of him. It's like he just up and disappeared, too.

"Good morning, Huxlee, here's your peppermint mocha." I hand her one of the cups. "And your pumpkin bread."

She takes the package with the bread and she squeals in excitement.

"Thank you so much!" She takes a big bite before moaning when she takes a sip of the coffee. "If you could work on the window this morning, I would be forever grateful." She bats her long eyelashes at me and I chuckle as I make my way to the back to get the window paints.

A few hours later, I stand back and admire the painting. This year I've painted a scene with Santa on his sleigh, all the reindeer, in order, and on the other window I've painted a bunch of houses with chimneys ready for him.

Inside the store, I see Huxlee giving me a thumbs-up of approval before she goes back to the shelf she was cleaning and decorating.

We spend the rest of the day joking around with each other before calling it a day and heading home.

This time, I pick up tacos on the way and turn on *The Holiday*.

THE BEAST

My arms close around myself, and I open my eyes to see Callie has disappeared. I clutch my head as memories start rushing into my brain. Almost three hundred years of being born, living, and dying suddenly flooded my mind at that moment.

I see the world through my eyes over and over again through the same stages of life. Visions of a changing world, over three hundred years of advancements, societal changes, and memories of some kind of magical flying machine overwhelm me.

I make my way to a nearby chair and collapse into it, still clutching my pounding head.

Kenna approaches me, "Sire, are you okay? Where's Callie?"

"I... need... you... to get... Zev." I grind out through more flashes of lives gone by.

Zev comes in and helps me to stand, supporting me with his weight while he leads me back down the staircase. "Ken... na..." I pant, using my other hand to press against where my temple throbs.

"Kenna, come," Zev says over his shoulder, and I assume she follows behind us.

"Study," I say and he leads all of us there, helping me to sit on the couch before dragging another chair to sit across from me. Kenna sits beside me quietly.

Finally, the onslaught of memories slows and I am able to breathe easier again.

"Are you okay, sire?" Kenna moves to sit as far away from me as she can while I slowly lower my hands into my lap.

"No, I really don't think I am."

"What happened?" Zev asks. "Where's Callie?"

"Gone."

I do my best to explain to them what just happened. The flood of memories that came back to me, the feeling of somehow merging with a missing piece of myself. But none of us have ever experienced anything like this before. The only memories we've ever had here have been the ones from the lives we were living when we were banished. But now, I feel like there are more questions than answers as to why we've been sent here.

Callie has been gone for too damn long. My staff avoids me at all costs. My attitude has left little to be desired over the almost year since she was taken from me.

I know I could have convinced her to marry me, but when she was ripped from my arms with our first kiss, it felt like my heart was ripped out of my chest and no one here is able to put it back together. Deep down, I know that only she is capable of doing that. And now that I have memories of her time with me in another form, as Mason, I'm somehow jealous of my own self.

Every night I wish I could hold her in my arms again, her body soft and pliant next to me. She fits against me perfectly, our bodies molding together even in sleep. Just her damn presence pulled me from the brink of death.

I drink more than I ever have, trying to drown the pain that resides in my chest. No matter how much I drink, the pain only seems to come back stronger than ever once I've sobered up. I've lost count of the number of times I've drunk myself into a stupor and woken up back in my room.

Minutes ago, I was by myself, drowning my sorrows again in the library before Kenna came in to give me a report on the war. Why she still puts up with my behavior, I'll never know. But she's the closest thing to Callie I have anymore. How fucking pathetic is that? My one spot of light is the woman who was kind to Callie.

I throw my empty glass against the wall in my library. Kenna flinches at my outburst. There have been no sightings of any of the occupants of the abandoned castle. Every day that goes by and we don't find them, I fear for the safety of my people. For all I know, they're burrowing beneath my damn mountains.

"Anything else I can help you with, Your Majesty?" Her voice sounds like she looks, small and like she's trying to hide within herself.

"That will be all," I growl out, turning back to my desk and slamming my hand down on its surface. A book falls off the edge and I reach over to pick it up. It's then I realize what book I'm holding. It's that damn book she never finished. The one she would sit on the couch for hours, reading. It's one of the longest books I own. We just didn't have the time. I would have preferred for me to show her the simple life she could have in the castle with me.

I never got the chance to show her what life could truly be like as my wife, my queen, my equal. My father was a tyrant, my mother a mouse to his lion. Callie, on the other hand, made me so damn proud, taking up the reins for the battle preparations. She would be the lioness to my lion. Queen of the domain, ruler of the pride. I would bow at her feet and beg her to never leave me again, if only I could be with her again.

And watching her take out the enemy with those arrows made me want to do just that. I would kiss her feet, if only she would let me.

The way she continued to fight and stay with our men, even after she had been tortured for far too long. How could I have let her be captured like that? I will regret those moments every day of my life.

If only this damn prison world wasn't so fucked up. If only I knew who was sending us here. If only I could get back to her. I grab another glass and fill it halfway with whiskey. Not that I need more to drink, but maybe this time it will help. If only I was so lucky.

I take the book to the couch and sit, opening to the spot where she last was, a now pressed rose acting as a bookmark. She smiled when I brought it in for her one day while she was here. Rather than start from the beginning, I pick up from where she left off, keeping the rose in her spot for when she returns. Because she *will* return to me, even if I have to burn down the whole damn world to get to her.

Images flash through my mind of me holding some faceless being against a wall, choking the life out of them for what they've done to my people. Their gasps are music to my metaphorical ears as the life slowly suffocates out of them.

I set the book on the side table when my mind won't stop running back to Callie. A sharp stab of pain hits my chest as I picture her with another man back home. I never thought to ask if she had someone already. But somehow, I know she wouldn't have spent all the time with me if she did. She doesn't strike me as someone to break her marriage vows.

One day, it will be me she vows to spend forever with, to have and to hold. I just hope it happens before it's too late.

My neck hurts like a bitch when I wake up hunched over on the couch in the library. I remember what I was doing here last night. I was imagining the demise of the prison world's creator, while hoping to have Callie back with me.

Every day I feel weaker and weaker, and I know it's because I haven't eaten, not truly since she left. I've been told I smell of booze by anyone who dares enter the room I'm in.

I'm sitting on the couch in the study with my head in my hands, drunk from the previous night's alcohol, when the door opens, and Kenna enters with Zev. If he's walking on two feet, it must be something serious. I have not seen him on two feet except for special occasions and holidays for years. "Yes?" I ask.

"Sir, I brought you something to eat," Kenna answers. It's now I notice she has a tray piled high with food. Zev carries a tray with a tea service.

"I'm not hungry," I growl.

"You're a damn stubborn fool is what you are," Zev says. It's the most I've heard him speak since I first met him. They set their trays down on the small table in front of me.

"Excuse me?" I balk at his words.

"Oh, I'm so sorry. Does the poor widdle king need his nappy changed?" Zev talks like I'm a damn baby.

I stand up, stumbling drunkenly over my feet. Getting up into his face, I stupidly reply, "What the fuck are you talking about, Zev?" My finger jabs into his chest.

"You're acting like a spoiled baby. Figured maybe I should talk to you that way. How do you think she would feel if she knew you're here starving yourself because you're such a damn stubborn bastard?"

"Yeah, and who gave you permission to talk to *your king* like such an ungrateful prick?" My hands shake as we stare each other down.

"Fine, don't eat then. Maybe the child and the pirate are through with her. Maybe we were mistaken about the missing weapons. Do whatever you want." He shrugs and leads Kenna with his hand on the small of her back out the door.

He's a fucking asshole, but his words have their desired effect. I finish every bite on the tray and wash it down with the tea.

The garden is where I feel the closest to her. I walk among the flowers, bringing each one to my face. But I can't seem to find one that smells just like her.

I dismiss the usual staff who takes care of the replanting out here and sit down in the dirt myself. Though I rarely saw my benefactress in the garden, she did teach me how to care for the flowers. How to properly plant the new plants. How to organize the different ones for best pest control.

My favorite was growing the food. Having something to eat at the end of the season always excited me. And there is nothing better than plucking produce straight off the plant to eat that day.

The garden right off the castle is strictly for flowers, and I dig my hands in the dirt, taking a fistful and watching it flow through my fingers. Our food is grown in the village. Several of the people who have been banished here were put in charge of making sure we are all fed.

We tried to make sure each person handled something they were skilled at in our world. Our kingdom may be small, but we have thrived in the time we've been here.

Until the battle, there had been no deaths here that I'm aware of. Even Zev has learned to control himself when in his wolf form, feeding only on creatures that have become overpopulated in this world.

I think back on my early days, when Zev would bring me rabbits, fish, squirrels, or whatever he could get ahold of. He would usually try to catch something extra to bring me to eat. That is, until he brought me the first human. Kenna was my first guest in the castle. Zev found her wandering among the trees one day. He shifted to his human form and learned she had been here for many, many years, arriving here about one hundred years before me.

I put up all the tools and go back into the mountain, my legs feeling noticeably steadier under me since I finally ate something. My head has started to clear from the alcohol-induced haze and I'm able to walk among the halls without stumbling into a wall.

Walking past the kitchen, I invite everyone to join me for dinner in the dining room and we spend the rest of the night enjoying each other's company; me doing my best to pretend everything is normal before finally making my way to bed.

CALLIE

My drive to my parents' house is less eventful this year. I gather myself for a second in my car before pulling out my phone and sending a text to Huxlee.

ME

Here safe.

HUXLEE

No Callie on ice show?

ME

Not this year. Mark from the cafe is supposed to bring you a huge mocha latte and pumpkin bread every morning. The store is open until I get back. It's already paid for.

HUXLEE

Employee of the decade!

ME

Merry Christmas. Love you.

I get my suitcase settled in my room. Jen comes in and wraps her arms around me. "How are you doing, Callie?"

Even though my story with the beast is fantastical, my entire family hasn't treated me like a crazy person. "It's almost been a year," I choke out.

"I know, sweetie, I know." She pulls me into her arms and rubs my back as I cry on her shoulder.

"Group hug?" Stacy suggests, coming into the room. She wraps herself around my back and the tears flow more.

When the tears finally stop falling, I say, "I love you guys." And with one last, big squeeze, we make our way out the door.

As soon as we leave my room, it's time to put on a fake smile and pretend like my heart hasn't been slowly dying over the last year. I join the kids in a new game Mom bought them this year. I watch as everyone opens their Christmas jammies. I listen as Mom reads the new Christmas book. I give all the kids hugs when they are ready for bed.

Once it's just the adults awake, I wrap myself in my coat and go onto the back porch. The snow falls around me and I inhale deeply the smell of winter. I tilt my head back and let the frozen flakes fall on my upturned face, opening my mouth to catch some on my tongue.

Walking down the steps, I hold my arms out to my sides and spin around. It's the most free I've felt in months. The further from the house I move, the more it feels like I'm back in the prison world.

I walk among the trees surrounding my parents' house and pretend I'm back with the beast, and he's giving me a tour of his world.

I imagine him standing next to me, holding my hand in his as we talk about our future together.

I smile as I imagine him kissing me, fingers entwined in my hair.

"Callie," my mom shouts from the porch. I heave a sigh as my apparition falls away. Turning back to the house, I make my way back up onto the porch. "Are you okay, sweetie?"

She moves to one of the chairs and sits down, patting the chair next to her for me to sit as well. "How would you feel if dad was suddenly gone?" The question falls out of my mouth before I can stop it. But once it's out there, I can't help but hold my breath, anticipating the response.

My mom takes my hand in hers before responding, "I imagine I would feel a lot like you do right now." She clutches my hands in both of hers and brings them up to her mouth, blowing warm air across my chilled fingers. "Why don't we get you inside by the fire? Everyone else has already gone to sleep. I'll make cocoa." She bats her eyelashes at me, which makes me smile, and we both stand to go inside.

I watch her flutter around the kitchen, pulling out the ingredients and pans she'll need. The noise brings Jen and Stacy both into the kitchen. "Girls' night?" Jen asks.

"I'll pop the popcorn," Stacy says.

Jen picks the most ridiculous chick flick from our high school days, and we laugh and let the world slip away for a few hours. In the wee hours of the morning, they make their way back to their rooms. I sit in front of the fire, staring into the dancing flames.

CHAPTER 33

When You Wish Upon a Star

I go into my room and read his journal, waiting for the house to get quiet.

Kenna helped me clean all the dust out of the castle. Zev continues to bring us people as he finds them on his hunts. People who have been here for varying lengths of time, some longer than me. Some only for days. But none have been here longer than Zev and the granny, Beatrice, who came with him.

We are excited by the people who know how to grow food, who know the terrain better than we do and have been teaching us the kinds of food we are able to grow ourselves.

Some of the people got to work building small homes in the valley between the mountains.

I forgot to mention, the mountain the castle is

underneath is actually a mountain range of sorts. Every day Kenna and I set out to explore more of the tunnels and see how many exits to the outdoors we can find.

On one of these adventures, we found a door that leads to the area in the center of the range. It was then we knew it was all built in a circle. Unfortunately, the center was completely empty, no buildings, and the dirt was unworked.

While I would not complain about having all of these people live in the castle, I understand that living with no view of the sky can be unsettling for some.

Half of us pitched in to build homes for the "villagers," as they have come to calling themselves. It didn't take long before every family who wants to live in their own small home is settled.

The rest of the group helped work the fields, getting them ready to plant. Soon we will enjoy being able to eat freshly grown fruits and vegetables.

Kenna prefers her room in the castle. She actually asked me one day after several homes had been built if it would be okay with me if she stayed. Would you believe she asked me if she would be a bother? Like I'm not the demanding beast in this scenario.

I assured her that she was welcome to stay

as long as she wished. She made quick work of inventorying everything in the castle. I've never seen anyone clean as thoroughly as she does, but I would never ask her to do that forever.

Over time, we have managed to house quite a group both in and out of the castle.

Placing a bookmark in my place, I listen for any noises in the house. Thankfully, I hear no noises indicating people awake, and I quietly and carefully change into my sweats and make my way into the living room.

On my way, I snag the thickest blanket off the back of the couch and move to the back door. Carefully, slowly, I slide the door open, cringing when the alarm makes a beeping sound. I hold the door open, listening for anyone moving in the house.

Finally, I step outside and close the door behind me. I use my hand to clear the snow off one of the chairs and wrap myself up in the blanket, every part of me is covered by its warmth, except for my face.

I turn my face up to the sky. The snow has stopped falling for the moment and being away from the city, I'm now able to see the stars. Using the names I made up for the constellations when I was a kid, I name all the ones I can see.

When a shooting star catches my eye, I immediately close my eyes as tight as I can and wish to see the beast. I keep my eyes closed and repeat my wish over and over again until finally my face is so cold I can no longer feel it and stand to go inside.

I set the blanket on the couch and sit in front of the fire to thaw out. When I can feel all of my fingers, toes, and face again, I finally make my way to my room. It takes me a couple of clumsy sleepy minutes before I'm able to get back into my Christmas jammies, and I climb into the bed, the journal hugged against my chest, and fall asleep.

THE BEAST

I sit on the couch, engrossed in Callie's book, as I have come to call it, while the castle grows quiet around me. When I've finally finished it, I set it down and make my way to the solarium we saw the fireworks together in so many months ago.

I push my hand against the pressure switch that opens the false mountainside. The snow falls outside, and I move closer to the windows so I can see the stars.

Making my way out of the room, I move down to the ground level and exit into the village. The lights are out in the village while families do their best to get some sleep, preparing for Christmas morning.

I make my way to the center of the square, where I was telling stories that first time Callie snuck out of the castle. It was never necessary for me to question anyone on who let her out. Immediately, I knew it had to be Kenna who showed her the way outside.

I think back on that day, and a smile comes to my face. I tilt it up to the sky, letting the snowflakes fall on me, the cold more prominent on the scarred part of my face.

When I stop feeling the cold flakes against my face, I open my eyes and look at the sky. I can see stars all around. The only boundary is the edge of the mountain cutting off the rest from view.

The constellations here are different from the ones I remember back home. I never cared to name them, the hope always being to make it out of this place.

When a shooting star flies by, I close my eyes and make a wish. It's a silly thing we did as kids and none of our wishes ever came true, but I wish with everything in me to be with Callie again. To see her face. To hold her in my arms. To kiss her pink lips.

When I run out of parts of her to wish to see again, or for the first time. When I run out of parts of her I'd like to touch. When I run out of the parts of her I'd like to taste, that list is the most extensive. And I finish off with all the things I'd wish to hear her say again. I make my way back inside. I stoke the fire in my room, strip off my outer clothes, and get beneath the covers of my bed, falling asleep to thoughts of Callie.

CHAPTER 34

When You Believe

CALLIE

I jolt up in the bed when something brushes across my back. Looking behind me, I suck in a breath when I see him in my bed. Immediately, I throw myself at him, wrapping my arms around him from behind. Slowly he turns in my arms, wrapping his around me. My head pillows on his bicep, and his other arm drapes across my waist.

"What... how... you're really here?" I question. His answering smile makes my heart flop over in my chest for the first time in what feels like forever.

He brings his hand up to trail his fingers down my cheek before his palm rests on it and his fingers tangle in my hair. This time it's not slow, it's not sweet. There is no second-guessing, no waiting for the other to accept. Our lips crash together, tongues tangling.

We jerk apart, and he falls off my twin-sized bed at the sound of the door opening. "Auntie Calth, are you coming down for breakfath? Mommy thayth we can't open prethenth until you eat," Macie says. I roll over to look at her while she rubs her eyes. One jammy pant leg hiked up on her calf. Reaching a hand up, I feel my swollen lips, and for the first time in what feels like forever, a genuine smile adorns my face.

"I'll be out in a few minutes, sweet girl. Save me some chocolate milk, will you?" She nods and leaves the door cracked as she turns around and heads back down the hall.

I hold my breath, pull myself to the side of the bed, and look over the edge.

"Good morning," he says. "We do have a slight problem."

"You're all the way down there?" I guess, a smile spreading across my face.

He sits up and rubs his elbow. "Damn, that hurt. But no, that is not the problem. I seem to be lacking clothes." He looks down at his old-timey undergarments, gesturing down his body with his hand, his brown hair falls forward as he does.

"That's my favorite part," I reply, giggling as he leaps onto the bed, tickling me. "Stop, stop, stop." I laugh.

"Callie, who's in there with you?" Andy demands from the doorway. The beast immediately pulls his hands away and I turn around, a guilty look on my face.

Quickly, I make my way to the door. "Hey, Andy, can you ask Jake for a set of clothes?" I ignore his question.

He rolls his eyes and makes his way down the hallway. "I knew there was something going on with you! All this time I've been questioning why you wouldn't come back to me. How could you move on so quickly? Are you some sort of harlot?" the beast whisper-shouts as soon as Andy's footsteps fade.

"What the fuck are you talking about?" I growl as I get out of bed and push my door closed so I can change. I yank my pajama top over my head, pulling my bra on and securing it in place. Grabbing a shirt from my suitcase, I tug it over my head and then slide my pajama pants down my legs. I stand staring at my jeans, trying to decide on what pair to wear today while I wait for his response.

"Does your *husband*," he hisses the word like it's dirty before continuing, "know that you've been parading around with men in other worlds?"

A laugh bubbles out of me before I can stop it. I clutch my sides as I convulse in laughter I can't get to stop. "You think... I'm married... and sleep in... that tiny bed?" I finish, gasping for breath.

He stands and looks down at the bed for the first time. My twin-sized childhood bed. "Then who is..." He trails off. I don't have a chance to answer before there is another knock on my door.

Quickly, I pull my pants on and move to it, opening the door and quickly grabbing the clothes from Andy's outstretched hand. "We'll be out in a minute," I snap, closing the door in his face.

"That"—I jerk my chin at the closed door—"is one of my brothers, you overbearing, idiotic, infuriating beast."

Setting the clothes on the bed for him, I angrily make my way across the hall to the bathroom to brush my teeth and hair. By the time I make it back to my room, he's dressed in Jake's clothes.

I close the door behind me and stand leaning against my door, arms crossed, waiting for him to say something. He looks at the ground, eyebrows draw down. "You should really stop doing that," I say and he looks up, multi-colored eyes meeting mine.

He takes one, two, three steps before stopping right in front of me. "I'm sorry, I've made an ass out of myself," he states.

"Yes, you have." I nod in agreement. Slowly, I bring my hand up to his face, his eyes close as I gently run my fingers over the scars. They're fainter than I remember. His hands move to rest on my waist, and he pulls me into him gently.

He moves his hands to my face and runs his nose along mine as he breathes out his next words, "I truly am an ass, and I'm sorry. I don't think I've truly breathed since you left."

This time when our lips touch, it's sweet, an apology. Gently, I push him back. "It's Christmas, and if we don't get out there to eat with the family, all the kids will break down my door."

He steps back from me, letting go of my face and trailing one of his hands down my arm to entwine his fingers with mine. I step away from the door and open it, leading him out to meet the rest of my family.

My dad stands when we enter the kitchen, looking between me and the beast. "Callie, who's this?" Dad asks.

Mom turns around from where she's getting plates loaded and drops the utensil from her hand. It clatters across the floor. "Mom, Dad, *this* is—"

"Honey, we've already met Mason," she says. "Though, and I hope you don't think me rude for saying this, he didn't have those scars the last time he was here. And his eyes were both brown, I think."

My head spins to look at him and it's then I see it, and how I missed it, I have no idea. If you take away the scars, the beard, cut his hair and his eyes were the same color, they would look like the same person.

He leans into me, wrapping his arm around my waist and breathes into my ear, "It's important to remember looks can be deceiving." I gasp, my hand coming up to my mouth as tears come to my eyes. Quickly, I make my way back to my room, ignoring everyone I see along the way. He follows close behind, blocking me from closing him out. "Callie, talk to me," he coaxes gently.

Reluctantly, I let him into the room and close and lock the door behind him. "Explain," is the only word that comes out of my mouth. Words have escaped me in the inner turmoil I'm feeling. How could I not have seen it?

He sits on the bed and it creaks softly beneath his weight. Running his fingers through his loose hair, he collects his thoughts while I stare down at him. He takes a deep breath before starting. "You already know I was sent to the prison world many, many years ago. You also know that we have no idea who's been sending us there." He looks at me for confirmation. I nod, acknowledging the information.

"When Zev first came to tell me you had entered the prison world. Something within him knew, I don't know if it was your scent or just the magic of the place, but he knew that you were the one from the prophecy.

"When I entered the dining room on that first night you were in the castle, when I met you, or, more accurately, when I caught you before you hit the ground at our first meeting." He holds back a laugh before continuing, "Holding you in my arms, seeing you, I knew then. I knew there was something different about you. It was like my heart started beating for the first time in my life.

"Every time we were together, I couldn't help but watch you out of the corner of my eye. Those first few days, those days you thought that I couldn't talk, I was afraid of scaring you away." He takes several breaths while he gathers his thoughts again.

"But it wasn't until the kiss, if that short brush of our lips can truly be called that. It wasn't until the kiss that something happened, which I don't quite know how to explain." He pauses for a moment before continuing. "All these memories started rushing into my brain. From what I can figure, from the time I was banished to the prison world, I have lived many lives here, in your world. Almost three hundred years of being born, living, and dying suddenly flooded my mind at just that one brief touch.

"From that point on, you've been all I can think about. Kenna and Zev have been incredibly unpleased with my behavior these last months." He looks down at his hands.

My chest rises and falls. I slide down the door to sit on the ground, keeping my eyes on him the entire time. "How can you be so sure?" I ask.

His eyes meet mine. "How can I be so sure of what?"

"That I am the one from the prophecy?"

"I can't, not really. Not until you truly destroy the prison world. But deep down..." He presses his hand to his chest. I mirror him without realizing it. "Deep down, I know. You can't tell me you don't feel it, too."

"Then why haven't you been here?" My words are barely a

whisper. I remember all the times Mason made promises he didn't keep. All the times he didn't call or text me back.

"Since our kiss, I have been trapped in the prison world. No matter how hard I tried, I couldn't get back to you." He rises and moves to stand in front of me. He holds out his hand to help me up and I place mine in his.

"But I passed my days remembering when you came back to me and I was able to get better. My fever broke, and I was able to walk again. With my memories, I know that's when I was here as Mason and spent the day with you and your parents."

I let him pull me into him as he again pulls me into his arms. I rest my head against his chest and wrap my arms around him in return, and he kisses the top of my head. "As for this last year... I have no idea what's been keeping us apart. But if I ever find out what or *who* it was, I'll tear them apart with my bare hands.

"But something else happened with that kiss. It's like two halves of myself finally merged back together. It's like the person who banished me to the prison world just banished part of me. And now, I'm whole again. I suspect that's why the scars are more faded than in the prison world, and why my eyes stayed two different colors. Both versions of me have now melded together to become one again."

I run my fingers carefully over his scars. "Do you remember now how you got these?"

He shakes his head before squeezing me tighter and replying, "Now, how about we go back out there and I can meet the rest of the family?" I nod against his chest before pulling back. "But first..." He tugs me to him, kissing me briefly before releasing me.

"So you're the boy-toy," Jen says when we settle at the breakfast table.

"Jen!" I screech. She laughs before taking another bite of her cinnamon roll. "Don't think just because you're holding that baby that I won't smack you," I threaten.

"Can you believe how violent your Auntie Cals is? Someone should really teach her manners," she tells baby Lily.

"I tried," Mom responds. "These kids never listened to their mom."

"Hey! What did we do?" Jake and Andy say at the same time.

Mom gives them her knowing look and they both shrink in their chairs. "That's what I thought."

I look over at Mason, and he shakes in suppressed laughter. Under the table, I pinch his thigh and he laughs harder.

"So, Mason, what are your intentions with our sister?" Jake asks.

I groan and rest my head on my crossed arms on the table. Mason reaches over and starts rubbing his fingertips up and down my back and goosebumps break out all over my body.

"I'm going to marry her," he states, fully confident in what he says. I lift my head slightly to see my family's reaction. Their traitorous nods tell me everything I need to know. He's completely won them over.

I sit back up and take my first bite of cinnamon roll. The perfect roll melts in my mouth and I moan at how good it tastes. Mom could put Cinnabon out of business, I swear.

When the kids come and start stalking us in the dining room, we quickly finish the rest of our breakfast and throw away our plates before moving into the living room. I sit on the floor in front of Mason, who sits on the couch. He plays with my hair as we watch everyone around the room.

Dad passes out everyone's presents and the kids' faces light up while they open both things they've asked for, and the things they need, like new underwear and socks. Tucker groans when he opens up his undergarments and the adults all laugh at how over-the-top he is.

When Mason's fingers drift to making small circles on my neck, I relax further into his legs. My head tilts to the side, leaning against his knee to give him better access. The kids run off to play with their presents. Adults clear away the trash and start organizing the presents the kids left to make leaving in the morning easier.

Reluctantly, I pull away from him, standing and extending my hand to him. "I want to show you something." He places his hand in mine and stands. "Hey, Dad, can Mason borrow your coat?"

"Sure, sweetie, you know where it is."

We bundle up, and he snags Jake's boots for his feet and we make our way outside. I lead him through the trees. The snow crunches under our feet and we leave footprints in the snow. He takes my hand in his while we walk through the trees. I know just the spot I want to show him.

We stop at the base of a large tree, one we helped my father build a treehouse in when I was a kid. "I used to come up here when I was a kid and spend the day reading. It's been years since I've climbed up there, but it will give us some privacy."

I grasp the tallest ladder rung I can and start to climb. "Well, I've got a pretty fantastic view. I may just wait here for you to finish. For safety reasons, of course."

Looking behind me, I see he's staring directly at my ass as I climb. Rolling my eyes and laughing, I focus my eyes back on the climb so I don't fall.

When I open the trapdoor, the dust flies around me. I lift myself the rest of the way in and wait for him to join me.

He makes it up, and I close the trapdoor behind us. Looking around, I try to picture everything as if I was seeing it for the first time. "It's cozy up here," he says before reaching out and pulling me to him.

His fingers tangle in my blonde hair as he brings my face to his and kisses me. I sigh when our lips touch and wrap my arms around him. He slowly unzips my coat and I shudder because the cold air is better able to reach me. I reach up and slide his coat zipper down, and wind my arms around him, slowly lifting the edge of his shirt so I can touch his bare skin.

Our lips stay connected, tongues dancing, breaths coming faster and harder. I start to move my fingers beneath the top of his pants and he pulls back. He holds me back with his hand and I take in deep breaths of cold air, waiting for him to speak.

"Callie... we... can't. It... wouldn't be... proper."

I can't help the laugh that bubbles up my throat. When I see his face doesn't change, I realize he's serious. "Wait, you're joking, right?"

"I am most certainly not joking," he replies, and I zip my coat back up. "Are things really so different in your time?" I glance up from my zipper, an incredulous look on my face. "I mean, I know they are. I have the memories. But in my time, it's so ingrained in us to be married *first.*" He gives me one last lingering kiss before leaning down and opening the trapdoor, leading the way out.

CHAPTER 35

Sweater Weather

While the kids hog the bathroom getting ready for bed, we wait in my room until we can do the same. Mason sits on my bed while I run my hand along the bookshelves with my childhood books. A volume of *Beauty and the Beast* catches my eye and I pull it from the shelf. "This is about you."

He looks down at the book in my hands and then back up at me. "What?"

"It's something I realized when I met granny and was chased by Zev. You guys left behind something else when you were taken out of this world, besides your journals. All of you have been turned into children's stories. Well, they aren't necessarily for children, but they've changed it over time to be for children."

"What are you talking about?" I sit down beside him on my bed and I hand him the book. Over the next few hours, I sit and watch him read the story left behind with his departure.

"How is this woman so familiar with my story? And it looks like she's embellished it some."

"My best guess? She must have had access to your journal at some point. Or maybe she was someone who knew you? Perhaps she's the one who banished you to the prison world? It's really all speculation. I have no way of knowing how someone who died a few hundred years ago got the information for their story. Have you never heard the story before?"

"Callie, boys don't exactly clamor to read fairytales."

He stands and puts the book back on the shelf before reaching out to me.

With the whole family here for the night, and all the children nearby, I make up the couch for Mason to sleep on while he gets ready for bed. When his heat presses against me from behind and his arms wrap around me, I breathe in his scent as it engulfs me, afraid that he won't be here with me for very long. We kiss good-night before I make my way back to my room.

His hand running up and down my arm is what makes me open my eyes the next morning. I'm facing him and am grateful that he's still with me. "We should probably make a trip to my house today, so I can get some clothes." He kisses me.

"We can do that," I reply. "When did you come in here?"

"Just a few minutes ago."

"You watched me sleep, didn't you?" I poke him in the side and he laughs.

"Maybe for a moment. How long will it take you to get ready?"

"Just a few minutes. In the meantime, though..." I trail off, gently pushing him onto his back with my hand, climbing to straddle him.

We spend the next several minutes kissing, his fingers in my hair before he gently tugs me back. "You are going to be the death of me."

"What a sweet death it will be, though, won't it?" I smirk and climb off of him. This time, I wiggle my ass as much as I can when I shimmy out of my pajamas and walk to grab my bra and clothes for the day. I hear him groan behind me as I cover myself back up. Looking over my shoulder at him. "What?" A wicked grin spreads across my face.

He stands and pulls me to him. "You're a little temptress, that's what. How long until we can be married?"

"Well, seems to me you haven't actually asked me," I smile and run out of the room, closing myself into the bathroom to get ready for the day.

We eat breakfast with my parents before loading up into my car and heading out for his house. He only lives about twenty minutes from my parents on a good day. Even with the snow on the roads, we make it in less than an hour.

His house is beautiful, with rolling hills all around covered in snow. In the distance, I see a barn. "What's in there?"

"This used to be a ranch. With my traveling back and forth, I never bought the animals to make it operational again, though. My parents in this lifetime passed away, leaving me a large sum of money and something compelled me to buy the place... come to think of it, it was also around the time you must have found the journal."

"I thought you grew up here?"

"Not too far from here. Maybe I can show you the place sometime."

I follow him to the wraparound porch. The white house with green trim looks straight out of a *Home and Gardens* magazine. I run my hand over the railing while I wait for him to unlock the door. He pulls a key from over the door and lets us in.

"That's not exactly a good hiding place," I remark.

"It's not like I can keep it in my pants pocket. I never know when I'll be here." He holds the door open and motions for me to enter before him.

Inside is covered in a light layer of dust, his time away apparent. He has me wait in the living room while he packs a suitcase. There's not much here, no pictures on the walls, or any knick-knacks on the mantle. His furniture even looks brand new.

"Did you ever actually stay here?" I yell toward where he disappeared.

"What do you mean?" he responds.

"All the furniture looks brand new."

He pokes his head out of what I assume must be his bedroom and I motion to the couch. "Well, before I met you, I spent most of my time with Annette, and after I met you, I was staying in a hotel near you unless you count my other half, which was stuck in the prison world." He goes back into the bedroom and comes out a few minutes later with his suitcase. "Ready?"

I nod and follow him back outside, waiting for him to lock the door again. He puts his suitcase in my trunk before closing it and grabbing my hand.

"I want to show you something." He pulls me around the back of the house. I gasp when I see the giant greenhouses. I look at him for an explanation. "I have someone come and maintain these for me, but I couldn't not have flowers here year-round. We have a bouquet delivery service set up and donate the extra flowers to some local establishments."

When he opens the door, my jaw drops. The giant greenhouse is heated and has so many different types of flowers. It reminds me of the greenhouse at the castle.

I walk down the rows, bringing my nose to each different kind and inhaling their scents. He follows behind me and is smiling each time I look back at him. "What?" I ask.

"Nothing, I just like seeing you smiling."

At the very back of the greenhouse is a small table and chairs with a tiny kitchenette. He pulls out one of the chairs for me to take a seat. Once I'm seated, he moves to the kitchen and makes us some tea. "I hope you don't mind drinking your tea out of a coffee cup. It's all I have in here."

He hands me my cup and takes the seat opposite me, holding my hand across the table. I sip the warm liquid and enjoy the warmth of his hand. When he starts to trace up and down from my palm to my elbow with his fingers, fire burns in my veins.

"My dearest Callie." He grasps my hand again. "From the moment I met you, I knew something was different about you." He stands and brings me to my feet, his hands resting on my hips. "And when you ended up in my castle, I knew you were the one, not only the one from the prophecy, but the woman I wanted to spend the rest of my life with. I want you to be my partner, my wife, and my queen." When he drops to one knee, pulling a ring from his pocket, tears fall down my cheeks, and my hand flies to my mouth. "Callie, will you marry me?"

I nod, my voice escaping me. He stands and slides the ring on my finger and then his hands grasp my face, pulling me toward him for a kiss.

Staring at the ring I ask, "When did you get this?"

"This"—he takes my hand in his, raising it to his lips and kissing my fingers—"was my mother's ring. It was in a safe place tucked away in my room."

When we're back in the car he asks, "So when would you like to get married?"

"How about tonight?" I respond. He looks at me like I'm crazy. "The courthouse may be closed, but my parents are friends with the judge who performs the marriages there. I'm sure they could convince him to make a house call."

"Don't you want a true wedding?" His whole body is turned to me as I continue to drive back to my parents' house.

"Mason, I just want you. We can throw a big party and celebrate with our friends later." He takes my hand in his and brings the back of it up to his lips.

"I love you, Callie."

Keeping my eyes focused on the road, I reply, "I love you, too, my beast."

Mom and Dad meet us in the front yard and Mom immediately notices the ring on my hand. "Oh, sweetie," she says, pulling me into a hug.

"What? What's happened?" Dad asks.

"They got engaged, Jerry." She wraps her arm around me and walks with me back to the house. "Do you guys have any idea when you want to get married?"

"We were thinking tonight?" She stops me in my tracks and looks at me the same way Mason did earlier. "Mom, we never know when we're going to be here or in the prison world. I don't want to have to wait another year to marry him if that's when the powers that be decide to bring us together again."

"Jerry, can you call the judge and see if he'll come over here tonight? Remind him he owes you for fixing his pipes last winter."

"Yes, dear." Dad pulls his phone from his pocket and looks for the judge's phone number.

"But what are you going to wear?"

"I was thinking I'd call Huxlee and see if she could bring the ballgown?"

"Oh, Callie, that sounds like a wonderful idea! Let me call your brothers and see if we can get them all back here."

Dad's off in the distance already on his phone and I pull out mine at the same time Mom does hers. It rings a few times before Huxlee picks up. "Callie?"

"Hey, Hux, I was wondering if you could do me a huge favor."

"Of course, what on earth could you need all the way over there in Jackson?"

"I was wondering if you could bring me a dress. Tonight."

"I'm going to need a little more to go on than that. Why do you need a dress? And why do you need it tonight?"

"I'll tell you all about it when you get here." I decide I would much rather tell her in person that I'm getting married. "Can you go to my house, into my closet, and bring me the beautiful ball-gown hanging there?"

"Girl, I think you might have had too much eggnog over the last couple of days, but sure, I'll be there this afternoon sometime, I guess."

"Thank you, Huxlee, I love you."

"Love you, too, crazy girl."

Mom hangs up and turns to me. "They'll be here in a couple of hours." She pulls me to her and says, "There's just a few more things we'll need to get you married."

"Oh, yeah, what's that?"

She leads me into the house and moves to pull down the attic ladder, and we both climb into its dusty depths. "I think I have just the thing." She opens a few of the boxes scattered along the edges. She makes it to the last box before exclaiming, "Ah hah! Here it is!" She pulls out an odd package of some kind. "I would be honored if you would wear my veil." She hands me the package and continues to dig in the box. "Oh, look, here's something old, something new, something borrowed, something blue, and I think.... Here it is, a sixpence for your shoe."

"Where on earth did you get a sixpence from?"

"Thrift store, of course," she answers with a shrug.

We collect all the items and sneak into her room to get me dressed. "First, you should probably take a shower, then we can have a lazy day of watching movies and manis and pedis until Huxlee gets here."

Mom pulls out all of her supplies, and we rummage through the kitchen, looking for snacks. Dad and Mason spend a lot of the day on and off the phone before we finally hear a knock on the door. My brothers and their families walk in and the kids immediately run to play games. Jen and Stacy join us in my parents' room.

"Ooh! Manis and pedis count us in!" they say as soon as they see our makeshift salon set up.

"So, Callie, are you sure Mason is the one?" Jen whispers in my ear.

"In this moment, I can't imagine being happy with anyone

else," I whisper back. She nods and places her hand back on my knee so I can continue painting her fingernails.

Out of the corner of my eye, I see Stacy and Mom suppressing smiles. "You two have something to say?" I ask, my grin stretching across my face.

"It's nice to see you truly smiling again, Callie," Stacy pats me on the back awkwardly, trying not to mess up her wet nails.

We've watched a couple of movies before another knock sounds at the front door. "I've got it!" Dad yells from the other room.

A few minutes later Huxlee enters, "Girl, you have some explaining to do."

"Surprise!" I hold my left hand up for her to see the ring.

"What. How. Who?" She stumbles over her words.

"Wouldn't you know, turns out the beast and lover-boy are the same person!" Jen says and Huxlee looks between the two of us before sitting on the edge of the bed.

"Someone is going to have to do more explaining than that."

"It's a long story, but the short version is... magic?" I shrug and she reaches down to remove her shoe and throws it at me.

"Hey! It's my wedding day!"

"Yeah, and you're making no sense. I thought maybe I could knock some into you." She laughs.

"Someone banished part of Mason to the prison world and the other part has been reincarnated over and over again in this world until I magically put him back together?" I respond quickly.

"Oooookay, I guess I'll just have to take your word for it."

"All right, it's time to get Callie ready. Sweetie, I want you to sit down at my vanity. I'm going to do your hair and makeup for your big day." Her voice cracks at the end, and she quickly wipes a tear away.

I grab her hand before she can run away. "Thank you, mom."

She squeezes my hand back before going to my room to grab

my makeup bag. "Now, are we doing soft and classy, or full glam?"

"I'll let you decide." I close my eyes and keep them closed as much as I can.

We hear noise outside the room but when we hear Dad yell, "No peeking." We chuckle and Mom returns to getting me ready.

The other women help each other while Mom focuses on me.

When she's finished with my face, she asks, "What about your hair?"

"Whatever you think would look best. I trust you. Thank you for all of this. I love you."

"I love you, too." Her fingers in my hair takes me back to when I was a kid and she would braid it. She uses a lot of hairspray and bobby pins to hold everything in place.

They all help me into my dress and Mom adds the veil comb into my hair before she slowly turns me around so I can see myself for the first time. Mom's hand covers her mouth while tears fall down her face. "You're so beautiful."

I pull her into me and hug her tightly. "Thank you so much." I release her and hug each of them. "Thank you all for being here."

Everyone else is already dressed and we watch Mom as she quickly touches up her makeup and changes into a fancy dress.

"You'll only get pictures at your only daughter's wedding once," she says. "Jerry! Get in here and change!" she yells and my dad enters shortly after.

He stops when he sees me, tears glistening in his eyes. "You look beautiful, my Callie girl," he tells me, coming to hug me and give me a soft kiss on the cheek.

"Jerry, do you have something that Mason can wear?" Mom asks.

"I think my tux from our wedding is still tucked in the back of the closet. He looks about the same size as I was back then." He locates the tux and takes it and his own suit out. We all wait for Dad to come back and tell us they're ready.

When there is finally a light knock on the door, we are bouncing with anticipation. "Let's get you married," Mom says and opens the door to let my dad in.

"Huxlee, wait," I say. "Will you be my maid of honor?"

"Oh, Callie, of course I will." She laughs as she hugs me, and they all go out the door after each of them kiss me on the cheek.

"Give me just a second and I'll be back," Dad says before leaving the room again. When he comes back, he's holding a beautiful bouquet. He hands it to me before taking my hand and looping it through his arm.

I bring the flowers up to my nose, inhaling the sweet scent. "How?" I ask.

"Mason apparently has some connections in the flower world. Don't we need to do something with your veil?" He motions to the veil that is currently pulled back behind me.

"Oh!" With my free hand, I carefully pull it over to cover my face and my dad helps me make sure everything is in place.

He opens the door and I gasp. On either side of the door is a trail of flower petals and candles. A tear falls down my cheek as we make our way out. The path through the house leads all the way to the back porch where they have strung Christmas lights over the porch. Bouquets of all kinds are in vases around the porch and I look up to the front and see Mason's face.

Behind him stands my dad's friend, the judge. His wife and family are also out here. I smile at them when I pass. On the other side of the aisle is my family, my brothers, and their wives and kids.

Then my eyes focus on Mason, a big smile on his face as I walk toward him. When we reach the front of the makeshift seating area, the judge asks, "Who gives this woman to be married?"

"Her mother and I do," my dad responds. Mason comes forward, extending his hand toward me. My dad lifts my veil back and kisses my cheek. "Give him hell, sweetie," he whispers before placing my hand in Mason's and joining my mom.

Since we didn't have time to write our own vows, the judge

reads the standard set and our eyes don't leave each other throughout the entire ceremony. When the judge says, "I now pronounce you man and wife, you may now kiss the bride," Mason twirls me around and dips me low before kissing me passionately.

"May I present, for the first time ever, Mr. and Mrs. Moreau!" We hold hands as we walk back down the makeshift aisle. When we enter the house, he pulls me into his arms and kisses me again.

"Moreau, huh?" I ask.

"Does my wife have a problem with my last name? We can take yours if you want. I really don't care."

"I just think it's funny. I just married you and didn't even know your last name until the ceremony."

"Regrets already?"

I press up against him, taking his face in my hands, his beard tickles my palms. Shifting my eyes back and forth between his, I answer, "Never."

"Just one more thing to take care of," the judge says, walking back into the house. "I need you two to sign the marriage certificate, and then we'll leave you all to celebrate on your own."

We share the pen and both sign where we need to and then the judge leaves as he said he would.

"Cake?" Mason asks.

"What? How on earth did you get cake on such short notice?"

"Okay, they're cupcakes, and from Mademoiselle Little Debbie, but they're all I could find on such *short notice*."

We share our wedding "cake" with everyone before Mason and I load back into my car, suitcases and all, and head back to his house.

"Well, I didn't expect we'd be heading back to your house so soon, but I can't help but be grateful not to be under my parents' roof on my wedding night. Especially with my brothers and Huxlee all there." I shudder at the thought. Mason holds my hand the entire way to his house, occasionally bringing it to his lips and kissing it on the drive.

CHAPTER 36

God Only Knows

When we pull into the driveway, I hold my breath. I'm not a virgin, but for some reason my stomach does flip-flops and I'm as nervous as if it *was* my first time.

Mason comes around to my side of the car and opens the door for me, extending his hand. I place my hand in his and let him pull me out of the car. He wraps his arm around me and places a too-quick kiss on my lips. While he grabs our suitcases, I wait by the car and follow him into the house for the second time today.

He unlocks the door and sets our suitcases just inside before reaching back to take my hand and bringing me into the house. He pulls me to him and slams the door shut as soon as I cross the threshold.

Our lips crash together, and he carefully removes the veil from my hair, pulling away only to set it across the back of his couch.

We continue making our way to the bedroom, and I help him get out of his tux jacket. I throw it behind me before unbuttoning his shirt as quickly as I can.

Mason struggles to undo the back of my dress and I flip around so he can see what he's doing. His fingers brush down my back as he slowly unlaces my dress. The sound of the laces rubbing against each other is the only sound besides our heaving breaths in the silence of the house.

Once my dress has been completely unlaced, it falls to the floor around my feet and he draws me to him once more. I quickly work to finish getting his shirt off, and as soon as I do, he lifts me and I wrap my legs around his waist.

I release his lips so I can trail kisses down his neck, nipping and sucking up and down. He lets out a growl when I nip just below his ear. He presses me up against the wall just outside his bedroom door while he reaches and turns the doorknob, opening it.

He holds me up, and I keep my arms and legs wrapped around him, running my fingernails through his long hair. His answering growls tell me he's enjoying this just as much as I am.

When my back hits the bed, he pulls back and slowly removes his pants and undergarments and stands completely naked, staring down at me. His impressive length stands at attention, and I have no doubt he's completely ready for me.

"We're going to have to get these off of you, aren't we?" He smirks down at me before twirling his finger for me to flip over for him.

Instead of simply unhooking the bra containing my breasts, he leans over me, completely covering my back with the heat of his body. Reaching around, he uses his hands to engulf each of my breasts, and as he does, he involuntarily thrusts against me.

"I should probably tell you something..." I start. Behind me, he freezes, hands releasing me when he pulls back. "I'm not exactly... I know you haven't... but I'm not a virgin..." My voice trails off as I finish the broken sentence.

"Is that all? I deduced that when we were in the treehouse," he says.

I look back and he has a smile across his face. Releasing the breath I was holding, I smile back at him.

"Let me assure you." He trails his fingers along my spine and goosebumps pepper my skin as he unhooks my bra, infuriatingly slow. "I may not have had sex in this body." I pull my arms out of the straps and he tosses it across the room. Leaning in close, he whispers in my ear, "But I have *all* of the memories of my past lives." I shudder in his arms.

Next, he flips me onto my back and I wrap my legs around him as he presses his lips to mine once more. The feel of his chest against mine, his length just where I want him, pulls a moan from me. His hair rubs against my sensitive skin, directly connected to more intimate parts of me, while those same parts enjoy the friction of his hard length.

The only barrier between us is my panties, and he pulls back to oh-so slowly drag them down my legs. Once I'm completely naked, his eyes roam up and down my body and an appreciative hum escapes him.

He climbs up onto the bed and carefully brings me up with him, my head resting on the pillow before he lowers his glorious weight on me again.

I position my knees up so my legs rest on either side of his waist. He holds himself up on his elbows, looking down at me before bringing his lips to mine once more.

My impatience to have him inside of me grows and, finally, I wrap my legs around his waist once more and drag him to me. He leans back and asks, "Are you sure you're ready? I don't want to hurt you."

"I've been ready since you popped up in my bed." I chuckle and drag him to me with my legs once more.

He kisses me again, and I run my tongue along the seam of his lips, asking for access. As soon as his lips part, my tongue darts out and tangles with his.

Oh-so painfully and blissfully slowly, he inches forward and eases just the tip in before pulling back again. I growl at the loss and use all of my weight to reverse our positions, so I am now straddling him.

He brings his hands to rest on my hips, and our tongues continue to dance. I make sure my legs are positioned where I want them before slowly lowering myself onto his length. We both groan when I completely seat myself, filled with his length. I stay where I am, allowing my body to adjust to the glorious invasion for just a moment before starting to move.

I lift and lower myself along his length, rolling my hips at the bottom, eliciting a moan from both of us. Quickly, I feel myself climbing toward climax, and when he releases my lips, I can hear his pants grow quicker. My own pants increase and I keep my mind focused on the glorious feeling of him inside me, the feel of his cock as it rubs against my most tender places.

He wraps his arms around me and reverses our positions once more. I bring his arm around my leg, showing him how best to allow for the deepest penetration. My breasts bounce freely as he continues to plunge into me.

I look up into his eyes and he smiles down at me, continuing the blissful assault on my long unused places. His movements start to change and I bring my fingers down to move in small circles on my clit and I shatter around him, followed by his release just a moment later.

He collapses on top of me and we breathe deeply, catching our breath. "That was, wow," he says between pants. "Is it always like that?"

I chuckle before answering, "I thought you said you remembered from your past lives," I tease, "but not always. A lot of women never reach a climax."

He looks at me shocked before rolling off of me and asking, "What was that you did with your fingers at the end there?" He props his head up with one of his hands and looks down at me while I answer.

"Uh, well, you see... when you changed our position... it kind of *distracted?* my lady parts. And I needed something to help build me back up quickly."

"So you helped yourself go off?"

"Go off?" Genuinely confused by phrasing I've never heard before, it takes me a minute to realize he's talking about my orgasm. "You mean orgasm? Finish? Fireworks?" I laugh as I think about the many other terms for orgasming I've read in books.

"Dear wife, are you making fun of me?" He punctuates each word with a kiss.

"Just a little bit." I hold my thumb and pointer up close together.

"I do believe..." A moan escapes me when he brings his hand to rest against the curve of my sex. "Like this?" he asks and two fingers dip inside me.

My eyes roll back in my head at the same time my back arches off the bed. "What about this?" he asks when he curls those fingers inside me. Quickly, I can feel myself building toward another orgasm, and I pant as he continues to pet that place inside me.

"Thumb," I choke out, needing a little pressure against my clit to get me there. Briefly I look at him and he looks confused. Reaching down, I use my fingers to show him what I mean, and he's quickly able to replicate the motion with his thumb.

His fingers alternate between curling and plunging in and out. My pants and moans grow in volume. He adds a third finger and I can feel myself tighten around him before everything explodes and I ride his hand as I come down from my high.

He pulls his hand out and brings me to him with his other arm. My arm rests across his abs and he runs his hand up and down my spine while my breathing slows.

Once I've caught my breath, I look down and see he's back to standing at attention. I run my fingers lightly up and down his length and he hisses out a breath.

"Callie, you don't have to," he starts. His fingers start to weave into my hair before the pins stop their entry into my blonde locks, and he gently tugs on what he can to bring my face up to his.

"I want to." I climb back on top of him. This time, when I lower myself on him, my insides feel gloriously used. I look down at him and prop my body up with my hands on his chest. Slowly, I rock back and forth and he looks down to where our bodies connect, watching the motion, and we can both feel the effects on our bodies.

This time I keep a slow pace, building us up, bringing both of us to the precipice before pulling back and changing position. Time and time again, I bring us both to the brink and pull back, both of our bodies building tension with the continual denial of what we're both ready for.

This time he lets me stay in control and I begin to pick up the pace a little. I squeeze my inner muscles along his length. A low moan escapes him and I roll my hips each time I hit the bottom. He brings his fingers to my clit and my body takes over. I start to move faster and faster, building us both to a climax so life-changing, I collapse on top of him, falling quickly to sleep.

I awake to his fingers running through my loose hair while he whispers sweet nothings in my ear. Tilting my face up to him, I smile and he says, "If I'd have known it was going to be like that... I may have let you take advantage of me in the treehouse."

"Oh, take advantage of you, huh?" I tickle his side and he jerks and twitches until I'm flung to the other side of the bed and he rolls onto all fours and stalks back over me. "Did you take my hair down?"

"While you were sleeping, yes. Dear wife, I do believe we should get something to eat. I'm famished." I look over at the clock and see hours have passed since we got to the house.

"What do you have?"

"Perhaps we should have thought about that on the way here. I'm afraid my options are limited to canned soup or mac and cheese."

"I can always go for some mac and cheese." He rolls out of the bed and marches out in nothing but his birthday suit. I shrug and move to the bathroom so I can clean up before making my way to the kitchen.

CHAPTER 37

Grown-Up Christmas List

Thankfully, he had some of the pre-made cheese kind, and the mac and cheese tastes divine after working up such an appetite. He leaves the food in the pan and has me sit beside him on the couch. My legs stretch across his lap and he alternates between feeding us some of the cheesy concoction. We spend the rest of the night talking about our hopes and dreams.

Maybe I should have known him a little longer, gotten to know him a little more before becoming his wife. But there's just something about the beast, my beast, that I know deep down he was meant to be mine.

"So, if you could have one wish, what would it be?"

He kisses my bare shoulder before answering, "I already got what I wished for." Tangling his fingers in my hair, he pulls me to him and kisses me deeply. While his tongue plunges into my mouth, I hold his face to mine and I climb to straddle him on the couch.

Slowly, I lower myself onto him, allowing him to set the rhythm with his hands on my hips. He pulls back and says, "You're going to be the death of me, woman," before flipping me to lie back on the couch and taking over, thrusting deep and hard. I bring my hips up to meet him with every thrust, and we both groan.

He holds himself up with one hand on the armrest and his other hand comes down to run lazy circles along my skin. His fingers graze the side of my breast and I inhale sharply, the contact sending a jolt to my core.

He moves his fingers closer and closer to one of the tight peaks before pinching one lightly. I groan at the contact, thrusting my hips harder to meet him. He trails his lips down my chest, bringing my nipple into his mouth and lightly biting down.

My movements become more erratic as he works me into a frenzy, alternating between my breasts and continuing to trail his fingers lightly across my body. When I can't take anymore, I weave my fingers into his longer hair and drag his face back to mine. When I kiss him again, his lips are moist from the attention he gave my breasts and I plunge my tongue into his mouth.

His breaths quicken when he gets closer to his climax. He slows his pace and brings his fingers back to the spot he now knows needs his attention. Closer, deeper, higher, he makes my body climb until we explode. He stays inside me while he continues to rub circles around my clit until I lay my hand on his arm, stilling his movements.

"I meant, what would you wish for besides me?" I laugh and he smiles down at me.

He looks down at where our bodies are still connected. "That feels very odd. But I guess I would wish that there wouldn't be another war." He kisses me deeply before continuing, "I would wish that the small battle we already fought in the prison world would be the end." He pulls out of me before saying, "But ultimately, I would wish that we could rescue all of our people and bring them back here."

"Our people?"

"You, my dear wife, are now a queen. We will rule our people with love and kindness. We will protect them from the child and the pirate," he replies through clenched teeth, glancing away. I lay my hand on his bearded cheek and gently run my thumb back and forth until he looks back at me.

"We will do all of those things. But first, we have to figure out how to get back there."

KAR

I open my eyes and immediately roll to my stomach on the mat they've given me to sleep on. Using the butter knife I stashed after they brought me dinner one night, I mark another notch at the base of the stone wall.

Today it's been one year since I've been living in these tunnels. One year since I was banished to this prison world and left in the care of the oh-so enjoyable Peter and Hook.

Growing up, I knew about this world and was always threatened with its existence. As a child, I was told I needed to learn my lessons, or I'd be sent here. As I got older, I had to do what I was told, or I'd be banished here. When I finally became an adult, I was threatened with being sent here no matter what I did.

Finally, I couldn't take the verbal abuse anymore and I talked back. The one time I spoke up for myself, I was banished here.

Peter and Hook immediately captured me and brought me down here. But they must see something in me, or why would they have cared for me over the last year?

I've been fed, allowed to bathe, and given the occasional trip into the sunshine where I take the opportunity to soak in as many of the sun's rays as I can because I never know when I'll get to go back out there again.

When I first got here, I could hear the moans and screams of another person. I could tell it was a female, based on the pitch of the screams. But after hearing more people traveling through the tunnels than I ever have in the rest of the time of my being here, the moans and screams stopped. I have only heard one or two people at a time since then.

I hear the sound of footsteps, and I blow out my candle and shrink into the corner, hoping that by making myself as small as I can, they'll leave me some food and leave me alone.

When I see the face of someone I know but have never seen in this world before, I know my luck has run out.

Acknowledgments

First and foremost, thank you to my family for always being supporting of whatever I want to do.

Thank you to my best friend, who was willing to read this first time author's rough draft and give me valuable feedback.

Thank you to my beta readers for kindly (or not) helping me make my book better. You guys are the real MVP's here!

Thank you to my editor, who had no problem telling me everything that was wrong with my book and being an amazing human with all the advice she gave to this newbie author.

Thank you to all of the authors in the BookTok Community, and those willing to come on my podcast, Freya's Fairy Tales. Your tips, tricks, and other advice helped me get to where I am.

And Finally, thank you to each and every one of you for picking up a book written by me. I will be forever grateful that you took a chance on me!

About the Author

Freya Victoria is a Texas native that has always wanted to write her own books and has spent countless hours attempting to write, reading books from every genre, and has been reading aloud, with all the character voices, since she was a kid. Growing up, Freya always struggled to come up with a storyline that she could develop into a full novel but, she finally found an idea that stuck. You can find Freya every day in the recording booth, working on someone's audiobook, working on more podcast episodes, or sitting on the couch reading and writing. She resides in Texas with her husband and daughter and hopes to one day move into the country where she can not have to edit out the sound of her neighbors mowing their lawn or the trash truck as it drives by!

Trigger Details

ALCOHOL

There is alcohol consumption in the book, no one is an alcoholic.

ASSAULT, BLOOD, DEATH, DECAPITATION, GORE, MURDER, VIOLENCE, WAR

During the battle there is a lot of war related scenes in which there is blood, violence, decapitation, lots of arrows being shot, sword fights and subsequent carnage.

ASSAULT, GORE, HOSPITALIZATION, HOSTAGES, KIDNAPPING, PHYSICAL ABUSE, TORTURE

Callie is kidnapped and held captive, she is beaten, and later spends time with healers to help her.

ANXIETY

The beast is shot and she's ripped back to her world, and the other MMC (Male Main Character) ghosts her leaving her anxious and scared.

CHEATING

The MMC's girlfriend admits to cheating near the beginning of the book, she rubs it in his face on page.

SEXUALLY EXPLICIT SCENES & LANGUAGE

The Forgotten Beast is a fantasy romance book. It is a slow burn and nothing sexually explicit happens until the end. Profanity is nothing more than you'd hear out in public.